The Land Baron

A Conspiracy Thriller

Elliot Chatima and Rumbi Chen

THE LAND BARON

A CONSPIRACY THRILLER

Elliot Chatima & Rumbi Chen

Acknowledgements

I want to thank God for the abilities he has given us both, I believe that without God, we would not have achieved anything at all. I would like to take this opportunity to appreciate my co-author Rumbi Chen for her commitment and dedication, patience, resilience and creativity, as well as experience and simplicity. Co-authoring a book has its own challenges, but when you add 9 hour time difference, things get more complicated, yet with all the layers of complexity, we managed to form a perfect team working in harmony. The Land Baron is our third book working together after The Storm and Landing in 15 Minutes. We have two more books, which are "The gods above" and "The Diasporan" to be released before end of year 2025.

A special thank you to my family, Jane, my wife, Oriana and Onabelle Chatima, my two daughters and Othniel Arthur Elliot Chatima for their unwavering support.

Without the engine, the team that works behind the scenes reading every chapter and providing the much needed criticism and encouragement, this book would have not seen the light of the day. Thus, we are deeply indebted to Tafadzwa Tamanikwa, Trudy Phiri and Diana Vito, the ladies who have been working so hard to review the book.

Chapter 1

Engineer Dr Shelton Makaza whistled and tapped the wheel as he drove from his house in Greendale. An unmarked tinted Mercedes-Benz SUV shot past and slammed to a stop, blocking his way. As he assessed the situation, a black military-type Hummer boxed him in from the left, while a Toyota Land Cruiser tailed him. The driver gripped the wheel with one hand, a shotgun levelled at the Engineer with the other. To his left lay an open drainage, at least 15 to 22 feet deep. The Engineer's heart raced, as his mind calculated vectors and distances at Mach 6 speed. As he pondered, the Hummer sped off with a roar. Breathing out in relief, he thought the team may have targeted the wrong person, or that they were racing. However, he could not escape. The SUV still trapped him. At that moment, a Toyota GD 6 with a makeshift rugged-terrain bumper hit the Engineer's car, sending it rolling into the drainage below. Three men jumped out from the Cruiser behind and rushed to the wreckage. The Engineer had sustained numerous injuries, but the trio ignored him and grabbed all the bags from the car. After retrieving what they wanted, they set the car ablaze and fled the scene.

It is 5 July 2010 in the capital city of Zimbabwe, and life seems to be normal. At 08:45 there was a meeting at the council of Harare. This was to decide on the application made by a prominent businessman Mr. Michael Paradzai, a multi-millionaire local business tycoon with vast tracks of land across the country. The meeting was to take place in the Mukuyu board room. The thirteen-member team was seated, save for one Dr Shelton Makaza, who had vast experience in water and civil engineering. The latter had communicated that he was coming to the meeting, it was not his habit of being late for a meeting, let alone not to communicate his position.

British-trained, he was aware that coming to meetings on time was an indicator of showing respect to other people. Seconds turned into minutes and minutes turned into hours just like in the "Round and Round" song by Justin Bieber. Yet still there was no sign of the Engineer. The chairman of the land committee decided to give the Engineer some time till lunch hour. The Engineer had prepared the environmental impact assessment report apart from the report normally produced by EMA, the Environment Management Agency. The EMA report was submitted in hard copy and only the chairman of the committee had sight of the report. This raised eyebrows, but no one was strong enough to engage the chairman and demand the report.

By 3:30 pm, Engineer Makaza could not be located, and the chairman decided to proceed with the meeting without Engineer Makaza. The chairman called the meeting to order and since this was a specific matter, there were no minutes of the previous meeting. The quorum was confirmed, with Engineer Shelton Makaza noted as absent. The chairman indicated that the purpose of the meeting was to discuss the application for land as submitted by Mr. Michael Paradzai through his Native Investments. The chairman indicated that he had seen the report from EMA, which he was willing to share after the meeting but was quick to point out that the councilors had not objected to the use of the report. A committee member a Mr Changunda raised a matter requiring the chairman to consider adjourning the meeting till the engineer's report was heard, but he was crushed by the chairman before other members of the committee could have a chance to consider the proposal. The chairman indicated that there was need to respond to the application in the spirit of maintaining a good relationship with the business community. Another committee member raised a point of order. He stated that the land applied for, was close to some aquatic life which could disturb its ecosystem. It was also noted that the land applied for, was considered to be wetlands, held some heritage sites and areas of national interest. The chairman informed the team that the meeting was confidential, and a vote was to be used to decide on those in favor and those against. There was a point of order raised by the chamber secretary, who queried the voting methodology proposed. There was a disproportionate and borderline threatening response from the chairman. He insisted that the law talks about voting and does not prescribe how the voting is done, and it was up to the councilors to decide. Some committee members were about to leave the room in protest having realised that there were glaring governance breaches. At that point, the chairman indicated that each of the committee members was to apply for one commercial property and one residential property maximum size of 2000 SM.

At that point, there was silence and the members started sitting down one by one. The Chairman indicated that the stands were to be paid for and that a 40% discount would be applied however the chairman had managed to secure a sponsor and that Native Investments was willing and standing ready to settle the 60% component of the purchase price. This meant that councilors were not expected to pay anything towards the purchase of land. The deal created a direct conflict of interest but nobody cared about corporate governance. The stomach was louder than the corporate governance codes all combined, be it the provisions of the constitution of Zimbabwe that demanded accountability and transparency, the provisions of the Public Finance Management Act, the Urban Councils Act as well as the corporate governance for public sector, together with treasury circulars, statutory instruments as well as directives from the Minister of Local government and the best practices in urban developments. No one was moved by any of the "worthless" documents in a nation where corruption was seen as the thing and bragging about ill-gotten gains became a socially accepted practice.

"You should have come clean that there were other matters to consider. Surely such a patriotic and well-meaning stakeholder cannot be punished through lengthy and unjustified processes. We ought to use our influence to reward this at once," one committee member commented with a height-pitched voice betraying his excitement.

The chairman indicated that there was a problem with the law, as there was a requirement that an auction be conducted and the highest bidder allocated the land. Rose Majaya interjected, making a point that there was a provision in the Urban Councils Act. This is where the committee could directly allocate land, if they believed that the development was in the best interest of the city. The chamber secretary refuted Lisa Rose's position, but the chairman was ready to rubbish the contribution from the legal mind.

"Find the part of the law that allows the committee to allocate the land without going to tender and fix this," the chairman demanded.

"Then you will have to wait till I give feedback," the chamber secretary responded.

The chairman glared at the chamber secretary with the look that parents give their misbehaving children, when there are visitors at home and immediately the chamber secretary got the message.

The votes were done, and all the members voted unanimously for the awarding of the land to Native Investments. The company had not submitted bank accounts and a bankable proposal. Instead, they had only stated that they intended to invest USD 2.5 million in infrastructure that would modernise the city. The market value of the land in question was USD 22,5 million, going by similar valuations done for property opposite the 300, 000 SM land. Native Investments was allocated the land at a cost of USD 3.5 million. The meeting was closed, and all the committee members went home with offer letters of the land they had been promised in the meeting. The offer letters indicated that the stands had been paid for in full.

Chapter 2

Michael Paradzai was 2.2 meters tall. He was a pale figure as is the norm with many people who have amassed wealth save for a few outliers. Some say wealth favors the slender while others believe that the statistic means nothing. The naysayers opined that just because a pattern exists, it may not always mean it should be ascribed to. A story for another day.

Michael was born in Shurugwi, a small town close to Gweru in the Midlands. He was the third born in a family of 8. Michael was an intelligent child who had been asked to skip grade 4 and grade 5. This was due to the intelligence he exhibited and the pace with which he could grasp concepts, in all the 6 subjects that he was doing. After attending one term, he managed to finish the syllabus for all the subjects and was registered to sit for. He managed to score four units. The following year when he was supposed to be in grade 7, but he was enrolled into form one. He demonstrated brilliance in grasping all the concepts prompting the teachers to approach the school head to try him for the form two ZJC examinations. He wrote 9 subjects and passed with flying colors. At that point, it became clear that a genius was born, he was the talk of the town.

Michael was highly regarded, having won many international debates and global mathematics competitions. At fifteen, he was awarded the presidential Medal of Honour for the most influential and the most progressive Zimbabwean, whatever that meant.

The year that followed, Michael lost his father, who was murdered by thieves he had given a lift from Gweru to Shurugwi. Michael did not process the premature death of his father very well. He struggled to accept that his father was indeed gone, it was a very difficult time for him. His father's death was a bitter pill to swallow. His mother was deeply hurt and depressed by how her husband died. She lived for 6 months after her husband's death. One day she was coming from Gweru and asked the bus driver to drop her at the scene of the accident where her late husband's body was found lifeless 6 months earlier.

Londiwe Paradzai, Michael's mother, was married to Kizito Michael Paradzai - Michael's father at the age of 15, as it was the practice at the time. Londiwe's parents had borrowed maize during a drought season and when they continued coming for more, they pledged their last born daughter as security since they did not have any cattle or goats that were demanded in exchange for maize. The timelines agreed lapsed, and Kizito's parents demanded the full settlement of the outstanding 25, 90 kgs of maize. Londiwe's parents in a heart wrenching encounter, withdrew her from class, packed her bags and surrendered her to the Paradzai family as settlement. Londiwe was in pain and agony, but she was submitted to the Paradzai family as a slave or whatever they wanted to do.

One day, on a Thursday night in 1983, Kizito's father announced that he had "married" another wife and that he was to wait till she was 16 years in the summer of the following year and then commence duties of a wife. This displeased yang Kizito who saw the plight of the girl and asked that she be allowed to go to school and finish her education. This did not go well with Kizito's father. After a few days, a meeting was called. Kizito's father, one Mr. Nyamugoneka Paradzai, was chairing the meeting. In the meeting were Kizito's mother Sibongile, Londiwe and Kizito. Nyamugoneka cleared his throat, lifted his staff and with narrowed eyes, pointed at Kizito like one who is identifying cattle from a herd. He was quiet for some time and when he spoke, his voice was firm. Nyamugoneka had an imposing structure which made Kizito tremble with fear.

"I have taken note of your displeasure in my decision to take Londiwe as my wife. You have challenged me in my own compound and you must now stand up and fight me. Whoever wins will take the girl." Nyamugoneka charged as he challenged his son.

Kizito was stunned and his mother begged for mercy while Londiwe was terrified looking at the monster of a man that was going to be her husband. Kizito knelt down and begged for mercy but his father took advantage of the close proximity and released his staff on Kizito's left shoulder. The boy wiggled with pain like a snake that was hit in the head. He screamed with pain. His mother was astonished but knowing her husband she knew better not to cross the red lines.

Nyamugoneka stood up and lifted Londiwe like one lifting a puppy. He looked at her and growled with a deep voice, "I had given you a grace period to grow till you are strong but tonight you will be my wife."

At that point Londiwe was shaking. Nyamugoneka then put her down like one throwing a cat.

Nyamugoneka frowned, lifted his roving index figure as if it were some kind of weapon and he charged. "Here is the deal. If you want this girl, you will work for her, I will not touch her. She will be going to school as you requested, but after she turns, 16 you are to take her as your wife and leave my homestead. But before you leave, I will be the one to have the honour of breaking the virginity."

There was silence in the room. Kizito stood up and shouted, "I will pay you whatever it takes to set her free."

The following year, Kizito was given Londiwe as a wife but had been deceived by his father who tried to rape the girl three times and threatened her with death if she dared bring up the subject. Londiwe was officially handed over to Kizito as his wife. That day, Kizito surrendered Londiwe to her parents. He was happy to hand her over, he had worked for two years for his father to repay his father the 25, 90Kgs of maize. Kizito asked Londiwe to marry her and when she agreed he took two more years raising the money to marry her. Though Londiwe and her parents were willing to surrender at no lobola consideration, Kizito insisted and they wedded. It was the first wedding in the village.

At the scene of the accident, Londiwe was thinking about all this history and how she was shown real love by her late murdered husband. She fell to the ground and a passerby Good Samaritan rushed her to the hospital where after running some tests, the doctors confirmed that she had stroked and that she had a blood clot in the head. She was in her last moments, and Michael came to see her after hearing the harrowing news. He looked at his mother who was in the throes of death. She managed to speak to him and only said, "Look after my children," before she gave up the ghost.

Instead of crying he screamed, it wasn't the screams of sorrow, but of determination. He had three objectives, to avenge the murder of his father, to look after his siblings, and to make sure that they go to school. Michael had to make money and make sure that his family will never suffer again.

Londiwe's burial took a week to be finalised, given that the husband's murder investigations had been ongoing. The police became even more suspicious. The provincial officer in charge was present at the burial. She was buried next to her husband. The burial was held on Saturday, and the mood was somber with some still grieving the loss of Kizito. Reverend Jonathan Mwale was given the task of conducting the burial arrangements. The previous night, Kizito's brother Jacob had given an announcement regarding the burial program.

At 9 am, the program started with the speeches. First to speak was Londiwe's father, as is the norm to show respect for the in-law. Londiwe's father allowed himself to be vulnerable as he narrated the circumstances that led to the marriage between her daughter and Kizito. He broke down in the process. He was, however, thankful to his late son in law who had been so good to them. Restoring the dignity and empowering them with a sustainable cattle breeding project. As at that date, Londiwe's father had 85 cattle, 120 goats and 350 pigs. He attributed all that wealth to his late son-in-law. He mourned him than he did his daughter.

Representative of Londiwe's mother was second to speak and so on.

At 10 am, the reverend stood up and instructed the church proceedings to start. The first song was "Lomhlaba" (this world is not our home), this was followed by, "Take it to the Lord in prayer', followed by There is a habitation, build by the living God, for all of every nation who seek they Grant aboard…." The songs kept pouring as the mourners sang from the heart. The singing was soothing, uplifting yet in the same code evoked sadness of the heart. Fellow church mates switched from singing to crying and back to singing, expressing emotional trauma and anguish.

As they sang "Hatina musha panyika" (this world is not our home, we seek a home that is far whose name is Zion), there were murmurings as mourners turned to the east road. The song leaders stopped singing and mourners burst into loud cries as a GD6 and a Mercedes Benz' were parking. Londiwe's elder cousin and her last born brother had arrived, they had not had a chance to offer their condolences to Londiwe in person on the passing of her husband. They had only talked over the phone. The two who lived in Australia, had been sent to school by Londiwe's husband. As for the cousin, it was a miracle that she managed to go to university. The two had lived with Kizito and had all their needs met. From the moment they disembarked from the car they wept bitterly for both Kizito and Londiwe. It was a sad sight to see. Both of them fainted upon entering the house and seeing the white casket of their sister, it was traumatic, and a devastating blow to the family. It was a turn of events, and vicissitudes was a better term to describe the occasion. The situation calmed down and they were introduced to the many elders. As is customary, the history of what happened to both Kizito and Londiwe was narrated, in-between the people would start crying albeit at lower voices.

The reverend started the preaching and in a rare show of maturity, he began by asking all the pastors from other churches to come forward and join him at the pastor's bench. The reverend acknowledged the Prophet from Johhane Masowe Echishanu, the group captain from the Salvation Army and the senior provincial evangelist from the Jesus is alive Ministries.

The reverend requested the choir to sing "Jesu Dombo Rakare" (Jesus the Rock of ages). How befitting was the song for those who needed comfort. The children were left as orphans, both parents had died. While death is the way for all, circumstances and timing made it difficult for the revered to preach the word. What was he going to say? How was he to tell the mourners that God cares? How was he to tell the children of the goodness of God? That God was in control? Indeed, it was a difficult message to preach. While everyone was feeling for the family left behind, everyone's attention was now turned to the man of God who was supposed to calm the people. Reassuring the people, conforming the people and giving hope to the children left behind. It was indeed a mammoth task ahead for the reverend. But the spirit of God was to give him utterances, all he needed to do was offer himself as a vessel and the Lord was going to glorify his name even at a sad, dim, dark and gloomy occasion like that.

Reverend Mark Mutumbwa rose to his feet, and everyone fell silent in an instant. He was a man who feared the Lord and had devoted all his life to Christ. He had preached sermons at funerals, but this was no ordinary task, considering the many complex situations where it was difficult to find appropriate scriptures and words to cheer the bereaved and the mourners. Yet here he was afraid, weak, grieving, and in need of encouragement himself.

When he spoke, his voice betrayed the sadness of the heart, his face down. "I call upon the group captain to open for us with a word of prayer."

The group captain immediately rose and sang a popular song "Ndicharamba ndichinamata" (I will keep on worshiping the lord in all instances, even if my father, mother, aunt, uncles, sister or brother shall not worship the Lord as for me I shall worship the Lord). The group captain, perhaps being moved by the Holy Spirit, decided to continue singing and the reverend gave a nod for him to continue singing. The song was deep, and for the situation at hand, it was a suitable song to sing. A man was holding four shakers in each hand, producing and sound that was in unison with the drums and the singing. After that, the group captain from the Salvation Army sang "Ishe vanouya" *(The Lord is coming, prepare for his coming),* another song that soothes the soul. The reverend still gave a nod for the song to be sung and it went on and on and people were really encouraged. The song gets one to reflect on the time when the Lord will call you and when your time here on earth is done.

The song is meant to help everyone reflect on the day they will give up the ghost and with the popular belief that one will stand before the Lord for judgment. The song achieves its purpose of getting people to reflect on their standing before the Lord and how they will be judged on the day of Judgment sooner or later.

The Sermon

"Dear family and friends, we gather here today to celebrate the life of Londiwe, a devoted mother, wife, and child of God. Our hearts are heavy with grief, and our prayers are with the eight children she leaves behind. May God's word bring us comfort and hope in this difficult time."

Bible Reading

- 2 Corinthians 1:3-4: "Praise be to the God and Father of our Lord Jesus Christ, the Father of compassion and the God of all comfort, who comforts us in all our troubles, so that we can comfort those in any trouble with the comfort we ourselves receive from God."

- Psalm 34:18: 'The Lord is close to the brokenhearted and saves the crushed in spirit."

- Matthew 5:4: "Blessed are those who mourn, for they will be comforted."

"May the Lord bless his word for it is Holy," the reverend added after the member of the other church had finished reading the scriptures. "Londiwe's sudden passing, coupled with the traumatic event that preceded it, leaves us with many questions. But even in the midst of uncertainty, we can find solace in God's presence. He is the Father of compassion, the God of all comfort. As we gather to honour Londiwe's memory, we remember her love, her laughter, and her devotion to her family. We remember how she cared for her children, how she supported her husband, and how she served her community.

But even as we celebrate her life, we acknowledge the pain and the fear that her children must be feeling. Losing a parent is never easy, and the circumstances surrounding Londiwe's passing make it even more difficult. Yet, as people of faith, we hold on to hope. We know that God is near to the brokenhearted, that He saves the crushed in spirit. We know that He will comfort Londiwe's children, that he will provide for them and that He will guide them through this dark time.

To Londiwe's children, I want to say this: "Your mother may be gone, but her love, her legacy, and her memory will live on through you. Hold on to the lessons she taught you, the values she instilled in you, and the love she showed you." And to all of us gathered here today, let us remember that we are not alone in our grief. We have each other, and we have God. Let us support Londiwe's children, let us pray for them, and let us trust that God will see them through this difficult time.

In closing, I leave you with these words from Revelation 21:4: 'He will wipe every tear from their eyes. There will be no more death or mourning or crying or pain, for the old order of things has passed away.' May God's promise of eternal life and comfort be our hope and our solace in this difficult time."

Prayer Time

"Dear Heavenly Father, we come before you with heavy hearts, mourning the loss of Londiwe. We pray for her children, that you would comfort them, provide for them, and guide them through this difficult time. May they feel your presence, your love, and your peace. We pray for the family and friends gathered here today, that you would give us strength, courage, and hope. May we find solace in your Word and comfort in your presence. In Jesus' name, we pray. Amen."

Message from the son

"Family, friends, and community, I stand before you today, with a heavy heart, to pay tribute to my beloved mother, Londiwe. Her passing has left a gaping hole in our lives, and I struggle to find words to express the pain and sadness we feel.

"My mother was more than just a parent; she was a symbol of peace, a unifier, and a shining example of love, care, and hard work. She dedicated her life to raising us, her children, and ensuring we had the best possible future. Her selflessness, kindness, and generosity inspired us all.

"As her son, I promise to carry on her legacy. I vow to work tirelessly to care for my siblings, both older and younger. I will do everything in my power to provide for them, support them, and guide them through the challenges of life.

"I promise to make my mother proud. I will work hard to achieve greatness, to become someone she would be proud to call her son. I will strive to be successful, to be wealthy, and to create a better life for myself and my siblings.

"But I also promise to seek justice. I will not rest until those responsible for my father's murder are brought to account. I will not rest until I have avenged my mother's death. I will fight for truth, for justice, and for the protection of my family.

"To my mother, I say thank you. Thank you for being such an amazing parent, for showing me what it means to love unconditionally, and for teaching me the importance of hard work and determination.

"Rest in peace, Mother. Your legacy will live on through us, your children. We will make you proud, and we will ensure that your memory is never forgotten."

After that, *sahwira* came and addressed the children, acting as if she was Londiwe, and it went on.

Message from Londiwe
"Vanangu, my children, do not cry. I am at peace. I have gone to join your father, and we will watch over you from above.

"I know that my passing has left a great void in your lives, but do not worry. I have taught you well, and you will continue to thrive. You are strong, intelligent, and capable.

"Do not forget the lessons I taught you. Remember to respect your elders, to care for one another, and to work hard. These values will guide you through life's challenges.

"I am proud of the people you have become. You are kind, compassionate, and generous. Continue to make me proud, and never forget that I love you more than words can express.

"To my family and friends, I thank you for your love and support. You have been my rock, my comfort, and my strength. I will always be grateful.

"Do not mourn my passing, but celebrate my life. I lived, I loved, and I laughed. I am at peace, and I will always be with you in spirit.

"Farewell, my loved ones. May God bless and protect you always."

Chapter 3

Kizito and Londiwe's 8 children were distributed amongst the relatives in a harsh reality that created a rift between the children. Tearing the once solid unity into pieces, the late-night stories that their mother and father used to narrate were now echoes from afar, it was forgotten. Michael was taken in by Londiwe's mother. Soon after the funeral, Kizito's elder brother Nyamusamba called for a meeting in which he nominated himself as the one in charge of his young brother's estate. He took over all the fields, the 300 cattle and 150 goats. He even took over the foodstuffs and the maize that was in the storehouse. Nyamusamba went on to sell the two houses that were in Gweru under the pretext that he wanted to distribute the funds to the children, to cater for their school fees but that did not happen. He instead used the funds to buy two houses for himself in Bulawayo. Londiwe's children struggled with life. They were used by the relatives as cheap labour in the fields. They would herd cattle, plough the fields and do the daily menial duties with no time to do school. During the rainy season they attended school less than 40 days out of the 56 schooling days.

Michael was deeply hurt seeing what was happening. One day he was coming from school when a car stopped and a man in his late fifties called out his name. Michael was not sure how to react, he did not recognise the stranger calling him. He decided to stop and hear him out.

"Afternoon son," the man called out in a relaxed tone, with one hand tapping the top part of the driver's door.

Michael looked at him with suspicion as if weighing whether he could defeat him in a first fight. "Good afternoon Sir, how can I be of help?" he finally responded, but did little to hide his frustration for being interrupted by a stranger.

"Are you not Kizito's son?, the man demanded.

"And if I am, what business do you wish to discuss with me?" Michael said, looking into the air as if there were some kind of ideas to be gleaned that were to be useful in the discussion matter.

"It's a beautiful weather isn't it?" said the man.

"Old man you obviously didn't stop me here to talk about the weather. Call the met department, they will be happy to discuss the weather with you," he yelled.

The old man pulled a cigarette, looked at it as if looking for some code to unlock some valuable treasure chest, before he offered one to Michael, "Smoke?", he said while holding up the case with an extended hand towards Michael.

Michael looked at it and with a dismissive look on his face, "No I will pass," he scorned the offer.

"Old man, what brings you to the neck of this bush? I have things to do."

"Easy, young man, see that the problem with you young men of today, you lack patience. Anyway I have a job for you, I want you to be a security guard at my business, I will pay you a fair amounts."

So it was, Michael started working the following Monday. He was trained for six weeks as a security guard and was further trained on how to use guns and various weapons. He proceeded to learn martial arts and graduated with Black Belt 5th Dan over time. He learnt sword fighting and became a pro.

The years that followed were defining. Michael foisted three robberies at the mine and recovered gold worth USD 22, 5 million. Understanding the weaknesses of the mine security system, Mike decided that he deserved more money than he was getting and so he demanded to be paid six times higher than the salary he was getting. When the old man a Mr. Diamond Gold refused to yield to his demands, he quit immediately and bought a bus ticket to South Africa. That night, there was a break in and gold worth 72, 5 million was stolen. Mr. Diamond suspected that Michael was involved, but could not prove. Michael had stolen the gold prior to handing over his resignation and what followed at night was a cover up. Mike had a solid alibi.

Michael was aware that he was being watched and for the six months that followed, he joined the South Africa robbery gang which performed many robberies in Zimbabwe and made good with the loot. They robbed banks, schools, supermarkets, wholesale shops and gold mines. They had informants in some of the robberies, while others were just based on studied information or information purchased from the secondary market.

It was on a Monday morning when Michael led his team to a high stakes armed robbery in which USD 7.9 million was stolen. The getaway cars were four GTi golf with a top speeds of 260. Everything went well but in the end they say in any game of hide and seek, clues can always be found.

The Zimbabwe Republic Police, known for its special investigative skills, managed to put together a pattern. The places that were hit belonged to Mr Diamond Gold or his close associates and a bank which he had significant equity. Michael became a key suspect in the matter. Interpol was alerted and Michael escaped to Botswana, where he was arrested but through his lawyers protected to be taken to Zimbabwe. He was finally transported to Zimbabwe in a convoy of six motor bikes in the front, three BMWs, three

VXV8 an ambulances and three Toyota trucks with 8 armed soldiers in each. A hit scope was hovering above them the entire journey. It was a triumphant entry for the nerd turned criminal. He was put in solitary confinement. Through emissaries he offered USD 1.5 million for his freedom.

Michael studied real estate and obtained a certificate with the University of Cape Town. He started buying land in high density through proxies and by the end of year one after prison, he had three hundred houses. While in prison, Mike developed relationships with some of the most notorious drug traffickers, human traffickers, money launderers and members of smuggling cartels. He was initiated into the gang's activities.

Chapter 4

There was a heavy knock at Nyamusamba's house. When he took time to open, a gang of 16 men broke the door open and retrieved Nyamusamba, who was wearing shorts. There were screams from his three wives and children, but that did little to deter the heavily armed team that was geared for war. They twisted his hands to bringing them between his legs and hung by the hands, suspending his whole body, being supported by his already twisted hand.

One of the gang members pulled a pliers and looked at him intently, though he was wearing a mask , it was clear that his eyes were full of hate. "Alright, old timer, are you ready for the Q and A? Here is how it's going to work, I ask the question, you answer the question. No to long speeches or explanations, any wrong answer will attract pain, we can do this without any pain or we can do it the hard way?"

Nyamugoneka was seething with anger, yet in the same code pain was making it difficult for him to think properly. In the end, he spat on the man.

The man simply wiped the saliva as if he was defeated in the contest. "I will take that you were practicing but hear me old man, this is not a spitting competition. The next time you do that, I will inflict pain that you have not felt in your entire life. Now focus as we are about to start!"

It was cold yet one of the gang members poured cold water on him. He shivered.

"Did you kill Kizito?" A beefy man with a scar on his forehead growled and the old man jerked his head.

"Please answer the question."

Nyamugoneka thought for a moment and then thought to dodge the questions. "My brother was found dead and I was the first to attend to the scene of the tragedy. I gave him a decent burial, release me from this madness and we talk like men," he demanded. "Yet you are the sole beneficiary of his estate, are you not?."

The old man screamed with pain and agony, but the embarrassment of his three wives seeing him in such a state was more damaging and demeaning.

He was silent for a moment and when he spoke, he was defiant, "The properties belonged to my young brother and I was the one to see that his wealth was distributed fairly. His children are well taken care of, so if that's what you are here for. then you story is weak and without substance."

The gang member who was interrogating him, in one motion, pulled out the biggest nail from his biggest finger, sending Nyamugoneka screaming, then another and another and another till they pulled out all the nails. They poured vinegar and salt on him, he screamed and tightly closed his eyes. The team looked at each other and nodded. They brought one of his young daughters in front of him. At that moment, they asked him to look at the girl and think before he could answer. The old man was defiant, he maintained that he was not involved, but when one of the gang members pulled a sword and put it on the shoulder of the little girl, he admitted to have killed his young brother. At that point, all the family members were asked to keep quiet.

"My young g brother was beginning to prosper and at first, I would assist him. But when he began to surpass me in business and offered that I should work for him and treat me as a shareholder with 25%, I did not like the idea of working for him. I did not like the idea of him being richer than I was. For a long time people looked up to me and the power balance was beginning to shift and I decided to kill him."

His narration painted a picture of a man who had a premeditated the whole act.

"He is lying," one of his wives protested, he did not do this alone. He was hired by Mr Diamond Gold to do it. They wanted to take his head and body parts for rituals, but when they disagreed on disfiguring the body they decided to leave the body and left. My husband is the one who pretended to have been called by someone, but he never left the scene of the murder."

Nyamugoneka was quiet, he looked at his third wife who had just narrated the story. Tears came flowing effortlessly as the old man regretted his actions. One of the men was recording the confession.

At that point, the family was asked to get inside the house and one of the gang members asked. "What did he say in his last moments before he died?"

Nyamugoneka answered, "He pleaded for mercy…"

"And you showed him none?" One of the gang members bellowed.

"Mr Nyamugoneka do you have any last words or last wishes?" Another gang member was pouring petrol on the ground beneath him and opening some bottles of highly effective acid. After that, there was a loud cry and a ball of fire. The gang members left.

Mr Diamond Gold's upper body was found floating in the swimming pool, half of it was eaten by the pit bulls that he kept at his house in Borrowable along Stonchart.

25

Chapter 5

Michael had decided against throwing a party to celebrate the recent purchase of prime land from the city. His wife, Candice Paradzai, had managed to talk him into it, in a move that cemented the notion that it is not power that is powerful but influence. And so it was. Men are powerful and are always seeking power and money, but women position themselves to influence decisions at the highest level, and they are not only to be recognised but respected and in some cases, feared as well.

The party was held at 6 Crouch Street, a street where those who have overcome their childhood dreams stay. They had conquered human basic desires, they operate at a level never dreamt of by an average men, and they had seen the "light". Their how was never a point of discussion as nobody had bothered investing time and effort into it. Number 6 Crouch was a place to be, whether you had business there or not, it was a place that many desired to be. It was like the state house, passing through, one would always wonder what was in there. That curiosity made it an achievement when one is invited. That is why many would post such an invitation on social media.

If you needed a place where your soul can connect with the spirit and the inner man can be explored. If you were looking for a place number 6 connected with the Carrick Craig Road, another road famous where the political elites dwell, albeit surrounded by trees and enjoying melodious live music from all sorts of birds. Further down, Glen Helen connected to the Crouch. This created a triangle, a shade of green connecting great roads. It was the people who lived there that made the roads great roads.

The drive walk at number 6 was made from a special type of material imported from South Africa. The design of the wall was meant to provide more than just security, it was meant to speak of the greatness of the owner. The designs had been made by a one Clement Metcalf from France for USD 385,900 excluding personal expenses paid to Metcalf for site visits and presentation of the drafts. Put together the cost can easily be in the region of USD 415 000. But who cared about such "small" amounts?. The driveway was made by James Greelish from Scotland a man known to carry out such work for high profile people. The obsession with foreign hands could be explained by two things, the desire to have the best thing done and the guarantee that the right thing will be done. Michael also liked bragging about throwing big names globally.

The driveway was illuminated with special bulbs that came at a cost of USD 950 each. It was designed to meander in a serpentine fashion with landscaping following and lilies on the edge of the driveway, while an assortment of pricy flowers curved through creating a wonderful site that one could not resist. The house was not visible from the gate at the 20 000 square meter property. The driveway pierced through a thick layer of trees, or shall we say a forest. There were friendly game in the form of a Deere, antelopes, zebras, waterbucks and eland. These were pious and a great sight to see. Their innocence had a healing effect. A male eland, fleshy and strong with long and pointed long horns, moved around with grace and with ease. It had a white stripe that was difficult to ignore, it was as if the white stripe was the quintessence of the animal. There was a water body that surrounded the house and a collapsible gate was erected. In the waters were sharks and alligators that were waiting to entertain any uninvited guest, perhaps the visual was more pronounced than putting a notice. A signpost that read "trespassers will be short, and survivors will be short again." Donald, the artificial intelligence robot, was in charge of vetting the guests before they were invited. Donald would use algorithms and search for detailed information about spending patterns, where and what was spent on and the behaviors of close friends on social media. Donald had done a great job screening controversial people who would have otherwise "tarnished" the hosts' image.

The house was protected by thirteen-member guards, a body of men as they were known and 7 pit bulls. Michael was always ready to show off the dogs to anyone who cared to see or shall we say it was his habit to showcase the vicious dogs as a deterrence measure. Even if one was able to overcome the sharks and the crocodiles and the pit bulls, there was another hurdle, 13 Laser beams that created a diamond shape. If by some luck one was able to overcome that, there was a system designed to create a live current on all door handles. The safe deposit room was suspended in water, it could be hoisted to dry ground only with a series of security features, including the full right-hand print, a pin code, a swipe card, and eye verification after which the system would send a one-time password to Michael's mobile phone. Once the safe is opened, a key is needed to open the safe deposit boxes. These keys were made in Mexico by a specific company that had signed a contract never to create another key like that again.

At exactly 7 pm dignitaries started arriving, accompanied monthly by their "spouses". There were VVIP and VIP tables and each guest would enter their invitation code and allocated a table and seat based on the system reservation. There was a live jazz band playing mostly songs from Zimbabwe's Oliver Mtukudzi, Hugh Masekela and Victor Kunonga.

The Land Baron

Oliver Tanaka, a Japanese-American, was the director of ceremonies, Rumors were swirling that he was paid USD 150 000, excluding travel, accommodation, and other feather beddings. Born in Japan in the city of Tokyo, Oliver was the public address system was specialist for private high-profile clients. The payments he received was to compensate for the fame he created through his social media posts, where he had been and whom he had hosted. Oliver had 2.2 million followers, good enough to boast the following and approval rate for any of his clients.

Oliver gave a sign to the performing artist to slow down. He grabbed the mike and when the sound was low enough he adjusted the mike to speak before he was handed a cordless mike.

"Ladies and gentlemen," he started, a few guests were still arriving and ushers were escorting them to their seats. Oliver remained calm, but his facial expression betrayed his frustration.

"We're gathered here to—" There were loud cheers as a group of four men and a woman arrived in a happy mood. They looked like they had a head start and were at a higher level.

Oliver continued, "We are gathered here to celebrate one of Africa's finest and a world-renowned. The majestic, the Jewel of Africa, the most eloquent, the richest man to have ever lived in the country of Zimbabwe. A leader, a family man, and a distinguished fellow, a great man full of wisdom. Kings come from far and wide to consult and get wisdom."

There were whispers from the VVIP table where one of the politicians commented. "This guy has taken boot licking to another level. We need him to train our juniors on how to appreciate their superiors. I need my campaign manager for my constituency to be trained this way, I can get used to being introduced this way."

The man seated next to him, who goes by the name Choga nodded in agreement, he was not only agreeing but in firm belief of the rhetoric that his colleague was uttering.

Meanwhile, there were cheers as other prominent businessmen poured in, dropping gifts at the gift table.

It was the mayor's time to speak. The mayor walked with grace, beaming with self-confidence and self-importance was written all over his face. The mayor was a poet and he got down to business.

Michael the Great Man of our time

Michael, a titan of industry and might,

A hero's tale, of hard work and endless light.

He earned his place, at the table of greats,

Through perseverance, and a heart that never waits.

With a lion's roar, he tackles every test,

A shrewd businessman, with passion that's truly blessed.

His commitment unwavering, a beacon in the night,

Guiding others forward, with a gentle, humble light.

A builder of cities, a maker of dreams,

Providing shelter, and spaces where businesses beam.

He brings ambience to the city's bustling streets,

A master craftsman, weaving a tapestry of unique treats.

The city's transformation, a testament to his name,

A legacy that will live on, long after the flames.

Of youthful energy, that once roamed the streets,

The Land Baron

Now harnessed and focused, thanks to his guiding beats.

A man of great humility, with a heart of gold,

Michael's story inspires, and forever will be told.

His impact on the city, a lasting, shining light,

A true hero's legacy, which will guide you through the night.

After the mayor's flattery poem came business associates, heads of government ministries, bank CEOs and so on. There was applause and ululation speaker after speaker. In what seems to be an act of taking bootlicking to another level, there was a lineup of speakers full of praises with some borderline blasphemy but nobody cared about a thing.

Chapter 6

Lisa and detective Mike are working as civil servants with a combined salary of USD 700 after deductions. Their family had grown to four members. The couple was struggling to pay rent as they needed USD 400, leaving them with only USD 300.

"Hey boo, don't you think we need to be serious about buying a property?" Lisa remarked while holding the detective by the waist and looking at him in the eyes. The detective had gazed at his wife's eyes a million times but the look never grew tired. Lisa was his happy place. The detective was getting frustrated that he was constantly failing to meet Lisa's expectations, but she was a great woman, beautiful and peaceful. She never stopped believing in her man through it all.

Detective Mike took time to respond to Lisa.

"Are you ok honey?" Lisa enquired.

Detective Mike was worried. He was in a place far away, and he snapped and looked at Lisa, then kissed her.

"I am so sorry honey, what did you say? I wasn't listening, do you mind if I ask you to repeat? Honestly, I was distracted?"

Lisa looked at him, frustrated but full of love as usual.

"Look honey, I know this matter affects you. Why don't we work together and raise money to purchase a stand? We can build a temporary structure and live there while building the house."

"Wow you have a great idea babe, you are very smart, that's why I love you." Detective mike remarked. Lisa moved closer to him holding him closer, while detective Mike kissed her on the forehead.

They both agreed to start a project as a way of raising money to secure a stand. The three months that followed saw the couple working on a chicken project, starting off with a batch of 100, managing to increase it to 300 by the 4th month. In the first month, 45 birds died due to various diseases. Detective Mike could not stand it and while he was still "helping" in some way, he had withdrawn from the fowl run. He was disheartened by the sheer number of losses, but Lisa kept going till she mastered the game.

The chicken project caused a standoff that left the marriage strained as Lisa felt that she was left to manage the project alone.

One day, Lisa was waiting for Mike in the living room.

"We need to talk Mike," Lisa said, almost yelling but lowered her voice almost immediately after raising it.

"Babe, I wanted to tell you that we now have USD 4900, we are however, short of USD 5000,. MMBZ is offering loans to civil servants and I was hoping we could apply and top up, what do you think?"

So it was, the following day, they went to the MMBZ Bank.

"Good Morning, how may I help you?" asked Nancy, the loans officer.

Lisa and the detective looked at each other before they both looked at the teller before Lisa responded by a flat, "we need to apply for a loan. We are Civil servants and we want the facility we have been told about," she added.

Nancy pulled some forms and laid them on the table and began to explain

"The loan is processed within 24 hours and will be credited into your bank account with MMBZ or paid directly where you desire. There will be a1% application fee, a 2.5% administration fee, a 1.5% loan draw down fee, our Interest shall be 19% per annum compounded. The loan shall be payable over 36 months. The total of the administration fee, application fee and draw down can be deposited as cash or withheld from the loan amount, this means there will be a 5% deduction from the loan."

Lisa was stunned as Nancy was explaining and in the end they signed for the loans. The following day, they went to the Down Hut Properties based in Avondale. The estate agent was selling the stands on behalf of Native Investments, a company owned by a well-known self-styled business tycoon. The stands were for the North View Hills.

Lisa and Detective Mike looked at each other, they smiled, believing that they were finally going to fulfill their long-standing desire of owning a house. Purchasing a stand was a first step.

They chatted while waiting to be served and when their turn came, they were ushered into a spacious office with maps all over the wall and rolled-up plans were scattered everywhere. The impression gave Lisa an instant feeling of accomplishment, she could almost see herself in a house. In a kitchen, a spacious one with material of her choice.

David Zisengwe and Michelle Mazwi were attending to them. Mike handed over the proof of payment and the cash payment receipts. There was a moment of silence, before David stood and handed over the agreement of sale documents.

They were given time to read through, the title deeds was said to be in place and were to be made available once the council had approved. They went through the agreement, and when they did not raise any issues, they were told to visit Chapwtitika and Chitsikidze legal practitioners. The Lawyers were on number 12 Stephen Conley Avenue and were responsible for the conveyancing process. They were the ones to sign the final agreement, as well as receiving conveyancing fees, which were demanded upfront. A fee of USD 1500 was paid for the conveyancing.

After that, it was time to get permission to occupy the stand. Native Investments required USD 50 fee for them to be shown the place, USD 450 to join the Residents Association.

The week that followed, Lisa and the detective moved into a temporary wooden structure that they had purchased.

It was on a Monday morning, while Lisa and the detective were preparing to go to work and the kids were readying for school. Four men stormed into their property holding guns. One made shots in the air before they went on to demand that they vacate the property as the property belonged to someone else and there were title deeds to show.

Detective Mike called the police, not just any police, but the Support Unit was dispatched to his house. When the police arrived, detective Mike had managed to calm down the intruders.

Lisa was in tears, she could not believe what was happening. The following week they were allocated another stand, but that too belonged to someone, and it went on six times till they were allocated to an isolated place with no other properties. The following morning, the maid came running after encountering a three-meter-long python that had caught a rabbit. The sight was frightening.

Three months went by and still there was no sign of services. According to the contract, the developer was supposed to make a storm water drainage system, power lines and water system. All this could not take place in a year or two years.

Residents came together and hired a lawyer, they made payments and submissions were made but all what the court did was to grant Native Investments time to fix the roads and all other related services. Over time, the residents got tired and took native Investments to court. The residents had a clear case against Native Investments, but for three straight years, the date for trial could not be granted. In the 4th year, the dates were set but kept on being shifted by three to four months.

In the 5th year, there was a court date that was set and the notice of the date was served at the wrong date, and the plaintiff did not attend court. That day Native, Investments submitted that they did not have any obligation to provide the services stated in the contract on the basis that the stands had been sold for a small amount and that the amount collected could not be expected to provide for services.

And so it was, the judge made the judgments on the same day and ruled that the residents were supposed to make further contributions for the purpose of developing the services stated in the contract.

When the judgment was delivered, the Lawyer who had been representing the residents called for a meeting to brief the residents. The lawyer had followed all the protocol but when the day came, there was a team of police barricading the place. The police had a letter from the nearby residents objecting to the meeting and as such the meeting could not take place.

Chapter 7

Dr Chigovanyika was one of the committee members spearheading the process of getting the developer to meet his performance obligations stated in the contracts. The evening after the court case, sixteen men pounced at the Dr Chigovanyika's residence. They broke the gate and went into the courtyard. There were three German Shepard dogs protecting the house, and they were all shot on site.

There were loud bangs as the team got busy twisting and wrestling with the bars. Dr Chigovanyika called neighbors to rescue but the sheer number of the robbers was frightening and nobody wanted to get hurt. The police from the nearby post were called but complained that they did not have fuel to attend to the scene.

"Open the good damn door sneaky pimp," one robber yelled on top of his voice.

There was commotion as Dr Chigovanyika's family was in panic there were screams of innocent children. Many phone calls were placed but this did not help in any way, it was a hopeless situation. One robber lifted his AK 47 and started shooting into the air. The entire neighbourhood was gripped in fear as the bullets were continuously fired into the air and the gunfire illuminated the dark night, in what looked like emasculate display of fireworks. Only that the fireworks were made of real fire, dangerous fire capable of killing.

"What do you want gentlemen," yelled the Dr. There was no response for a moment, there was total silence. A deafening round of gunshots this time targeting the house where he was, rang out, and at the first sound, the doctor ducked along with his entire family.

"I am a psychiatric patient who has come for treatment I, hear you are the best in town aren't you?" one robber yelled on at the top of his voice.

"I'm sure you are aware that I don't attend to patients at night, you need to come during the day," yelled the doctor in response.

"Wow!" The robber responded, "finally a man worth killing. I have killed many men. Weaklings, men who had no pride and no ego, fearful and wasted, but I have not come across such a rare, bold and strong-willed men."

The doctor responded almost instantly.

"You are damn right I am no pushover skunk stink, you better be ready for the storm that's coming your way baby girl because I can be pretty rough."

The robber was stunned.

"You know you are just one of us hey?" the robber responded. "I bet it won't hurt having a Dr in the team," the robber continued.

The doctor had to think fast.

"You know I don't want people who waste my time baby girl, I don't waste time with men who go to waste on a woman," remarked the doctor playing psychological games.

"Ouch stop right there babe girl, you know that's my line hey, how do I go to waste on a woman when all my entire time in prison I had all the men I wanted," the robber went on.

The doctor's wife gave him a look that says, "When all this is over, you shall explain all this to me. But the war was not over.

"What was your crime that locked you in prison forever?" the doctor tried to change the subject after the gaze from his wife.

"Babe girl don't change the subject," responded the robber.

"You know I am going to open this door and wrestle you down and cuff, I can be very rough you know," the doctor yelled but with limited authority and originality in the voice but it was passable to the robber.

"Babe girl, that's what I am talking about, come here I am all yours I can't wait," the robber responded with a loud voice.

Initially, the other robbers thought that it was another game plan different from what they were used to, but later realised that the doctor was managing them. Cooling them down and slowing their anger and possibly appealing to the leader.

There was commotion as the robbers argued amongst themselves and what started as a small matter grew to a full-scale argument and in the end the doctor got a small winder. He took a 45 Caliber magnum with a silencer slipped through one of the windows and wearing night vision goggles, he started eliminating them one by one.

The doctor had been taught well that in a moment of crisis one should not draw the weapon if they do not intend to shoot and they should not shoot if they did not intend to kill. So it was a massive shot out and seven men went down. The doctor jumped to the robber he had been talking to and wrestled him down and shot cuffed him and he was very rough as he had promised.

"You said you are a psychiatric patient didn't you?" the doctor enquired. "Well my friend I am going to give you a psychiatric treatment."

The doctor dragged him to one of his working rooms and sat him on a steel chair. He pulled another chair and looked at him intently.

"Here is how it will go, I ask the question and you answer the question asked, do you understand?" the robber who was at this point identified himself as The Big Papa looked at the doctor into the eyes then after sizing him up he spat on his face The doctor carefully wiped the saliva as if collecting it for future examination and continued.

"Do you really mean this or you are just wasting my time?"

The doctor ignored the Big Papa's questions and instead asked him questions. The Big Papa decided to keep quiet, the doctor took a whip and started whipping him anywhere he so desired.

"We have been given a contact and were asked to cause maximum fear and damage, we are told you are interfering with the business of a high profile businessman, you are playing with fire man."

The police came while Big Papa was being interviewed, they arrested the doctor and freed the Big Papa, the doctor spent 40 hours in the cells. After that the man himself Timothy Garwe, the runner boy and ruthless killer for Native Investments showed up. He wore cowboy boots with steel stars and a cowboy's hat. When he entered the room where the doctor was sitting he touched the hat in a sign of sarcastic act of respect.

"Howdy, Timothy yelled with a Texan voice?" He pulled a pack of cigarettes and offered one to the doctor who refused.

Timothy lit one and started smoking, waiting till he had made three pulls and exhaling everywhere in a provocative manner.

"Doctor you are a well-known figure in society, your work is greatly appreciated, we need to resolve this matter once and for all, there are two options on the table, either you forget this and we all act like it's a bad dream and move on with our lives or we do it the hard way."

Timothy exhaled in the doctor's direction perhaps to emphasise the matter.

The doctor looked at him until the gaze was uncomfortable for Timothy, if the meeting was not happening at the police station Timothy would have punched or done worse things to doctor Chigovanyika.

"What is the harder way?" the doctor enquired.

Timothy stood up and walked around the doctor as if he were a policeman inspecting a shipment of illegal goods.

"We can charge you with murder and kidnapping and torture of Big Papa. The men who visited you were harmless but you fired 33 bullets from an AK47 recovered at your house and not to mention the 45 Caliber you used to kill the innocent civilians that we sent just to scare you. Big Papa tells me that you had a great conversation and out of nowhere you started shouting. We have seven witnesses from the neighbors, they are all willing to witness.

The doctor stood up and looked at Timothy into the eyes.

"Get these chains off me and clear all the charges if that's what you want. I can change my profession to be a paid for serial asset target killer any day I chose, but for you I will gladly kill you for free."

Timothy was frightened by the remarks made by the doctor but decided to downplay the fear.

The police officer came to release the doctor and when he was leaving the charge office Timothy yelled "stay out of trouble."

Chapter 8

On a Monday evening, it is raining in the City of Harare and residents of East View are lined up going home. East View is one of the suburbs that Native Investments had "developed". It had been ten years since purchasing the stands and the promised development was still a pipe dream. But that was not the concern for the day.

The subject matter at hand was on how to navigate the treacherous red soil dirt "roads". Branching off from the main surfaced road were steep edge drops that required careful navigation, as many low-clearance cars struggled, with some damaging their sumps and gaskets in the process. There were open ditches filled to the brim and these continued to fill up with water posing challenges to drivers with small cars. Many small cars struggled with some needing to be pushed as the engines stopped midway in the water.

Panic gripped the residents, and a team of rescue personnel was assembled. Several cars veered off the road with wheels stuck in the fine dust, sending the front tyres skidding in the process.

There was a deafening sound of cars revving as drivers were frantic in trying to come out of the mud, but the more they revved the cars the deeper they sank. Choking smells of skidding tyres filled the air, and in the end, many cars were left by the roadside either due to being stuck or running out of fuel in the process of high raves. Some cars burnt the clutch plates. By 11 pm, residents finally gave up left the cars and started walking to their homes.

Many cursed the developer, with some blaming themselves for not doing enough due diligence in the process of purchasing the stands.

The site was once again a reminder of the idea that Zimbabweans were a divided people. A divided society, which one opined emanated from the hunter-gatherer culture, not able to work together as the stretch of the road could have been rehabilitated and made passable had the residents agreed to work together but many committees were put forward and people could not cooperate for one reason or the other. Even as the people walked in the rain, on slippery roads, with some falling in the process. Year after year, the idea of working together and cooperation never crossed their minds, or they did not just see it necessary to cooperate in such an endeavor.

The following morning, at least 14 cars were broken into with batteries stolen. It was a hive of activity at the East View Police station. Children could not go to school as the roads were not passable, and there was no public transport due to poor roads. The few buses that had started coming through pulled out when the roads kept deteriorating, with no clear plan for rehabilitation.

The developer was nowhere to be found. In a "Kabuki" dance style with the residents, the developer had always come up with a "road works ahead," each year always promising to rehabilitate the roads but it always turned out as a gimmick.

Chapter 9

The week that followed proved to be a busy one, Native Investments was taken to court. The Municipality of Greendale was accused of parceling land belonging to Greendale Municipality without the consent of the council.

The matter was before the High Court Judge, Justice Marivadze, a seasoned judge of the High Court. The Greendale Municipality was represented by Thomas Thorn, a lawyer with a reputation for winning cases even with very limited evidence. He was indeed a thorn to his adversaries.

A very thorough and articulate lawyer. On the other hand, Native Investments was being represented by Jonathan Chirwa, a lawyer known for taking up cases that are borderline criminal commercial cases. Most of his cases were dead ends but he was able to hold off, buy time through bribery, technicalities, plea for time, and related skirmishes. In other words, his services were more of managing the impending losses, but there were cases he pulled a fast one and won the case or caused a negotiated settlement to take place.

"Your Honour, the matter before us is that of fraudulent misrepresentation of material facts. The Municipality of Greendale invited property development for developing certain piece of land situate in Greendale into housing stands. This invitation to tender was made in line with the Urban Councils Acts, which stipulate that any land development agreements between an urban council will be decided through a competitive bidding process."

The judge was gazing at both the plaintiff and the defendant,

"Do you have the tender advert and the tender bid documents?" the judge interjected.

"Yes Your Honour, the documents are part of Appendix C44 and C51 respectively."

The judge called for an assistant to help him navigate the voluminous documents and after a few moments of studying them he gave a nod for the plaintiff's attorneys to proceed.

"Your Honour, my client went on to shortlist three firms for interviews after which they proceeded to perform detailed due diligence. The tender committee after following due process, my client maintains that Native investments failed to meet the bid bond requirements, which had been stipulated as a condition to operationalise the contract," he proceeded.

The defense council erupted from his chair shouting.

"Objection Your Honour, my client was in the process of raising the required bid bond, I have with me a letter seeking extension for the deadline which the Council acknowledged and signed for."

The judge requested to see the letter in question and after careful examination he submitted it to the Clerk, admitting it.

"Your Honour, may I submit the letter of response from my client sent via a registered mail, in which my client declined the request for extension sought."

The judge examined the letter and ordered him to proceed.

"Your Honour, my client was made aware that there were some activities on the piece of land earmarked for development. We immediately entered into discussions with Native Investments to stop all forms of development and first meet the contingent conditions in the agreement."

"Despite many promises and assurances made to my client by the defendant, there said development continued with more equipment being mobilised on site. My client continued exploring all the available non-litigation-based engagements. However, the efforts did not yield any positive results."

"Objection Your Honour, the parties to the contract were still engaging, they even engaged two weeks ago."

The plaintiff's attorney frowned at the defendant, the anger in him was so visible that if he was within reach, he could have thrown a punch at him.

"Our urgent application has three prayers which we seek your honourable court to grant. And these are as follows;

1. That the plaintiff be granted the right to protect their property by demolishing the properties on site within 24 hours and further issue orders that the illegally settled residents be warned not to reconstruct at the said property.
2. That the contract between our client Greendale Municipality and Native Investments be terminated in full for the reasons that the Native Investments failed to raise the requisite bid bond, and that they failed to act with integrity by fraudulently allocating land and causing construction of houses without my client's approval.
3. That Native Investments pay for the cost of demolition, cost of litigation on a client and attorney scale.

It was the defendant's time. The judge called for a recess.

When the court was back in session, the defendant's barrister rose up and swore to tell the truth.

"Your Honour, we have listened to the case presented by the plaintiff's attorneys and we believe that there are material facts that the plaintiff's attorneys did not state. These material facts go to the core of the contract. And are as follows:

1. My client has a legitimate contact, and this contact is not under any threat as my client is in the process of meeting this requirement;
2. My client has decided to commence the development on the dates stipulated in the contract pending meeting the bid bond. The inability to meet the bid bond was due to the change in policy and country risk assessment for the bank. This position was communicated to the plaintiff;
3. The development process was done in good faith given the backlog in housing units and the need to offer decent accommodation to the residents.

"Objection, your honour, new information has come to our attention that the said bank was not able to offer the bid bond due to the default on existing loan commitments."

All arguments were presented before lunch hour, and the court was adjourned. Judgment was expected at 3 pm.

It is 8 am at Greendale Municipality, a total of 22 JCBs were assembled and fueled. The court had granted all the prayers by the council.

At 9:55 am, the JCBs went into action. It was a sorry state witnessing houses being demolished, razed to the ground, the drivers meant serious business. They did their work with no feelings or attachment, just demolishing the houses.

A Mr Majoni knelt down begging the drivers, his entire family joined him, but that did little to dissuade the man on the mission.

So it was, houses that had cost hundreds of thousands were destroyed, the work of the Land Barons. A total of twenty nine upmarket properties were destroyed.

Chapter 10

Michael was enjoying his ever-increasing dominance in the real estate development sector. He had invested in many other businesses as well. At 10 am all his team members were seated. Michael opened the meeting with a prayer before chairing the much-awaited meeting.

Michael had long promised that new business ventures were in the making, and they were going to be more profitable. The team had been speculating as to what that could entail, but the meeting was there to put to rest all the speculation.

"We thank God for all the blessings that he has showered upon us. We are not deserving of his grace, whatever we have had has been through hard work, perseverance, careful planning, and above all the Lord's blessings."

Michael had graduated with a diploma in Theology. He wasted no time achieving a degree in the following two years that followed. He had been awarded advanced learning credits which cut his course from four years to two. He wasted no time enrolling for a Masters in Real Estate which he passed with a distinction. All these qualifications and publicity that came with it gave him the credibility that he needed.

Two years ago, he had donated prizes worth USD 950,000 to a local university and as if returning the favor he was conferred with an honorary doctorate in Business Management and Real Estate. So it was Dr Michael who was making waves. A self-made businessman, a doctor, a philanthropist, a youth coach, and a community builder. The wall of good deeds made it difficult to criticise him publicly or in private. Yet these deeds were made specifically to conceal his true character.

"I am sure we all have watched the *Men Who Built America* documentary, and you will agree with me that having a company is about having new ideas. It's about finding new ways of doing things."

He paused to see if everyone was on the same page with him. And when he saw that everyone was nodding in agreement. he went on.

"Timothy my head of operations will be in charge of the unit. We have recruited ten men who will be in charge of "operations" and these will be reporting directly to Timothy."

He paused again to see if there were any objections or suspicion to the plan. He needed everyone to be on the same page, the nature of the business required that he take staff step by step and allay their fears. He did not want them to see the bigger picture.

There was a hand from Jennifer, but the chair was not taking questions as yet.

"Has anybody heard of global mobility?" The chair looked around to see if there was anyone to respond to it. A cousin of his, Marshal, raised his hand and responded.

"Sir it's about facilitating the movement of people from one country to another one continent to another, in search of work."

There was an awkward silence in the room.

"Well done," Michael broke the ice.

"We will be facilitating people, especially young girls to get jobs overseas. We have constructed our airport that meets the international standards."

There were three hands in the air and the chair realised that the staff was getting excited, he allowed only one, Steward, to ask.

"Do we have our own aircraft for this business?" Steward asked, his legs shaking and hands sweating.

The chair looked at him and looked up as if he had overlooked that when one builds their airport they will actually require the actual airplanes to fly. But Michael was no fool.

The chair moved to the front and beamed three customised Gulf Stream 55-Seater planes. "Say hello to our new planes."

These will carry our international guests, and if not in use, we have a wet lease arrangement with Sahara Africa Airlines to cover their routes.

The meeting ended after that, but three people remained in the room. Michael, Timothy and Steward.

"Gentlemen, we are going to have a formal human trafficking business. We will have three categories; willing participants who will be our assets and will work overseas meeting at most two high-profile men per night for USD 5900. The sharing ratio shall be 40% for the girls and 60% for Native Investments. The agreement with the girls shall be for a period of 5 years and for this, we require girls who are virgins and with no tattoos, nose rings or visible scars. For those who have met men before, we will make an assessment on a case by case basis."

There was no objection to that. The second layer was for beautiful girls who were to be recruited under the guise that they will be working in the cruise ship and airlines as hostess. These were to be airlifted and sent to forced sexual slavery but allowed to send money back home, and forced to send videos showing that they were well taken care of and that life was going on well. These would meet at least 5 clients per night for USD 399 per client. Tips were to be theirs.

The third and final layer was local sex slavery, where girls would be kidnapped and used for a week, meeting as many as 20 men per night before they are released or killed.

And so it was, the first week saw 150 first-level being dispatched and started their night life. 75 of the second level were treated modestly, but due to the demand for sex services, the rate went up, and this prompted an increase in their expected number of sexual encounters.

The local brothel project took some time to take off, but in the process, instead of kidnapping, Timothy tried a trick, and it worked. He would go out to places like Greencroft , Five Avenue, and offer guaranteed clients at the agreed rates. This turned out to be a better deal. And so it was.

The numbers for the first month after all the costs of VISA processing came to USD 590 000. This pleased Michael, and he wanted more.

There were rumors of girls missing but subsequently, each missing girl would call home saying they were ok. They were even sending money back home. The police was concerned about this trend but did not do much but kept their suspicions.

The Zimbabwe Republic Police, a revered police service in the world ,known for its special skills, decided to get down to investigate the disappearance and subsequent emergence of these girls in foreign land, with only videos being sent home. Alarm bells were sent to INTERPOL and AFRIPOL.

One officer once vocalised his suspicions about Native Investments, but he was silenced and ended up dying in mysterious circumstances in the three weeks that followed.

#

One Thursday morning in the summer of October, a wave of pharmacies were opened selling end-to-end products. This was another project that Native Investments had embarked on. The Pharmacies were 24 Hour and sold mainly cocaine, fentanyl, and other related high-potency drugs. The youth had a code used when one wanted drugs. The pharmacies also sold prescription drugs as OTC, which usually happened at night when the Medical Controls Administration would not have dispatched the officers.

This business was highly formalised and the police could not understand where the drugs were coming from. They raided the streets but they could not find anything.

The following Monday, there were at least 22 cases of girls missing, one girl had escaped and among the 22, 2 girls were of British origin. No further information was shared. The list of suspects kept growing by the day. While the relations between Zimbabwe and the UK were cordial, there was still tension over the isolation of Zimbabwe from the Commonwealth. The UK had maintained economic sanctions on several key leaders in Zimbabwe.

Chapter 11

It is a Wednesday on the 5th of October 2024, Charles Mandi left the offices of Borrowdale Town Council. He moved to the nearby upmarket restaurant. He was due to meet Timothy, the head of operations at Native Investments. Charles was a council employee working as a janitor, his position, though seemingly low, it allowed him unrestricted access to the highest offices of Chief Engineer, Director of Housing, the Finance Director, Estates Manager, the Chamber Secretary, the Town Clerk, and even the office of the mayor himself, his Worship Councilor Machiridza.

Timothy had arrived an hour ago and his three boys were looking to check if Charles Mandi had not been tailed.

"Charles, Charles my man, how have you been?" Timothy opened the discussion before Charles could sit down.

"What's up my man? I hope you are not the one responsible for the disappearance of the girls. I hear you guys are now into anything and everything these days," Charles commented.

His comments seemed to have disconcerted Timothy but in an attempt to dismiss them, he laughed out so loudly, attracting the attention of the nearby tables.

They both laughed, and the waiter who was standing close by could not help but catch on the vibe, though she was not aware what it was they were laughing about.

They placed the orders and when the waiter had left them, Charles was the first to speak.

"So what brings you here Timothy?" Charles spoke with so much authority and firmness that surprised Timothy. I suppose the fact that he speaks or witnesses top leaders at a council speaking with authority, he may have caught the vibes or the proximity to power had made him arrogant. Whatever the case, there was no time to focus on that, yet ignoring the man's boldness in a transaction-making process was foolhardy.

"We need you to sign an agreement of sale for a land measuring 22 hectares and backdate this agreement to the previous administration at the council. You are to forge a council resolution dated any day in the year 2019. Forge an agreement with all relevant approval signatories that existed at that time. If you are in doubt, you need to go to the council minutes, you will find details of who existed around that time. There will be requirements for a direct sale without going to tender. A condonation from the procurement regulation with no objection from the Minister of Local Government, is all that we have," Timothy explained.

"You are very greedy, and I like that in a man. Especially a business partner, What's in it for me?" Charles asked without wasting time.

Timothy was stunned that a janitor could speak to him in such a manner, but that was not the reason for the meeting. "We will give you 20% of the land acquired plus a fully constructed house."

Charles looked at him in disbelief. "Don't waste my time, I don't do real estate man, only cash transactions. I live in the now, not these long-term transactions. Anyway, I accept your terms and here is a little change to it, though 20% market value of the proposed land will coast you USD 1.9 million, but mine is valued at a 20% premium. One week from now, we will meet here with all your documents, and you shall be ready to transfer USD 2.28 million into an offshore bank account of my choice.

The next seven days that followed, the two were seated at the same place. Charles was holding onto a folder with some documents, and when he handed them over for review, Timothy looked at him, then slowly looked at the documents, and after some 30 minutes, he was satisfied. He poured some wine and made a toast before paying for what was agreed.

Charles drank the wine in a hurry and immediately started shaking, and an ambulance was called but it was a little too late for him. Native Investment Trust, an NGO serving the underprivileged and orphans took over all the educational needs and all the sustenance for the family left behind. It even offered Charles' wife Jennifer a job as a consultant interviewing the applicants.

Chapter 12

Michael's wife, a beast in bed, overworked him the few nights he slept at home. She had an insatiable appetite. She often teased that if he left her unsatisfied, she would search outside. She had the money and means to do so, the only woman who made him cower and whimper like a puppy. After a night of rigorous activity, he worsened his leg injury. He tried to push through the pain, but it intensified, edging towards unbearable. He trudged forward, trying hard to hide his limp.

He stood in the doorway of the warehouse, his silhouette casting a giant shadow. This warehouse, off Old Mapereke Road, was where the real business went down. Hosted shady deals, hushed whispers and transactions sealed in smoke and shadows. Michael let out a whiff of smoke from his cigar. He glanced around, squinting in the dim light. Only half the overhead lights illuminated the vast space, as that's what Michael preferred. It kept everything in the shadows, quiet and controlled. The low light cut jagged lines across the concrete floor. His shadow, tall and imposing, stretched across the floor swallowing the faint glow. A thin wisp of smoke escaped his lips, rising like a warning, curling in the damp air.

He stepped inside, each footfall calculated. His limp went unnoticed, hidden beneath his slow pace. Every movement had a purpose. Nothing about him looked hasty, yet his presence filled the space. His men were scattered around the warehouse, then stood to attention. Some tossed their phones back into their pockets at lightning speed.

From the far corner, a figure emerged. Her boots clicked on the concrete as she stepped forward, a smirk tugging at the corner of her lips. "Michael," she said, her voice starting smooth, almost silky, like she already knew his next words. "I was starting to think you wouldn't show up."

Michael's eyes remained fixed on the floor. He raised his head with a slow motion that paused time. His eyes traced the empty space ahead of him, weighing its dimensions. At last, he spoke, his voice low and rough as gravel. "You never know with me."

Finally, he met her gaze, his eyes hard. "You always show up when things go south, don't you?"

She raised an eyebrow, not phased, her voice now raspy. "I don't mind a little chaos."

Michael stepped closer, his musky scent filling the space between them. "Chaos is fine, as long as I'm the one who controls it."

"You and your men have created trouble, again," she chuckled shaking her head.

Michael tilted his head slightly, watching her with cold precision. "Trouble? I'm here to clean it up before it gets out of hand."

She raised an eyebrow, amused. "You really think you can tame Mike?"

His eyes flicked to her for a moment, steady and unblinking. He moved forward, his breath warm against her skin and whispered, "I don't intend to tame him. I'm going to make sure he is silenced forever and that you don't make the mess worse, R-o-s-e."

The name landed like a slap, forcing her to look sideways. In an instant, he spun on his heel, eyes already on his men, leaving her with her mouth aghast. Rose shoved the chair beside her back, the metal scraping against the floor with a jarring screech. "Since when did you start giving a damn about danger?"

Her sharp voice hung in the air. Her eyes narrowed, waiting for him to speak, her patience wearing thin with each passing second. Her boots scraped against the ground as she shifted her weight, eyes locked with a fierce intensity. She cracked her knuckles. Her jaw clenched and muscles coiled like a spring ready to snap.

Michael froze, the words she threw at him hanging in the air. Without a second's hesitation, he turned around to face her, his gaze hard and eyes narrowed. "I've always cared about danger, Rose. Just not yours." His voice grew colder and sharper like a blade.

She leaned forward with a straight face, not a hint of fear. "You always say that. But you never stop me."

Michael's closest henchman reached for his shotgun, eyes fixed on Rose, but Michael's hand shot out, stopping him. He turned to her, his voice cold. "This time... I'm not here to stop you." He tapped his cigar aside, the embers fizzling out mid-air. "I am here to make sure it doesn't blow up."

He stopped in front of her, pulling her closer to him. He slammed his lips against hers but she shoved him hard with a force that made him stagger back, his eyes narrowing with fury. The henchmen dotted around the warehouse froze, eyes wide, unsure whether to intervene or not. In a blur, she darted past him with an icy stare till she reached the door. The men remained frozen, waiting for Michael's next move.

Chapter 13

Outside, the engines of approaching vehicles rumbled in the distance, growing louder with each passing second. Minutes dragged on, but the engines only seemed to grow closer, until it felt like they were right outside the building. The roar of heavy trucks shook the concrete, punctuated by the screech of tyres. Michael's men still stood like statues, their eyes glued to the door where Rose had exited. A great calm followed, unsettling in its stillness like the eerie silence before the eye of a cyclone. And then, with a forceful boom, the cyclone's fury hit. The rumble of engines surged again, this time accentuated by the thrum of low powerful motors. SUVs rolled in, their heavy frames groaning under pressure as they approached. The cyclone's eye had matured. The storm was ready to break. Then, as if on cue, the door creaked open. Michael's men barely breathed, every muscle tensed, their fingers hovering over weapons but not yet moving. Their eyes flicked over the warehouse seeking for signs of movement.

Rose stormed in first, her presence cutting through the room. Four beefy men with squared shoulders flanked her, eyes dashing over every inch of the warehouse. They were ready for anything. Rose's gaze swept the room, sharp and quick, sizing up the scene in a heartbeat. The air thickened. The seconds stretched and every muscle in the room tensed, waiting for what came next.

Rose glanced at Michael with a sly grin. "Miss me?" she asked, her lips curling into a smirk.

Michael stood there motionless, a slight twitch at the corner of his mouth, the only sign of acknowledgment. "You took your sweet time," he said, his voice cool.

She stepped closer, her boots clicking like a ticking clock. "I never said I'd give up. You think I'd walk into your den of rats without a plan?"

Michael's eyes narrowed as he scanned the room. He didn't trust her, not even for a second. His men, calm and composed, watched her every move. They'd seen her before, too many times. She was a wild card, and Michael didn't like playing hands with too many unknowns.

"You've got backup. I don't care," Michael said. "Your people know the deal. I don't know why you protect Mike so much."

Her lips curled into a smile, but it didn't reach her eyes. "Is it? Or is this just about your ego, Michael? You've been running this game for years, but you don't know everything."

At that point, Michael took a step forward, his boots scraping against the concrete. His eyes were piercing, unflinching. "You think I don't know what you're up to? I know every corner of this country, every deal. I know who you're working with and I know you're not stupid enough to pull a fast one."

"I'll take care of Detective Mike. He is useful to us, you don't know yet. We need him alive. Agree to my terms. You don't have much choice, do you? I want land. Give me 35% of Greendale and Mabweadziva," she said, pouting but keeping her face straight.

Michael chuckled and threw a sidelong glance at Rose. He took a long drag from his cigar, letting out a funnel of smoke. "That's a dream. Bury it. You will have no stake in my land. What I gave you is enough to feed your pathetic clan," Michael went on, boasting about his control and authority.

"Don't tell me you control everything, crap, because if you did, riot police wouldn't have been unleashed in our backyard. Keep to your lane. And I'll stick to mine. See what happened in Eastview and Greendale?"

Pointing to the four men behind Rose, Michael asked, "Why are these men here?"

"Where else should they be?"

"I like it when you are fiery. So hot Rose."

She shot him a disdainful glance, fully aware that he had dismissed her just like that. As soon as he finished speaking, a noise shattered, a sharp, metallic clang. The sound of a door slamming open echoed through the warehouse. All the men tensed, hands slipping toward their guns. Michael's eyes snapped toward the sound, his pulse quickening. Out from the door, a staggering figure stepped forward. It was one of Michael's men, Steven. His shirt was torn and blood-stained, his eyes wide and frantic.

"Boss... boss," Steven gasped, struggling to catch his breath. 'It's a setup..."

Before Michael could react, the hum of engines revved outside.

"They're coming," Steven said, his voice shaking.

Michael's jaw clenched. His eyes shot back to Rose. "You were never here for a deal, were you?"

She stepped back, raising her hands in mock surrender, but the glint in her eyes was cold. "You never ask the right questions, Michael."

"You set this up, didn't you?" Michael's voice was sharp, his eyes locked on her.

She shrugged nonchalantly, still unfazed by Steven's announcement. "I told you, Mike. You never ask the right questions." Her lips quirked. "Stick to your lane. With all those degrees, they didn't teach you that?"

His hand twitched toward his sidearm, but before he could draw, the warehouse doors banged open. Harsh lights flooded the warehouse as armed men in uniform poured in, dozens, all in black jackets with the same insignia. His men, still frozen in place, exchanged uneasy glances, waiting for Michael's instruction.

One of his men, the ever-reliable Ngolo, came up to him, whispering urgently. "Mike, we're outnumbered. There's no way—"

Michael cut him off with a sharp glance. "Bullshit. We're not backing down. Get ready."

As the first gunshots rang out, Michael's instincts took over. His hand was on his gun, the cold steel familiar in his palm. His men, trained and loyal, dropped into position, moving swiftly to return fire.

His eyes snapped at Rose. "Move," he commanded, jerking his head toward the back exit. "You're coming with me."

She hesitated, then shrugged. "I don't take orders."

"Then you'll stay here and die with your little army. Your choice."

She studied him for a moment. Then, with a sharp nod, she turned and sprinted toward the back door. Michael's men held the line for as long as they could, but he knew it wouldn't be long before the odds tipped against them.

They reached the back exit just as a barrage of gunfire rattled the door behind them. The battle raged, but Michael looked ahead. They had one chance to escape and it was slipping away fast.

Rose glanced at him, her face unreadable. "You really think you can outrun them?"

Michael's eyes were sharp and his expression hard. "I've outrun worse."

She smirked, her lips curling into a dangerous smile. "We'll see."

They moved fast, darting into the bushes behind the warehouse. Michael knew the place too well to need light. No stars, no moon, just a dark August night. Their footsteps hammered the dry grass. He dragged Rose along, gripping her wrist tighter with each step.

"We need a plan," Rose said, panting.

Michael threw her a glance, his breath coming hard. "I don't do plans, sweetie. I survive."

As soon as they emerged onto a clearing, they found Ngolo waiting with a black BMW X7, its engine revving. They heard the screech of tyres, more men in SUVs coming in fast. Michael cursed under his breath.

"Get in the car," he barked, pointing toward the door.

Rose hesitated for a second before she slid into the passenger seat. Michael jumped in, slamming the door shut.

Before they could even drive off, the first round of gunfire slammed into the rear of the car, sending glass shattering into the interior. They sped off, the engine roaring as they raced into the night towards the city centre. Michael's eyes were locked on the road. The light traffic in his direction kept him moving fast.

He raised his middle finger at Rose. "You think this is over?" she asked, her voice barely audible above the screech of the tyres.

Michael's lips curled into a hard smile, though they held no trace of humour. "No. This is just the beginning."

They exchanged a few obscenities until Rose shouted that she could end the chase with a phone call, if he agreed to work with her, not against her. She demanded he agree to her terms. She told him he wasn't invincible after all. He had to make his security stronger. Those were rubber bullets her team had; she was flexing her muscles. Michael cursed and slapped the wheel while she guffawed. He agreed—for now.

"Do you remember when we first met?" she asked, breaking the ensuing silence.

Michael's grip on the wheel tightened, his knuckles aching. A different time. A different place. "I remember," he said, glancing at her. "Two weeks ago. Feels like a lifetime." His foot pressed harder on the accelerator.

Chapter 14

Two weeks earlier, Michael had arrived at Mutorashanga Growth Point to donate $15000 of the $30000 earmarked for a community mushroom project. The full amount would fund a professional-grade setup, complete with climate control systems for optimal growing conditions. But on that day, he brought only $15000, secured in two cash-in-transit (CIT) vehicles. He aimed to show that the money was there, but ready to be transported elsewhere for safekeeping and disbursed as needed. The growth point teemed with activity as throngs of people gathered, fully aware that lunch would be served afterwards. Community leaders graced the occasion with the chief offering his blessing. Plainclothes police provided security for the event. They were tasked to protect Michael, the man of the people, at all costs. But someone of his stature, enemies and opportunists were always on the prowl, waiting.

As expected, the donation concluded with an invitation to lunch. The villagers gathered behind the local store, where a group of women served lunch. Meanwhile, Michael and the community leaders posed for photos, exchanging casual chit-chat. But in a flash, a gang of armed robbers ambushed the CIT vehicles. The police moved fast, but the masked robbers in balaclavas opened fire. Guns blazed. Panic swept through the crowd behind the store. People screamed and scattered in all directions, knocking over chairs in a desperate bid to escape. In that chaotic shootout, Michael stumbled as he tried to take cover, his foot catching on a rock half-hidden in the dirt. He hit the ground hard. His pelvis took the brunt of the impact and pain shot through him. For a moment, he lay there, disoriented.

Now, Michael limped, his pelvic injury flaring with each step. The fall had nearly torn his ligaments and could have resulted in a pelvic fracture, but his strength had kept him from needing surgery. He joked that eating lots of barbecue steak had saved him. At least his kids would love that excuse. His wife, rolling her eyes, would no doubt scold him: "What are you teaching the kids, huh? Can't you say veggies?" He tried to mask the pain, like a wounded bull pretending to be strong in the ring. With every move, he hid the limp from his workers. He had to maintain a face of authority. Any sign of weakness could trigger rebellion in the group.

Michael had planned to recruit Rose and nothing more. She struck the perfect balance of strength and stamina, enough to earn his nod. She came from the initial round-up of girls at Greencroft Shops. Hostile men and a few inexperienced ones harassed the girls, lining them up to inspect them and seize their national identity cards (IDs). The men only retrieved a handful of IDs. With the hassle of replacing IDs, most people guarded them like treasure, stashed safely at home. They were as prized as the Black Pearl, the fabled treasure-laden ship from pirate legends.

During the amateurish round-up, chaos broke out. Alert passersby tipped off the police at Avondale Station, the nearest police station to Greencroft Shops. The operation was foiled, though no arrests were made.

"Did I send boys to do a man's job?" Michael roared, pacing with a subtle limp.

Heavy fast breathing filled the warehouse. His men avoided looking at his legs or his face. Looking at his limp would be like sizing him up, and meeting his eyes would stir his anger. No one wanted to be on Michael's wrong side. He was the rugby forward you never wanted to face, ready to tackle you like a prop charging at the scrum. He never hesitated to pull the trigger if he felt triggered. Of late, his anger flared like it was on steroids, probably a side effect of the pelvic injury medication.

A mischief of mice scurried past empty drums, their frantic movements catching the corner of Michael's eye. They ruffled crumpled papers, then darted off.

"Want to play games?" Michael reached for his pocket. Ngolo jumped to respond.

"No boss. It's the mice. We put traps, but they sense them."

Michael shook his head in slow motion, his glare locking onto his men. "I want every mouse gone today. Clear?" he bellowed in Ngolo's face. He then resumed scolding them about the recent incident with the girls. He laid out a plan that shifted their approach to a willing seller model, focusing on the girls in the Greencroft and Five Avenue areas. From that point on, Timothy took full charge of the operation. However, Michael insisted on inspecting the 'merchandise' first.

All the girls were lined up in single file. He spotted a girl with four fingers on her left hand. Something about her unsettled him. Her look was unnerving, a heaviness he couldn't quite place. She didn't even look up, chewing gum. Michael's patience thinned. What's her name?" Michael asked, pointing at her and looking to Timothy.

He hesitated, glancing at the girl before muttering, "Don't know. Never seen her before," Timothy stammered, caught off-guard.

Michael's eyes narrowed. "Keep an eye on her," he murmured, turning on his heel.

"That's a limp? Ask me yourself," she snapped, her raspy beer-strewn voice slicing through the air, to his shock.

Michael, undermined in front of the girls and his men, rushed toward her. He raised his hand to slap her, then stopped mid-air his anger simmering. He turned and headed to his office, gesturing for Timothy to follow him. The warehouse had a small office tucked in the back. All shady shenanigans were conducted away from his business premises. He had a reputation to protect.

After talking with Timothy, Michael figured out the girl was Rose, a 29-year- black belt and clothing runner, buying from China and Turkey to sell locally. But her real money came from escort services and other short-term stints. That's how she got entangled in the round-up. She'd been lounging around at the shops.

With all that detail, Michael's face lit up. He sent for her. When she arrived in his office, she flat-out told him she wasn't complying with anything. The fieriness in her eyes and tone intrigued him even more. He leaned forward in his chair and spoke with her in a calm voice. After a few gentle exchanges, he ordered Timothy to take her off the list. She was a special one to him. That fiery look. The charisma. The nerve. The disdain. The attitude. The attraction. The silent provocation. She was fierce. A challenge he could use. A fox. Michael nodded at Timothy. "Leave us," the door clicked shut.

Chapter 15

Olivia, daughter of Londiwe, never forgave betrayal. Her life had always been marred by betrayal. It wasn't about the abandonment after her mother's death or being split from her siblings and shipped off to relatives like unwanted luggage. It was the relentless cruelty she faced at her aunt's house in Highlands, Harare, where luxury came at a cost. A cost forever measured in emotional and physical scars. Her aunt's house was a fortress. Security everywhere. A place where affection was scarce and discipline ruled. Her aunt's presence hovered like a dark cloud, even in her absence. A woman with eyes sharp enough to spot a speck of dust from miles away. She demanded perfection, bellowing instructions daily. Olivia's cousins? Free to do as they pleased, playing on Xbox, PlayStation, or chatting on their phones. But Olivia? She was the one forced to shoulder the menial work of the house, under 24-hour surveillance, every move scrutinised.

Her aunt, a woman of wealth and pride, ran her home like a military camp. She was as cold as the marble floors Olivia polished, and as unforgiving as the two-metre perimeter walls that surrounded her. Every day was a battle to survive in her house where nothing could be earned through kindness. Her aunt was meticulous in her control. She made Olivia play with the dogs, cats, even the odd rabbit and those two peacocks or any pet she could find. Olivia was terrified of peacocks, but she had to overcome her fear for the sake of her own survival. Aunty's insistence on pets wasn't out of kindness but another way to keep her in line. The animals were nothing more than tools in her aunt's twisted version of discipline. "Get the animals to play with you," her aunt would order. "Show them some love." And Olivia, reluctant, would sit on the floor, fingers tugging at their fur, knowing any sign of disinterest would bring punishment. Pets were distractions, to keep her in place. Protection and discipline were all that Olivia knew. The only thing her aunt believed in was toughness. There was no space for warmth. Love had been discarded the day her husband left.

While Olivia's cousins lived freely, she bore the brunt of her aunt's rules. She was the one who had to endure the pinch of the cold floor, where she slept each night, even as the air in Harare grew bitter with the chill of winter. Years of sleeping on it had left her numb, both physically and emotionally. The cold seeped into her bones, but it wasn't the worst part. The worst part was knowing she had a bed in her room but was never allowed to lie on it. Not even a pillow to rest her head. Only the floor. And the cameras. She never understood why she had to suffer. Over time, her body weakened. Her skin grew pale and flaky. But her aunt ignored it all. It wasn't enough to sleep on the floor, she had to do it in the coldest part of the house, under the watchful eyes of security cameras. She was never free.

One particular event cemented her fate: the death of Buju, the bulldog. Buju, a large, muscular English bulldog with a scarred snout and soulful eyes, had the look of a fighter. His broad chest and stocky frame were imposing, but his gentle gaze suggested he carried the weight of Olivia's aunt's memories. Buju represented more than just a pet. He sat deep in her heart, symbolising her lost love. Her estranged husband had bought Buju as a gift to her on their last wedding anniversary together. His leash had a diamond pendant, small but elegant enough to catch the eye without being too flashy, with their initials engraved on it. The aunt had always treated him with tenderness reserved only for the man who abandoned her. His gruff demeanour and silent loyalty reminded her of the husband who had left years ago. A man she could never forget, no matter how much time passed. But when Olivia's aunt, still in Sun City, near Johannesburg, learnt about Buju's death via video call, the fury was immediate. She had been told during her daily check-in, a call to see him, that Buju had been killed in a hit-and-run.

Buju's death was a tragedy, yes, but in Olivia's world, such incidents invited severe punishment. It was the gardener's responsibility to look after Buju and all the pets. In fact, only Buju had a name. That's how important he was. When the accident occurred, Olivia wasn't the one watching him, but it didn't matter. Her aunt's voice boomed when she returned from Sun City. The gardener stood frozen, guilt and fear written on his face. But Olivia was the scapegoat. It felt like the ground had shaken beneath Olivia's feet. Her aunt's wrath was uncontainable. No explanation could calm her.

"You—." Her aunt's eyes were flames, "This is on you!"

Olivia didn't even get a second to explain. Her punishment was swift and merciless. She would eat nothing but dinner for an entire week. No water. No snacks. Not even an ounce of sympathy. A week of empty stomach and silent tears. The cold May nights made her shiver, but it was the emptiness inside her that stung the most. The emptiness of not being enough. The emptiness of being an orphan, thrown to relatives like an old bag and treated like a rag. In that one week, her body had withered away. She was a girl left with little more than memories of what could have been, and the harsh reality of what was. The gardener, who was too scared of his master's wrath to intervene, could only watch in helpless sympathy. That's when she ran away.

Chapter 16

Now, Olivia was no longer the same innocent girl who had slept on the cold floor in Highlands. It would have been better if she'd been made to stay in the workers' cottage. At least then, she wouldn't have been forced to see how different her life was from her aunt's children. But then again, if visitors saw her there, they'd have reprimanded her aunt. Her aunt was vile and strategic like that. But Olivia, at 35, had become someone else. A woman driven by a strong desire for retribution. She became her brother Michael's protégé, with him teaching her the tools of the trade. But Olivia had her ulterior motives, ones she kept hidden deep within her heart. The years of torment, years of rejection, had forged her into something unforgiving. She was no longer a victim. She was a predator. The hunted had become the hunter.

She had spent years building a network of trust, hiring people who she thought would stand by her when the time came. She surrounded herself with loyal henchmen, people she trusted to carry out the most crucial tasks and Jack led her team. Via mutual agreement, she and Michael resolved to work separately with each focusing on their own areas while complementing the other's strengths. She had her luxury spa, Paradise Spa, for high-end clientele. Then her logistics company, Famba Ltd, coordinated all the transport requirements for Native Investments, key government institutions and a range of top private clients. Whether it was securing freight for classified deals, managing intricate supply chains or providing last-minute deliveries, Famba was the go-to place for seamless logistics. The company was known for efficiency and reliability, able to adapt to any request no matter the scale. Even the prevailing forex crisis didn't affect its operations. Famba Ltd controlled the Beira Corridor, managing the Beira–Harare pipeline for both oil imports and exports. It also led major gas and solar projects across Southern Africa and East Africa. And, Jack was a key man in all these operations. He knew well enough that loyalty meant everything to Olivia. It brought them close. Some people rumoured that their relationship went beyond business and overlapped into romantic escapades. The loss of her parents in her formative years broke her belief in happily-ever-after. She was only six. That tragic memory had shattered her belief in fairy tales, in love that lasted. There were no happily-ever-afters in her world, only harsh realities. She envisioned that the loss of a partner brought unparalleled pain. It wasn't only the loss of her parents that had broken her. After witnessing her uncle leave her aunt in a brutal act of neglect, she vowed to remain single. She had learnt that lesson the hard way. The pain was a bitter reminder that love wasn't worth the cost. She had sworn she'd never let anyone close. The idea of trusting another with your heart, of depending on someone, had always been impossible for her. Yet, she found companionship in Jack.

For nearly five years, her personal fitness trainer was there to entirely pleasure her whenever she wanted, after an intense workout session. They had time for thrilling private steamy sessions. The trainer's touch, once electrifying, had become mechanical over time. What had once been exciting was now empty. She needed more than mere physical pleasure. Finally, she realised he was too shallow to match her depth. Along came Jack. Her long-standing business partner and father of five.

Jack moved with precision in business and in bed. He always did. His intellect was unmatched. He offered the depth and reasoning she had longed for, matching her own in ways her trainer never could. The kind of man who operated with efficiency, making sure everything ran smoothly. Ensuring she felt comforted and safe. Always. The trusted partner. The man behind the curtain.

But today, Olivia had been betrayed.

She stared at the message on her phone. Olivia's fingers clenched around the phone, the edges digging into her skin as her whole body tensed. Betrayal. It stung like a knife through her ribs, quick and sharp. The words were simple, but they twisted in her gut. The room was quiet except for the hum of the air conditioning. But to Olivia, the silence was deafening. She stood still as stone, eyes scanning the message again. Jack. It couldn't be real. But it was. Her jaw tightened. She grabbed her black leather coat, slipping it on with the practiced ease of someone who had long ago learnt how to move when things fell apart. The betrayal was fresh, but it wasn't unfamiliar. She'd felt this pain before, buried deep in her chest where it festered. It was a wound that never fully healed. Trauma.

Someone she had trusted had turned against her, sold her out. This betrayal was worse than any she had endured in her childhood. It resurfaced the hurt she had buried long ago when she ran away after Buju's death. Her hand shot into a fist, ombre stiletto nails digging into her palm. This wasn't the same helpless girl from Highlands. She'd learnt long ago how to protect herself, and she'd make sure no one ever undermined her again. She dialled Michael's number. When he answered, she snapped, "Tell me you didn't know about this!"

Chapter 17

Jack was still breathing deeply, blood dripping onto the concrete floor. He was tied to the chair on all limbs. His eyes darted between Rose and Olivia, who was now standing off to the side, watching with an unnerving calm. He wanted to speak, to apologise, to make her understand. But there was no redemption. Not now. Not anymore. Game over. His actions had sealed his fate and he had underestimated the extent of her wrath. The consequences of his betrayal were more severe than he'd ever imagined. Olivia's hatred was palpable, but it wasn't the fear of losing her that hurt most. It was knowing he could never fix what he had destroyed, her trust. It took years to build but it all shattered in seconds. Worse, dying at her hands felt more real than any apology he could offer.

His hands trembled, straining against the ropes that held him to the cold metal chair. His breath came in shallow, labored gasps, sweat beading on his forehead. Fear. The seconds stretched on. With each breath, he struggled to hold onto the last bit of control—his mind. No escape. You reap what you sow. The nylon ropes dug into his skin, his limbs numb from their harrowing hold. But nothing compared to the suffocating pressure of not knowing how Olivia had found out. She would never tell him. An inkling tugged at him that she might have suspected him for a while. How else could this be explained? What could have triggered this nightmare?

Olivia's jaw tightened. Betrayal ripped through her, every cell screaming in hate. Jack.

She wanted to rip Jack apart with a chainsaw. It howled in her hands, its roar deafening but Rose grabbed her wrists behind her, forcing the saw to the side. With a grunt, she wrenched it from Olivia's grasp, letting it fall to the ground with a heavy thud. Tears welled up in Olivia's eyes as she stood there, shaking. She was oblivious to the muddy mess on her face as thick layers of foundation washed off. Her breath hitched and a choked sob escaped. She threw him a cold look, her eyes like daggers.

Seeing her like that, Jack bowed his head, unable to look at her. He could hear her hurt in every sniff and deep breath she took and the sigh that turned into a whistle.

Olivia never cried.

Whether happy or sad, her rough upbringing had toughened her. She had cried when she was six at her mother's funeral. Michael had hugged her and reassured her that he shall be there for her, no matter what life brought. Then, she cried all those lonely nights at her aunt's house. And now, Jack made her cry. How cursed was the man who could make her shed tears of sorrow!

Rose whispered that Olivia should keep focus. "Move fast and get Timothy to pay, too. After all, they were in cahoots."

Olivia pulled a shotgun and pointed it at Jack's head, wiping her tears away with a careless wave. "The only reason I'm not pulling the trigger is because of your five kids. I am ruthless, but not heartless. I suffered as a kid, and I'll be damned if I let your kids suffer the way I did. But you…" she tightened her finger on the trigger.

"But you, I'm giving you 24 hours to leave Zimbabwe. Alone. Your family stays. You send them money, I don't care. But you don't see them. Any silly moves, and you know what I'll do."

Jack nodded. Powerless. Any word from his mouth could fuel her anger. His greed had overtaken him when he offered Timothy intel on Olivia's Paradise Spa empire's expansion bid. That meant Native Investments could anonymously auction and take over the company. Olivia and her brother Michael had always worked as complementary forces, never direct competition. But Jack had betrayed her by going to Timothy, making a hostile takeover possible. For Timothy, it meant more money, more favour from Michael and a 5% stake in the new empire. For Jack, it was the price of keeping up with his wife's extravagant lifestyle. She always wanted more. A gleaming Range Rover Autobiography, Christian Louboutin heels and exclusive vacations to the French Riviera. No matter what he gave her, she always demanded more. PDO threads for her sagging jawline followed by PRP facials for glowing skin. Her fanatic obsession with perfection never ended. A vain, senseless slay queen who flaunted her apparent wealth on social media. An influencer worshipping at the altar of status, attention and validation. A social media influencer for a depraved generation. A socialite who demanded more than he could ever give her, with kids he'd do anything for. His struggle to maintain a 5-star life clouded his judgment, pushing him to make a deal that would destroy everything Olivia had built. Let alone, her trust.

Jack's actions weren't only about business. Olivia's spa empire, like many similar enterprises, served purposes beyond luxury treatments. It was a front. Her brother, the community role model, had his hands in illicit dealings. He laundered money through her legitimate business. The cash-only transactions, the spa's profits and inflated expenses were all part of the scheme. And blinded by greed and desperation for his flashy wife's sake, Jack had unknowingly dug his own grave. Six feet. His life is buried. No mercy.

Olivia's hands clenched. What angered her most was not only the betrayal, but the way Jack had undermined everything she had fought for. He knew her story. Her struggles. Her desires. Her aspirations. Her bond with her brother. She had other siblings, but Michael was life's gift to her. Above all, he knew what loyalty, love and betrayal meant to her. This shady deal would alienate her from her brother, the one person she trusted the most. It was the greatest form of betrayal. Unscrupulous. It was unforgivable. Her childhood trauma had taught her to never believe in love again and to never trust again. And yet, she had allowed Jack into her life. A man she had trusted, one she'd let into her life after vowing never to let anyone in again. He had to pay. He had to feel the burden of his actions for the rest of his life.

Jack's body shuddered as Olivia's eyes locked onto him. She signalled her men to drag him outside and into the car. She knew he loved children, Jack had always wanted many kids enough to form a football team. It was the one thing he cared about most aside from himself. And now, that would be his punishment. He would never be able to father another child again, artificially or otherwise. Olivia ordered that he be castrated. The cost of loyalty. The pain of betrayal. His betrayal would cost him everything. He would never see his kids again either.

Chapter 18

An orange hue set over the skyline, throwing a warm glow across her office walls. Olivia stood by the window, eyes scanning the parking lot. Cars trickled out. The water fountain danced in colours from the dying light. Then, her brother pulled into the lot.

Olivia had dealt with Jack's betrayal. His punishment shook even her. But now, standing alone in the silence, she missed him. But she had to move on.

The spa empire she'd worked so hard to build was at risk. That hostile takeover had been set in motion despite everything she'd done to prevent it. Timothy had been the main player but it was Jack who had initiated the deal. She had opened her life to him and trusted him completely. Now, that trust lay in ruins after the betrayal. Her anger had driven her to extremes. After having Jack castrated, she even considered keeping his scrotum as a twisted memento. But the doctor refused, citing health risks even in a sterilised environment. Some things couldn't be kept. She had to keep the memory of knowing his punishment was forever. Castration.

Five days later, the doctor's refusal still haunted her. The twisted impulse to keep Jack's scrotum felt like a cruel act of justice. It was a way to hold on to the punishment she'd delivered him. Jack's betrayal had reopened old scars, and maybe keeping a piece of him was the only way to regain control over the pain.

Her childhood trauma had resurfaced like a jagged scar. Long-buried horrors emerged. For a moment, Olivia wondered if she had become as cold and ruthless as her aunt. Could she ever open up again? Should she? Could she still rely on Michael, the only other person she'd ever trusted?.

A knock at the door snapped her out of her quiet moment.

"Open up, Liv. We need to talk," Michael's voice came from the other side.

#

Olivia and Michael muttered about Timothy's involvement in the scandal with Jack. Michael promised to clean the mess by all means and protect her business. However, the sudden ring of Olivia's phone interrupted the moment. She glanced at it, her business instincts kicking in. Eve's name flashed across the screen. She picked it up in a flash.

"Talk to me," she said, her tone shifting instantly to the businesswoman she was born to be.

"We've got a problem," Eve said on the other end. "It's that influencer again, Xo. She is a big name in the wellness space. Claims she had a terrible experience at the spa. Her reel's gone viral on all socials."

Olivia's hand tightened around her phone. "Details."

"She's saying we gave her horrible service. Says the facial last Monday left her skin irritated and the massage was so amateurish it only increased her stress. Also claims we botched her microblading, saying she looks like Mary Poppins with those thick dark brows. Other socialites are chiming in her favour. And of course, the 'Name and Shame' hashtag is blowing up."

Olivia's eyes narrowed. A crisis. And a public one at that. "I'll handle it."

She stood, straightening her magenta dress, her eyes locking with Michael's. He knew that look. She was about to take control. No words were needed.

"I've got to go," she said, her voice sharp. "You will retract the deal, won't you? Then Timothy."

Michael nodded, his jaw tightening. A silent confirmation, that's all she needed.

#

A disgruntled influencer with a platform could ruin her reputation. The world of luxury spas was cutthroat. She wasn't about to let one bitter client drag her reputation down and ruin everything she'd worked for. Perhaps it was time to pray. To repent. First Jack and now this. A catalogue of disasters. A series of unfortunate events. Fight or flight. Die hard or die trying.

Olivia's PR team would need to work fast. And so would her security team. Where treats failed, threats always worked. Michael had trained her well. The influencer might think she had the upper hand, but Olivia had been through worse. She knew how to turn a problem into an opportunity, how to control the narrative before it went ballistic.

"We're going to put out a statement," Olivia said as she entered her small warehouse, her voice calm and sharp. "But no apologies. We don't back down from this. If she wants attention, we'll give her something to keep her awake 24/7."

Eve raised an eyebrow. "What's on your mind?"

Olivia smiled, a sharp glint in her eyes. "By the end of tomorrow, she'll be the one apologising."

She leaned against the stacked pallets of supplies, eyes scanning the screen in front of her. The influencer's post spread like wildfire. With every passing minute, the situation worsened. No time to waste.

Eve paced in the background, her anxiety palpable. "We're getting hit on all fronts, boss. Instagram, X, TikTok, and even her YouTube. She's hosting a live on Facebook tonight. The comments are turning into a full-on war against us."

Olivia took a deep breath steeling herself. She had faced worse than a disgruntled influencer. This wasn't only about a bad review. It was about maintaining control over her empire. She had built Paradise Spa from the ground up and no entitled influencer was going to bring her brand down with a few hashtags.

"Do we have all the details on this lunatic?" Olivia said in a calm but authoritative voice.

Eve handed over a tablet with the influencer's account open. "Her real name is Monica Meyrick. Big following in wellness and beauty, and she's known for being outspoken. She's claiming the spa's service was bullshit. Also, we should pay her dermatologist's bills. She says we're all about the money and not the customer. The guys sent her intel to your phone."

Olivia nodded and scrolled through the initial post, her jaw tightening. "So, it's a direct attack on our reputation." She rested her arm on the pallets.

"First thing," she said, her voice cool. "I need a statement from PR. But no apologies. No grovelling. We're not in the wrong here. She's a broke ass trying to make a name and some cash off us."

Eve blinked, surprised by the confidence in her boss's tone. "But she's got over four million followers. That's no small thing. That kind of influence can make or break us."

Olivia let out a small laugh, biting her lower lip. "Exactly. Which is why we're turning this around to our advantage. They don't call me Liv for nothing."

Meanwhile, in the heart of the Paradise Spa empire, Olivia wasn't only facing a disgruntled customer, she was tackling a business challenge. One that, as Michael would put it, needed to be 'squashed before it turns into a liability.'

"Get me Xo's manager," Olivia ordered. "She's looking for a fight. She'll get one. My way. Not the kind she expects."

Michael had taught her an important lesson about real estate. It was more than buying properties, it was about controlling the space. He always said, "He who controls the narrative, controls the market." Olivia had learnt the same rule applied to public perception.

Half an hour later, Olivia sat with a few of her trusted PR team members.

"We've drafted a response," the team leader said, handing her an iPad. "It's a standard apology, acknowledging her dissatisfaction and offering a complimentary treatment of her choice."

Olivia glanced at the iPad but pushed it aside. "No. We're not apologizing. She doesn't get to dictate our story."

The room fell silent. They were used to Olivia's assertiveness, but this was different. She was ready to use every tool in her arsenal.

"We need to get ahead of this," Olivia continued in an icy sharp voice.

"We'll offer her something, but only on our terms. Reach out to her manager—an exclusive deal. Paid endorsement, but we control the whole thing. We'll put her in a wellness campaign that fits our brand, got that, but we call the shots. She gets the payout, but we owe her. That intel from security? No. I want all the dirt, past deals, scandals, everything. We'll remind her who's in charge. And when we're done with her…"

One of her team members added, "We drop her." Olivia's lips curled into a cold smile. "Exactly."

Eve's eyes widened. "You're flipping the situation, I see."

Olivia's smirk deepened. "When the going gets tough, the tough get creative. Don't try this at home."

"Empty vessels make a lot of noise. She wants to make noise. We'll make it louder. We'll spin her into our web and turn her into our food, whether she likes it or not," Olivia said in a stone-cold voice. "A well-timed press release, a few high-profile events and just enough whispers behind the scenes to make her look like she's chasing clout. In this business, perception is everything."

"And what if she refuses?" Eve asked.

Olivia leaned forward, eyes narrowing. "Then we do what Michael would do: we bring her down by all means. Her credibility. Her brand. Her audience. We get people talking, not just about her, but about her involvement with us. If she wants to play dirty, we'll give her a mud pool."

Later that evening, Olivia stood in front of a glass wall in her study, staring out at the treetops. The glass wall reflected her world, exposed, yet under her control. As the night sky settled in, moonlight bathed the distant city in a soft, cold spark mirroring the fire in her eyes. Even more, the breeze in Colne Valley always refreshed her especially after dealing with the PR mess earlier.

Michael's ruthless approach to real estate had always been about seizing control. To him, the world was one giant chunk of land to buy, sell and flip whichever way he pleased. All he saw was land, endless land. Olivia knew the lesson by heart and she'd twisted it to fit the brutal world of the spa business. The luxury spa business was ruthless, dominated by devious church leaders and moguls, with wealthy clients using it for status. But Olivia didn't need to tear people down to win, she only needed to rewrite the rules. And when she had to, she tore them apart.

The next morning, her response was ready. The statement would be bold. No apology, but a clear message that Paradise Spa controlled the situation. Xo's claims would be buried under a powerful PR push, forcing the influencer with no choice but to accept the partnership or lose everything.

By the time Olivia received the call from Xo's manager, the influencer's hold had already shaken. She'd seen the press statement, the media coverage and how her followers were beginning to question her, making memes in response. Olivia, daughter of Londiwe, never backed down. Those days ended the day she ran away from her aunt.

Xo's manager hesitated. Then knowing they were cornered, he gave in. The deal was sealed. Olivia had taken her first step.

Chapter 19

Once a month, Michael invited Olivia to his house. His family adored seeing 'Aunty Liv' but that day, the house was unusually quiet for a Sunday afternoon. Michael sat at the kitchen table with newspapers spread before him. His eyes were fixed on the classifieds and obituaries, staring into oblivion. Across from him, Olivia swiped through photos on her Google Drive, her fingers brushing the screen of her laptop. The images passed by quickly, but her fingers froze when she saw photos of her late parents.

"We used to hate Sundays," Olivia remarked, clearing her throat. She glanced up at Michael, a half-smile tugging at her lips. "You remember?"

Michael didn't look up from his papers but let out a soft chuckle. "Yeah, you were always the one whining about it. You couldn't stand going back to Highlands with Aunt Cruella, a Miss Havisham type straight out of Great Expectations, dripping with venom and grudges."

Olivia leaned back in her recliner, tapping a staccato rhythm against her latte cup. "Guess I never really appreciated the quiet. Didn't even know what it was like to have a real family back then. Not like this."

Michael looked at her with endearing eyes. "We were all we had. And still are. The others settled well in Kwekwe. Lucky them. The outskirts did them good. I wonder what Mum and Dad would say if they were still around."

Olivia locked eyes with her brother. For the first time after the Michael Junior incident, she let her guard down. The walls she kept up, the ones that shielded her from any sign of weakness seemed to dissolve in that moment.

"You ever miss them?" she asked in a murmur.

Michael's eyes hardened but lit up in an instant. "I never stop thinking about them. Kizito. Londiwe. But they're gone. And we are here now."

Olivia nodded, swallowing the lump in her throat. "I know. Just...sometimes I wonder how life would have turned out if we had a normal upbringing. Did we miss anything? People admire you. They love you for all the work you do. But the real you—"

Michael stood up, his oak chair scraping against the floor. He paused, looking down at her, his voice softer than usual. "Normal doesn't exist for us. But we're doing fine. It's just us, kid."

She forced a small smile. She understood. They'd built their empires from nothing. But sometimes, the price of power was higher than she wanted to admit than the surface.

#

Michael's office at Native Investments was just as imposing as he was, a modern fortress of glass, steel, and black leather. At home, he was soft as wool. The sharp edges of his office were replaced by the comforting warmth of soft rugs and mismatched pastel cushions. His laughter came easily. His gestures were gentle and the imposing man from Native Investments transformed into a father who leaned down to tie his child's shoelaces. At home, he was a family man, not the CEO of Native Investments.

Laughter spilled out of the kitchen, blending with the clatter of dishes and the quiet voice of the HomePod. It was playing gentle old-school R&B, filling the room with soulful melodies just the way his wife, Candice, liked it. Michael's eyes softened the moment he heard it. He slid through the door, wrapping his arms around his wife from behind. She giggled, leaning her head on his shoulder before moving away to resume dinner preparation. At the sink, Candice washed tomatoes. Their two kids argued over setting the table. Meanwhile, Michael stood back, smiling, out of his element but content.

"I get the fork!" Michael Junior, his son, shouted, his hands full of cutlery.

"No, I do!" Jasmine, his daughter, retorted with a pout.

Michael leaned against the doorframe, watching them with a rare smile playing at the corners of his lips. "Hey, hey," he called out, his voice low but warm. "What's all this fighting? You two are on the same team, remember?"

His wife glanced over her shoulder, giving him a soft smile. "I swear, you put them in a room with a plate and they'll argue over who gets the biggest piece of food." She wiped her hands on her apron, stepping over to him. "How was your day, honey?"

Michael's eyes lit up as he wrapped an arm around her waist, pulling her close. "You know, the usual. Deals, pressure. Same old." He kissed the top of her head, something he rarely did in front of anyone else. "But now it's better."

She smiled up at him, her eyes filled with affection. "I can tell. You've got that look about you."

Michael Junior and Jasmine, sensing the sudden shift in the room, stopped their arguing and looked up at their father with wide eyes.

"Daddy, what's for dinner?" Michael Junior asked, grinning up at him.

Michael chuckled, his tough demeanour slipping for a second. "You'll see in a minute. Go set the table, both of you. Quick."

#

Every day, Candice ensured the maid wrapped up work by 5 PM and went to her cottage. From that point on, she insisted on handling household duties herself as the lady of the house. Once her husband returned home, she wanted him all to herself. Candice was all about undistracted family time, just him, the kids and her. During the day, she didn't mind, but evenings were sacred and reserved for their closeness. And in bed, she owned him. The one place and time he let someone else run things. Elsewhere and everywhere, he commanded the show. But now, with the house quiet and the kids scattering to finish their chores, Michael's fingers tightened around his glass of whiskey, the amber liquid swirling in a piano-like rhythm. His eyes drifted over the table, unfocused. A muscle in his jaw twitched, and he exhaled a sharp sigh. His wife noticed the slump of his shoulders. He always sat up straight. Unless…

Candice sauntered towards him, wiping her hands on a hand towel. She had seen this before. The way he suddenly withdrew, pulled inside himself like something was gnawing at him. He had been quieter of late, harder to read. But it was too erratic to establish a pattern. Businesswise, Michael was still on top of his game. Conquering it all like Julius Caesar.

"Everything okay, babe?" Candice asked in a low tone, her eyes squinting as she leaned against the kitchen island, watching him. "You've been off lately."

Michael looked into his whiskey, avoiding eye contact. He couldn't. "Yeah," he mumbled, his voice rough and distant. "It's nothing, really."

His words were hollow. Michael knew she wasn't buying it, but he wasn't ready to explain. His phone buzzed on the table startling him. He grabbed it and gave a quick swipe. Another business lead, Alvaro the Portuguese. His gut twisted.

Candice watched him for a long moment, her brow furrowed. She knew this wasn't about the kids, his siblings, the house or the dinner table. "You can't keep pretending everything's fine," she murmured.

Michael looked up and for a fleeting second, his eyes entreated her, breaking the mask he wore so well. But the look vanished as soon as it appeared.

"I'm fine," he said, quieter now, but cold. "You know me. I'll handle it."

Michael sighed, running a hand through his hair. "It's just...work. You know how it is. The pressure is always there."

Candice's hand reached out to his left hand, giving it a gentle squeeze. "I know. I can see it in you. I'm always here for you. For better or worse. You know, they say if you marry a drunkard, it's for life," she chuckled.

Michael pulled his wife closer, leaning forward to kiss her forehead. No words, only the comforting quiet connection between them. In moments like that, he found peace. With Candice, he was more than the man who ruled the world, he was wholly himself. The empire, the power, the danger, none of it mattered. Only the two of them existed. And, in that quiet, simple peace, Michael had everything he needed.

"Let's just enjoy tonight, okay?" Candice whispered nibbling at his ears. "For us. For the kids."

Michael nodded, his eyes closing as he savoured the warmth of her breath and the soft brush of her nose against his neck.

Chapter 20

Being a Saturday, Michael stood in the centre of his living room, admiring his latest portrait, a celebration of his honorary doctorate award. He watched his son, Michael Junior, wrestle with his younger sister, Jasmine. Some peace and quiet while he let Timothy handle any trouble over the weekend. The dust had settled for a while and no issues in the news, the police or angry residents. Besides, he always showed up as the saviour. Create a problem to solve it and you turn up as the hero. It was one of his trademark moves. They all loved him. In fact, it was perfect time for a family holiday.

With a few phone calls to his team, he arranged a trip to Australia. Candice and the kids danced with joy at the idea of going to the Melbourne Cup, which Michael always attended solo. Normally, the school term would've kept the kids from such travels, but this year, they'd been spoiled. Michael had arranged for their early release from school, and with the end of term still a month away, the school arranged online lessons. Besides, it would only be a 10-day excursion before flying back to Zimbabwe.

Each year, with school in full swing, Candice stayed behind to mind the kids. It didn't bother her much, though. She always looked forward to the Abu Dhabi Grand Prix. The roar of the engines sent her adrenaline into overdrive. The Melbourne Cup took place on the first Tuesday of November, as it did every year. But the excitement didn't end there. The entire week was filled with races and festivities leading up to the finale race. Three weeks later, the Abu Dhabi Grand Prix took over the last weekend of the month. And that's when the real excitement kicked in for Candice, hearing engines roaring. Both offered the thrill of noise, but the roar of car engines ignited her inner child in a way galloping hooves never could.

#

The opulence of the final race was matched only by the warmth of the applause as Michael stepped onto the podium. Draped in a bespoke navy Bottega Veneta suit, he flashed a disarming smile as he handed a cheque to the event organiser. Michael donated a staggering amount to the Melbourne Cup's charity, an act of generosity set to dominate the headlines. No fanfare, only the quiet power of his presence.

"Racing isn't just about horses," Michael declared, his voice a rich baritone that commanded attention. "It's about community. It's about giving back."

The crowd erupted into applause, captivated by the image of a generous supporter of both the arts and sport. Yet only those closest to Michael knew the truth. All his philanthropic gestures were a smokescreen, a grand performance to launder his reputation in the public eye. Charity disguised his bloodstained business.

The racecourse buzzed with energy the following day, November 7th. The Melbourne Cup, known as 'the race that stops a nation,' was in full swing. The sun beat down on Flemington Racecourse, the energy of the Melbourne Cup pulsating through the air. Michael sat in his private VIP box, a glass of scotch in hand, scanning the chaotic elegance of the scene below. To the world, this was his stage, an arena where power and luxury converged. To Michael, the Melbourne Cup wasn't just a race; it was a manifestation dream. A dream for brighter days, the kind he was denied when his father was killed. Murdered by thugs. It was the life he wished he could've had, playing with horses, living on a stud. With all his money and influence, he poured both his wealth and time into the Cup.

For several months after his parents' death, Michael's primary school teacher took him to the local community hall, where old films were often shown. One, in particular, *The Horse and His Buddy*, was repeated frequently. It became his favourite. The storyline was about Vince's father, an Australian bookmaker whose life had been entangled in the world of horse racing. It was a dangerous yet thrilling industry that fuelled both his fortunes and his demons. His success in the betting world inspired a young Vince to pursue horse breeding, where he could control the sport from the inside. Horse racing ran in Vince's veins, an undeniable connection to the man he once idolised, even as he sought to surpass him.

For Michael, the film was more than a story. It reflected his struggles. Back then, it was the thrill of the track and the intoxicating roar of the crowd that drew him in. But as he had watched Vince's rise in the movie, he now saw the cost of such ambition. It took a toll on those who were willing to sacrifice everything for success. It reminded him of how far he'd come and the ruthless price he'd paid to get there. No going back.

From the vantage point of the private VIP box, Michael sipped his scotch, eyes fixed on the track below. This year, Michael had more riding on the race than ever before. His favorite to win, a sleek chestnut stallion named Ruby Inferno, was neck-and-neck with a fierce rival.

"Come on, boy," Michael murmured under his breath. His fists tightened as the race reached its fever pitch. The crowd's roar lit the racecourse. Ruby Inferno was a thoroughbred he'd backed with millions, both clean and not. A victory would cement his power, further legitimising his empire in the eyes of investors and the public alike.

The race continued and Michael leaned forward, his normally composed posture slipping. Ruby Inferno was a beauty on the track, his movements sleek and controlled. He reflected the precision Michael demanded in every aspect of his life. The chestnut stallion surged ahead, matching Michael's expectations. The crowd roared causing a wave of energy that seemed to lift the horse forward.

But as Michael's eyes tracked Ruby Inferno, a ripple of unease spread through him. Across the grandstands, in a sea of jubilant spectators, a figure caught his attention. Mina Santoro. He passed through the throngs of spectators with calculated poise. A man in a tailored cobalt coat. When he reached his seat, he turned deliberately to face Michael. Michael's jaw clenched, his scotch glass trembling in his hand. He forced a neutral expression. A thousand questions. How had Mina Santoro escaped the clutches of the Thailand prison system? A bribe? A tunnel? A trail of bodies left behind? The timing!

As the final stretch of the race unfolded, Michael barely registered the outcome. His world had tilted on its axis, his carefully controlled facade threatened by the ghost of a foe he thought defeated.

"Find out how he's here. And who let him out," he hissed in his built-in mic to Timothy. For security and strategic reasons, they sat in different private booths.

Mina didn't belong there. His gaze locked with Michael's again. For a moment, the roar of the crowd faded, replaced by the pounding of Michael's heart. The enemy he had neutralised was back. Taunting him in a place where Michael felt untouchable.

Every instinct told him to act, but he was frozen. With his role at the cup, he had to watch till the end.

After the race, Michael descended into the private room allocated to him beneath the stands. He found Timothy waiting and pacing about.

"You saw him," Michael said, his voice low and venomous.

"Yes, boss," Timothy replied, in a whisper. "I don't know how, but—"

"You don't know?" Michael slammed his fist onto the table, sending papers and a half-empty glass of wine scattering. "Do you think I pay you for nothing?"

Timothy fidgeted with an unease that caught Michael's eye. Michael's paranoia flared. "Unless...you already knew." His voice was quieter now.

"Boss, you know I'd never—."

Before Timothy could finish, Michael grabbed him by the lapels and shoved him against the wall. "Never?" Michael growled. "Never? That man was supposed to rot in prison, even dead by now. Do you understand what this means? For me? For us?"

Timothy stammered, blood trickling from his lip as Michael's grip tightened. Desperation clawed at the edges of his voice. "I'm on it boss. I'll give you details."

Michael released Timothy, letting him collapse onto the floor. "Mina Santoro. Free." Michael muttered to himself. "I should have killed myself that day. He dies today."

Michael poured himself another drink, the amber liquid catching the light from the window. He gulped his scotch in one mouthful. Timothy nodded, still crumpled on the floor, wiping blood from his upper lip. Michael turned to the surveillance monitors, replaying the footage of the race. He spotted Mina Santoro again, but this time, his attention shifted to the man sitting behind him. A face he couldn't place, but one oddly familiar.

"Mina Santoro," Michael said, his voice steadying. He turned to Timothy, who scrambled to his feet, making calls. "Get my family. Get the jet ready."

Chapter 21

All is well, that ends well. Michael and his family flew to Qatar that same day, November 7th. Mina Santoro's sudden resurgence saw them flee to Qatar. Michael planned to stay in Qatar for a while to figure out Mina's motives. Going back to Zimbabwe could mean walking into a trap. Clarify the target. Eliminate the threat.

Good news for farmers meant bad news for consumers, and vice versa, a common rule of economics. Mina's sudden reappearance meant bad news for Michael, they had to flee. But for Candace, it was also good news. Suddenly, they had an unplanned three-week holiday and the detour meant she could attend the Abu Dhabi Grand Prix. She'd finally enjoy the best of both worlds—the Melbourne Cup and the Grand Prix. Not by choice, but by fate. A twist of fate. A blessing in disguise for Candice. A catastrophic development for Michael. He busied himself with calls, but Candice soon worried about the kids' schooling. She arranged with the school to extend online classes due to 'unforeseen events.' A 10-day trip stretching into weeks. The kids were indifferent but excited to play at Disneyland Abu Dhabi. A quick flight from Qatar, and they'd be there.

Time was of the essence for Michael. Mina Santoro was capable of anything. Whatever had driven him out of prison fuelled his thirst for vengeance. Michael failed to understand how a man sentenced to life imprisonment without parole could be flying around the world, let alone attending sporting events. No doubt, his appearance was well-calculated. Mina Santoro wasn't hiding. He made sure to be seen by Michael, his nemesis. When friends become foes, it's worse than never having been friends at all. Michael's contacts in Phuket informed him that Mina's defense attorney had appealed to the Thai Supreme Court, petitioning for the ruling to be reviewed and citing unconscionable grounds. Even more appalling, the public prosecutor and his counsel were fired for incompetence, sending an innocent man to jail. Mina had played the system. Michael listened to the intel with exaggerated calmness, sitting back in his chair, his fingers tapping on the armrest. After a long pause, he spoke. "How much did he pay the? And how? Man is dead broke."

He was informed that Mina had bribed officials. He paid them 5 million Thai baht each by selling the remote islands north of Phuket, territory once co-owned by him and Mina. Those islands in Phang Nga Bay, like Koh Panyi and Koh Hong, were not only luxury properties; they were the crown jewels of Michael's portfolio. They represented years of hard work, trust and shared ambition between the two men. Leveraging their past business partnership, Mina paid a shady lawyer who exploited their shared history in the luxury resort islands to make his case. The court ruled in Mina Santoro's favour.

Michael's eyes burned with fury. His grip tightened on the phone as he hissed in eerie calmness. "What bull is this?" He squeezed the paper in his hand until it crumpled.

"You weren't informed?" Michael's contact said, almost dismissive. "Your consent wasn't needed for the sale. Big flaw in that contract."

Michael sank into his chair, fingers still tight around the phone. With a slow, wary motion, he rotated, his eyes narrowing and brow furrowing as he faced the window. Unbelievable. Ridiculous.

Damn trust. Damn friendship. No one had outsmarted him like this in years. Not even Dr Chigovanyika.

Michael's gaze hardened as he stared out at the city. He spun the chair back around, brow still furrowed. Mina Santoro and everyone tied to his release had to be terminated. By all means. He made calls to his contacts in Phuket, Koh Panyi and Melbourne. Then, he waited.

#

In his absence, Michael let Timothy run the show. The landmark Monday meeting couldn't be delayed. Timothy led the session with EMA officials, local council members, Chumachavazungu & Partners' lawyers, traditional chiefs from Mashonaland West (Mash West) Province, conveyancers, mining chamber executives and engineers, all packed into the Native Investments boardroom. Despite the heavy presence of stakeholders, the meeting failed to reach quorum, but it proceeded anyway. Native Investments respected no protocol. It was their way or no way. All key players had a generous financial incentive to comply and stay silent.

Within a few minutes, the attendees signed the lease agreements. The Great Dyke passed into Native Investments' hands. Michael's signature, already on the agreements, acted as an unspoken command that compelled everyone else to follow suit. Deal sealed. Native Investments had yet again grabbed land. This time, in a landmark deal along the Great Dyke, stretching up to Lake Kariba. The Great Dyke is a spine-like ridge that stretches over 500 kilometres through the heart of Mash West Province. It's one of the richest geological formations in the world, with extensive platinum and chromium deposits. A fierce battle raged over its mineral wealth between a Chinese company, a Portuguese tycoon only known as Alvaro, Native Investments and three local companies. Native Investments emerged victorious. This deal had the potential to transform the lives of local residents, bringing prosperity to the region. But as always, only a select few elites, the mafia, and the well-connected would see the profits. Meanwhile, bogus Chinese companies dominated the mining operations while local residents languished in poverty. These companies worked in cahoots with corrupt officials, worsening the situation. Worse still, the environmental damage was devastating, with rivers poisoned by toxic runoff and the landscape scarred by excavators.

After the meeting, the men lingered in the foyer chatting. Moments later, a voice called and said that the press conference area had opened. The attendees trickled towards the conference area. Amid the casual chatter, Dr Chigovanyika appeared. His smile stretched across his face, dimples popping, a bit too wide to be genuine. He walked straight to Timothy without hesitation, like he belonged there.

Timothy's eyes narrowed. How had Dr Chigovanyika bypassed security? Nobody invited the Doc. Before Timothy could react, Dr Chigovanyika grabbed his hand in a tight grip, almost painful. "Congrats, Timothy," he said, stretching the words, his voice smooth but hollow.

Timothy stayed calm, looking nonchalant as the eyes in the room remained on him. Why was his enemy here celebrating with him? The Doc leaned in, lowering his voice.

"Tonight," the doctor murmured, his grip tightening, eyes glinting brighter than his smile, "it'll be like a stray bullet. She won't see it coming. Neither will the police."

"What are you talking about?" Timothy hissed between gritted teeth.

"Helen. Your wife. The one with an octopus tattoo on her right thigh."

Timothy's Adam's apple bobbed but he forced himself to remain calm. He'd learnt to hide his emotions during his army enlistment, which he never completed due to illness.

"You—"

A voice called through the door, summoning Timothy to the conference. The final call. Everyone else was already waiting. The timing. He walked to the podium with a stealth that hid everything that had transpired with the Doc. Was his wife safe?

#

A packed press conference room buzzed with reporters, cameras flashing. After the usual formalities, Timothy announced that his boss and owner of Native Investments, Michael, was overseas on business. He explained that Michael couldn't attend the live stream due to a meeting that clashed with the event and played a video message from him. Timothy then provided a brief background on the deal.

Long ago, the government struggled with deforestation. Now, they faced depleting mountains, with some Chinese companies harvesting entire mountains, extracting the soil for export and further processing. Entire mountains were vanishing. Worse, wetlands were being encroached upon for development, with every available space transformed into buildings.

During the presser, journalists raised these concerns. Timothy reassured the public, emphasising that Native Investments, led by Michael, a true visionary, had always prioritised both people and the environment. His work proved that. Timothy also explained that they had consulted with EMA, environmental experts and even received the green light from traditional leaders. He stressed Native Investments' commitment to sustainable mining, land reclamation and job creation to uplift Mash West and the entire country. He acknowledged that the land belonged to the ancestors and was a legacy to be preserved and passed down.

Unlike other companies, Native Investments promised to employ people along the Great Dyke through responsible practices, not exploit them. They would put an end to the tragic paradox of locals living in proximity to wealth, yet unable to benefit from it. Timothy wrapped up the presser, framing the landmark deal as a win for the people of Mash West Province.

Applause filled the room, and cameras flashed. Timothy, eager to finish, only posed for one photo. He noticed the Doc eyeing him with an uncanny smile. The Doc was a moving chess master who could never be underestimated. Always unassuming. Always plotting. He never played by the rules, he made his own. He could turn anyone into a pawn. And when you least expected it, he'd say checkmate. In that instant, the Doc slipped out. Timothy reached for his phone to call his wife and security team but a strange SMS flashed. The sender was a mere string of numbers: 1-2-3-4.

The SMS read: *"Tomorrow's headline in the Sunday Paper: 'Corruption and bloodshed at the heart of Native Investments. Timothy exposes his boss, Michael, amid a heated internal power struggle.' Reply 1 to agree to a settlement, and I won't send it to the media. Reply 2 to have it sent to the media. You have 30 seconds."*

No time to call his wife or security. The room was still filled with reporters and cameras flashing everywhere. Timothy stayed calm, but his pulse raced. His fingers trembled. As he tapped the screen to reply, a strange symbol appeared: a loading circle followed by an error. The entire chat vanished. He checked the network, a strong signal. The texts? Gone. Like they'd never existed.

Sweat beaded on his forehead. He swore under his breath. He called his wife, but it went to voicemail. Then he phoned his security team, who informed him she wasn't at home. Checking her location, he saw she was at Paradise Spa, the home of luxury treats.

Timothy slipped away from the crowd, besides, the business of the day was over. He dialed his wife again. Was the doctor behind the unnerving message?. Trying to cause a rift with his boss? That malicious fake headline, where had it come from? Timothy had racked up plenty of enemies since working for Michael. His phone rang, and his heart skipped a beat. It was his wife. Relief.

"Hi, honey," his wife's bubbly voice came through.

"The heck?" Timothy fumed. "Why weren't you picking up?."

"Aww, honey I feel so fresh. You really miss me that much?

"Leave the spa. Now. Meet me at 105. You hear?"

"But honey, my brows are—"

Timothy cut her off, his frustration growing. "You want to die, Helen?"

His voice became sharper and urgent. She understood in that instant he was dead serious. No banter, no flirting. His words were terse, laced with danger. One moment, she was being pampered at the spa, getting her brows done: the next, a blow to the face. She held the phone tighter, heart pounding as she listened to the rest of his instructions.

Timothy sped in his car. His phone rang again. An unknown number. The hairs on the back of his neck stood as he answered, voice low. "What now?"

Michael bellowed on the other end, "What's this bull? You saw the text, right? Who's behind it?."

"I'm on it. But my wife's in danger—"

"Think I care about your wife? I pay you, not her."

The line cut abruptly. Timothy's heart hammered. His wife, in danger. The SMS. Michael, his boss. Every second mattered. He floored the accelerator. His phone buzzed again, this time, a text from Helen. One line.

"I will always love you."

His stomach wrenched. He slapped the steering wheel and cursed aloud. Was it the Doc? Or had someone else reached her first? His grip tightened on the wheel as he sped along Seventh Street. His phone rang again. He answered in a hurry.

The caller spoke, "Wrong move."

The line went dead before Timothy could reply. The sound of tyres screeching behind him prickled his skin, making him shiver.

Someone was following him.

Chapter 22

Michael was as fast as a chameleon when it came to reacting to his opponents, he was razor-sharp intelligent, his heart was deep waters, even those who had spent time with him were kept guessing as to who he really was. There was no pattern, no logic or theory, some say there was madness in his methods others believe that there were methods in his Madness.

He was a master tactician, though he loved family, but he was like Elon Musk whose famous quote about money and power he had internalised and it goes like, "Give me money, give me power, I don't care." Michael had learnt that there was no better loyalty than Loyalty to money and Power. Money and power was the ultimate goal of life. Everything that he did, the church, business all the relationships he had with people were aimed at getting money and power.

Michael had all cell phones of his associates, family member and adversaries bugged, he was aware of their movements, all the phone calls they made and what's app messages they sent each other. All the email correspondence and any other online platforms they used to communicate. Jack was Michael's asset and now that he was far from Olivia, Michael Realised that Jack knew a little too much and while he appreciated the punishment given to Jack, he considered the punishment cruel, gruesome meant to inflict maximum pain and fear to the team members, however a punishment like that left Jack with nothing to lose, he was a dead man practically. A man with no balls, can't father a child and can't have access to his family, the man had nothing to lose. He was a blank cheque, a blank page and Michael figured such a man could climb a mountain barefoot if there was need.

Michael met Jack in Sandton, South Africa. Jack was milling around the shopping mall, admiring the statue of Nelson Mandela and the surrounding modern designs. He was still reeling from the emotional pain of his two boys being taken out by a woman and the idea that Olivia could be having them. Jack was handsome with a six pack, he was two meters and change high his lips were a real draw, it maybe that Olivia was attracted by that. Jack could forgive the sins committed against him by Olivia, he had vowed to work hard and avenge for his two boys. The physical pain was still lingering. At times he was suicidal, and he did not expect such a painful ending.

Michael arrived at Daviel Restaurant, and they both ordered some eats which they rarely touched.

"How are you holding my man?" Mike enquired

"Nigga don't waste my fucken time, why do you come all the fucken way with your shitty ass to ask me such a stupid question? What's with your family?" Jack responded, he was shaking and had his first clenched the entire time.

Michael found it interesting and in a normal day he would have done worse things to him but he had to admit that after meeting Jack in person, the punishment chosen by Olivia was the most painful one, far from children and can't make more and the dick can't stand up anymore, what a shame, what a waste.

"Jack, listen here, I was about to say you have such balls to speak to me like that, but then I realised that my sister, a girl, outsmarted you and in the end she took them away. So let me just say you have such guts, but then where do they come from for a man without balls? Let's just say you are an angry loser wondering in the dark, confused and needing help, yet when it comes, you are too blinded to see it."

Jack responded with such a sharp mouth. "Well, you seem to forget one thing, that I have valuable information which can take Olivia down. I have much more damaging information on your little sister. I need a good deal here Michael." Jack frothed with anger as he spoke. Mike had a rare smile, which quickly faded.

"You know what if I told you that I have exactly what you need?" Michael responded casually and without much effort to it.

"Michael, you are too playful hey, what do you have, spit it," Jack said immediately almost cutting him short.

"Don't show weakness in a transaction my dear, you will get a bad deal," Michael snapped.

"I did not come to see you here for a lecture. I stay close to Wits and the University of Johannesburg. I could have gone there if I needed lectures, and many others are offering online, so I may not have needed to go anywhere to do that." Jack responded to Michael, who was almost standing up, but when he realised that he was getting out of control he sat down.

"What if I tell you that I can give you everything that you want in this life. What are you willing to do for me?" Michael asked with little effort to convince Jack.

"I want my two balls back, then we will talk," Jack answered in a hurry.

"You know that's not possible if they were destroyed, you are such a jerk you know that? So you are concerned about being able to fuck again instead of your family?" Michael answered back almost immediately.

"Michael what's a man if he cannot fuck? The purpose of a man, all his accomplishments culminate into fucking," Jack said with a smirk on his face.

Michael looked at him then looked sideways before he answered back.

"What if I told you that the doctor has saved your two balls and you have to be in surgery in the next 24 hours? There is a 50% chance you will make it alive due to underlying conditions and a 25% chance of success in the procedure?" Michael remarked.

The next 24 hours that followed saw Michael paying USD 80,000 for the testicle transplant, which was a delicate procedure. His Blood pressure was high, so they delayed till he had stabilised. At 14:50 on a Tuesday, the operation was given the green light.

The operation took one hour and thirty minutes. When the operation was over, Jack was put in the HD ward as his blood pressure was too high, he was being monitored.

Upon hearing that the surgery was a success, Michael left instructions to the doctors to contact him personally and never to allow any visitation. The doctors followed the instructions to the letter.

Michael had a meeting with one of his staff members who was working undercover and they agreed that Jack was supposed to be replaced immediately, and the plan was in motion. Stone was to hit now when Olivia was at her weakest.

Chapter 23

That day, Michael arrived at the Robert Mugabe International Airport, his team of elders from his Healing and Deliverance Church was there to receive him. They all took turns to kneel before the man of God and bless his name.

"Well come, man of God. We are blessed to have you amongst us. We praise God for giving us such a wonderful man like you," Elder Thomas remarked.

Michael touched their heads and prayed for them, they all got up and brought gifts of money ranging from USD 1000 to USD 3500 per person.

A convoy of six Toyota GD6s spade off to central town in Zimbabwe's Capital City Harare. There were billboards everywhere concerning tonight's event, it was a great night, a night of bliss. According to the program the Man of god was supposed to heal the sick. People had come from countries such as Kenya, Malawi, South Africa , Mozambique, and Botswana. It was promising to be a great night.

Michael was a man of perfection, he had been following all the developments, having video calls to see the decorations. The deco was top-notch designed by artificial intelligence and fitted by a team from China. It came at a cost of USD 105000 with the exclusion of costs and accommodation.

A quick meeting was held at the venue and all was set. First praise and worship was to start at 6 pm and was to go on for two hours till 8 pm, during this time people were arriving and taking places and immediately joining the singing. The event was being beamed live at the church's TV channel, i.e. the Native TV from 8 pm.

There was a new team of praise and worship. In between there was a TV show where the Elders were being interviewed live regarding the programme for the night and what people should expect from the man of God when he finally steps up on the stage.

"Elder Manenge, can you tell us what we are to expect from today's service. What are the key events that will take place tonight?" asked Brother Norman Nyika a church presenter at Native TV. He was beaming with confidence and excitement from the event ahead and the preparations had given him the reason to do so.

"Thank you Brother Norman for having me at Native Christian TV. We are blessed to have our father Papa Michael. A man sent by God to deliver his people from the bondage of slavery, poverty and sickness," Elder Manenge responded with emphasis and great conviction displayed all over his face.

Brother Norman was not convinced and he sought to have a different answer.

"Elder, perhaps you could elaborate more, we have people who have come all the way from different countries. What are they to expect in the sense that they can carry hope with them?"

Elder Manenge gave the mike to Deaconess Joyce.

"We bless our man of God Papa Michael and I greet you all in the name of Jesus. Tonight is going to be a wonderful night, the lame shall walk, the blind shall receive sight, the sick shall receive healing, the deaf shall hear, the barren shall receive the blessing of bearing children, the weak shall be strengthened, *maskerebosaka,*"

Deaconess Joyce responded and by the time she finished she was standing and raising the other hand. An atmosphere of "holiness" filled the room.

There were callers who called in to express their anticipation of tonight's programme and all of them were happy and looking forward to the church service.

Elder Manzini was given the mic.

"Hallelujah," he started. "Tonight we expect to have a great night, and I am here to remind you that you should be prepared to come and give to God. The work of God needs to continue spreading to all corners of the country and to all nations as it is commanded to us. Bring your best gift, bring the sacrificial money, not small money, if you bring small money, you will receive small blessings. Those that give in abundance shall reap in abundance, they shall have title deeds and legacy of wealth to pass on to the next generation, their names shall be written in heaven, and God shall remember their great work."

At exactly 11:45 pm, there was a familiar song being sung and boom Michael walked in, flanked by six men, and three of them went to the foot of the stage while three were positioned at strategic places to protect the man of God.

There was silence as Elder Pasi walked to the stage, He asked the people to stand as he introduced the Reverend doctor. Michael.

"Tonight I have the overwhelming task for which I prayed to God for strength and wisdom. That is to introduce the man that God spoke to and sent to us .He is here to deliver us, to prosper us, and to bring hope to us. I stand here to introduce our Papa, Dr, Reverend and man of God Michael Paradzai. A businessman par excellence, a giver, a man of God, full of the spirit, a humble yet mighty and powerful, advisor to nations and a healer. BSc, MSC,

DSC, DD and PHD, a professor in the making. A man full of greatness, truthful, pure and upright before God. Ladies and gentlemen, please put your hands together for our man of God Papa Michael." This was said to wild cheers.

Michael had a piousness about him, his tears were close by, and he frequently broke down when preaching. Some said he meant it, believing that he takes those times to genuinely speak to God and ask for forgiveness for his many sins.

The time for healing came, and this time, three people on wheelchairs were brought before him and he prayed for each of them. They stood up lifting their wheelchair celebrating their healing. There was a moment of praising God, and then a streak of testimonies came through, mikes were distributed and it started. "Papa, when you were praying, I received my healing, I have been suffering from a severe cough, and it stopped there and then." One member testified to wild cheers.

The roving mike in bay C was handed to a woman who started by singing a hymn. "Papa, when you were praying my leg that was born twisted and could not function properly was restored, and now I can walk, I can run, we praise God for you for you are a blessing to us." The confession went on and on, and there was praise and worship after which Michael came back to the stage.

"I am going to pray for the gifts, and the choir will sing for us as the money will be collected," Michael directed.

Chapter 24

It was on a Tuesday morning, a BMW X5 was speeding at 240 km per hour. The police were in hot pursuit, but when they got into rugged terrain, their low-base BMW struggled to navigate the pothole infested Bulawayo-Victoria Falls road. The police signaled that an X5 BMW was being pursued and they needed the Hwange police to intercept the robbers before they could cross the borders into either Namibia, Botswana or Zambia via Kazungula at the Quadripoint.

At exactly 60km peg the car was halted, money bags were taken out and packed into tourist backpacks, the X5 had a light bomb attached to it and the bomb self-detonated after 45 minutes.

There was a tour guide van that had 13 people in it. It was travelling to the mainland, Nyangani mountain to be specific. It was to pass the park at Leopard Rock hotel in three days' time. The robbery had taken place at the Ecological Bank where USD 6.5 million had been taken at gun point and the CIT team did little to resist. It was the cleanest robbery that took place, after the Ecobank robbery where an excess of USD 4 million was taken by a pick-up truck. By value, the city of Bulawayo had become the leading robbery hotspot.

Jack was the leader of the bank robbery team that operated under Michael's order. They used information from corrupt central or commercial bank officials. They would be notified each time an amount above USD 3 million was being transported and the team organised the hit.

The week that followed, Jack and his team walked into the central bank and went to the safe room, knocked and then the team opened the door thinking that it was their colleagues. They pulled out pistols and demanded pure gold. They took a trolley and pulled the 25 bars of pure gold in a sack exiting through the front entrance and left. Jack was repaying Michel for every transaction they had. Jack and his team would get 50%, of the deal was great. Michael had his boys dealing with all the logistics including the use of drones to track trucks. The amount of cash and valuables would be determined by the nature of the entire distance from the ground to the safety precautions. The larger the amount, the easier it was, as the team of CIT would be required to downplay the transaction, treating it as a normal small cash movement.

That night, Jack was in his hotel room at one of top-notch lodges in Nyanga when a woman knocked at his door. "Room service."

Jack had not ordered anything and hence decided to ignore but eventually Olivia opened the door.

"Did you miss me?" Olivia remarked.

"Olivia, what do you want? Let's get to that part and be done?" Jack responded.

"I want my two balls, and you will never hear from me again," Olivia shot back.

"And if I refuse what are the implications?" Jack responded with legs spread, chin up, showing no sign of fear whatsoever.

Olivia looked at him and remarked, "You have to work for me, keep doing what you are doing and remember that I want 10% of the loot from your share which means you and your team will get to enjoy 40% after paying my brother.

The mention of a precise split worried Jack, he had thought that he was ahead of Olivia, but he was not.

Olivia looked at Jack from top to bottom and reached for the door. She closed the door and grabbed him by the balls and while looking at him she yelled, "If I find out that you are fucking me in the sharing of proceeds, I will remove these myself."

Jack looked at Olivia, "Why don't you test them now? The dick is now firmer and crispy, and you will cheat on him if you test it."

Olivia looked at it. It had swelled, and in the end, she kissed Jack on the forehead. "Keep it in the pants, let's do only business. I have a loyal dick waiting for me in the next room, good night." Olivia left.

Chapter 25

Liza Paradzai is a beautiful and intelligent girl. She was Michael Paradzai's second daughter. She was studying for a degree in engineering. She was worried about her father and initially Michael was able to answer her daughter without struggle, but in recent years, he was beginning to struggle to answer her satisfactorily.

She was developing and she was revisiting all the answers she was given when she was still young. One particular subject she was concerned about was the alignment of persons. She wanted to understand if her father had multiple personality disorder. So she booked a session with the psychologist asking the mother to pay as she indicated she had questions about life.

Her appointment was at 10 am with Dr. Mwanza, a well-known family psychologist.

"Good morning Liza. It's great to see you in person," Dr. Mwanza started the conversation.

Liza stretched her hand, offering a firm handshake looking at the doctor straight in the eyes. The doctor immediately took a mental note to remember he could not bullshit her. He was here for a straight talk and she wanted answers to real matters.

"Good morning Dr. Mwanza, How are you doing? I have heard great things about you," Liza responded.

"Doctor what is the alignment of persons and is it possible that one person can have different and multiple personalities?" Liza enquired.

"Liza do you want me to understand the context of your questions or you want me to just answer the questions?" Dr. Mwanza responded rhetorically.

"Doctor, at this point I want you to be assisting me with some answers to the background questions that I have," Liza clarified.

"What is dissociative identity disorder?"

The Doctor took some time to respond, he was trying to start a file in his mind as he was also writing down some notes.

"Dissociative identity disorder (DID), formerly known as multiple personality disorder and split personality disorder, is a mental condition where an individual can have two or more separate identities. These manifest in different situations depending on the circumstances," the doctor explained.

The Dr. Stopped to check if Liza had a question and after a moment of silence he continued.

"Dissociate," means to separate or disconnect or better still to detach from. People with dissociative identity disorder may experience several different personalities, usually referred to as alters. Each identity may have different behaviors, memories, thought patterns or expressions. The identities might have different ethnicities and ways of interacting with their environments," the doctor expanded.

Liza was quiet for a moment, she took a pen and started writing some notes, the doctor attempted to look at the notes but they were written in modern shorthand forcing the doctor to mind his business.

"So tell me about the memories, are these bad memories or good ones?" Liza followed up with another question.

"They differ."

"Ok, so why can't all the memories be in one character or personality?"

"These personalities may take control of your behaviors at different times. Memories may not transfer from one identity to another, which can cause amnesia (gaps in memory). The presence of amnesia is often an important symptom that raises concern for the diagnosis."

"I see, so when you say diagnosis, you mean it's a disease?" Liza narrowed her eyes as she asked.

"It's a condition," Dr. Mwanza clarified.

"What's the impact of DID to a school child and a fully grown person?" Liza enquired further.

The doctor made a few notes before he responded.

"DID interferes with your ability to function in your day-to-day. It can impact your relationships with others and performance at school or work, DID is one of several dissociative disorders. These disorders affect your ability to connect with reality," he elaborated.

"Are there different types of personalities and how can these be noticed?" Liza sought clarity.

"You are onto something aren't you?" Dr. Mwanza asked with a smirk on his face as if to get her to talk about the underlying reason for a set of questions she was asking, but after seeing that the girl was not in the mood, he went straight to answering the question.

"Anyway, there are two types (or forms) of DID. Possessive and non-possessive. Possessive Identities present as if an outside being or spirit took control of your body (loss of control). You might speak or act differently in a way that's obvious to others. It's an unwanted identity, and the personality switch is involuntary."

Liza looked at him with a plain face difficult to decode before she responded, "Ok what's the second one?"

"Liza at this point I want you to tell me if you are facing any challenges at home or at school, if you give me that information, I will gladly assist you," he demanded.

"Doctor, I am fine. Can we move to the next one please," she responded showing some signs of frustration building up about being asked what she was going through.

"Non-possessive Identities are less known to others. You might feel a sudden change in your self-identification, as if you're watching yourself in a movie (an "out-of-body" experience) instead of being in control of your speech, emotions or behaviors."

"What are the symptoms of dissociative identity disorder?" Liza quizzed.

"The symptoms of DID include, having at least two identities (personality states). These affect your behavior, memory, self-perception and ways of thinking. Amnesia or gaps in memory regarding daily activities, personal information and traumatic events. Different identities affect your ability to function in social situations at work, home or school."

"What causes dissociative identity disorder?" Liza asked again.

"Look Liza, I am afraid I am going to have to insist that you let me in on what it is we are looking for?" Dr. Mwanza replied but

Liza did not see the need to upset the momentum of the progress that had been made so far.

"Very well DID causes may include, stressful experiences such as trauma and abuse. These events typically happen during childhood. DID is a way for you to distance or detach yourself from the trauma. DID symptoms may trigger (happen suddenly) after removing yourself from a stressful or traumatic environment (like moving homes). Close relatives or your children reaching the age at which you experienced trauma. A recent traumatic or stressful experience (like a vehicle accident). An abuser passing away or experiencing a life-threatening illness," he explained.

"Then they both need therapy, I was sure of it and this is confirmed."

"Who are these people?" Dr. Mwanza asked. At that point Liza realised that she had been shouting, she had thought that she was talking to herself but it turns out she was too loud.

It's not important doctor, we are almost done here.

"What are the complications of dissociative identity disorder? What are the risk factors for dissociative identity disorder?" Liza asked as she fixed her eyes on him creating an uncomfortable, eyeball to eyeball connection."

"You're at an increased risk of suicide with DID. More than 70% of people diagnosed with DID attempt suicide or practice self-injury behaviors. You may be more at risk of developing DID if you experienced, physical abuse, sexual abuse or neglect," Dr. Mwanza responded.

"Dr. Mwanza I would like to thank you so much for the clarity with which you have answered the questions. I am now knowledgeable," Liza said thanking the doctor and rising up instantly to leave, giving no chance to Dr. Mwanza to respond or ask questions.

In the end he managed to say, "My pleasure I am here to help if you need anything at all."

Liza called her father immediately after the interview and asked him and his sister Olivia to meet. This request was treated with urgency as Liza had not made such a request before.

At 3 pm Michael and Olivia were seated.

"Good afternoon Daddy, afternoon aunty, I will go straight to the point here. I think you two need to help. Based on your upbringing you need to see a psychologist before it's too late, here is hoping it's not too late," Liza remarked.

Olivia and Michael looked at each other before Olivia moved closer to Liza to offer support and help her say whatever that was on her heart.

"Baby girl, what's going on here. What are you saying? Talk to me now," Olivia pleaded.

"Aunty please do not be upset," she was in tears. "I have learnt of how you both grew up and I have a reason to believe that you went through rough treatment and you never managed to get any form of professional help. You may be at risk of self-destruction behaviour, you may have already been on a self-distractive path unknowingly," Liza continued.

Michael was shocked, he wanted to be tough and hard but it was too late. The voice of Liza, his favorite girl, had cut through and pierced his stainless fireproof layers of protection. Mike and Olivia broke down, each was sure the child knew what she was talking about.

In the end, both Olivia and Michael agreed to go for therapy. It was also agreed that Liza would sit in the sessions and all the 30 hours of therapy were agreed to be supervised by her. This was a condition that Liza gave for joining Native Investments after school or else she would leave for overseas.

Chapter 26

Olivia was mourning the separation from Jack and the circumstances, she had mixed feelings about the whole issue. Olivia had not been in a relationship that started from nowhere, it had always been an overlapping of situations. She never had anyone of her own. Olivia's upbringing had activated her masculine side, and all along she had struggled to act like a woman. The constant harassment and ill-treatment created a complex woman with strong attributes of a man. She had learnt to think like a man, endure hardship and put others ahead of herself. She grew up in luxury yet she never got a chance to enjoy anything. She was not a commoner but not a rich person either. Somewhere in between, a dangerous place to be.

Olivia was nestled on a couch at the DeCasami in Borrowdale when a man stood right in front of her. A tall, handsome man with six-pack and a protuberant chest. The kind that ordinarily put Olivia off, she had a preference, slim, quiet and polite ones.

"Good afternoon ma'am, my name is Stone," the man started.

Olivia looked at the man, and in an instant she wanted to slap him. She did not want the idea of a man disrupting her peace, any intrusion into her personal space was always met with a disproportionate response.

"And who are you?" Olivia replied pulling her glasses peeping at the man over the sunglasses, making a very limited effort to hide her disdain and lack of respect for the man.

The man did little to acknowledge the demeanor, deciding to focus on the subject matter at hand.

"I am a man of many talents hey," Stone responded, treating the matter lightly and ignoring the fact that he was talking to Olivia, a household name, a woman that many would not dare talk to let alone cross paths with. Yet here he was, a daring one.

Olivia wanted to rise up and perhaps spit on Stone. Shout at him or even slap him, but there was something about Stone. He was different, he was nice, gentle, yet steady, and showed no sign of fear. Stone addressed Olivia like some ordinary girl. Ignoring all the layers of complexity, deciding to focus solely on the girl.

"You must have serious balls of steel to come up to me and start a conversation with me here," Olivia responded.

"You are right ma'am, I have serious balls, and I'm telling you, the moment I saw you, my balls started dying to make babies with you. See, you are the kind of a woman that I like to take home and make love to every single day and put you to bed. I bet you are fertile, I want four children. Soon we will be going on vacation, the six of us. What do you say we get married?"

Upon hearing this, Olivia was boiling with anger. She wanted to explode but then again she decided that it was a great day and she wanted to enjoy the show.

Olivia looked up, sizing up Stone and looking for words to say, but she could not figure out how to deal with this situation. It was a unique situation. She had not had a man come to her speaking so baldly like that.

"I suppose you know what you are looking for, and you have found that in me?" Olivia enquired shifting her gaze and tapping the sunglasses in.

"Yes ma'am, I know who you are, you can hide behind all the thick layers of toughness, dismissive language and a scary stare but that won't scare me a bit," Stone responded almost immediately.

There was an awkward silence as both parties were probably trying to calculate their moves.

Stone was the first to break the silence.

"People speak of you as if you are a god, yet all I see here with my two eyes is flesh and blood, and no more god than the couch you are sitting on. Some say they see a monster or a beast, perhaps that's what you want them to see but I see beyond that."

Olivia was stunned, she was not sure how to respond to Stone's boldness and gentle yet firm grip on her conversation meant that another strong response was no longer possible. She had to try to be soft, but that was not her area. She was a hardened bitch who did not give a shit about anything. She was fired, cut, and forged in the furnaces of hell and did not give a damn. But there was something different here.

Olivia looked at Stone and looked aside, and looked at him again as if he were some kind of child trying to decide whether or not to trust him.

"Sit down," she finally said.

"Tell me, Stone, what do you want from me? Look at me and tell me what you see in me. Give me a reason why I should not break your leg right now and right here," Olivia demanded.

"I am Stone babe girl and that gangster thing doesn't worry me. All I see is a small little girl orphaned and taken to live with an aunt that treated her like shit. We grew up in the same neighbourhood and my father was a friend of your father. We tried several times reaching out to you, but your bitchy shitty ass aunt wouldn't let us get to you," Stone explained.

Olivia looked at him and was again having conflicting emotions, she didn't want to let anyone in and so she had developed a thick skin. But she had to admit that this Stone guy was here to crash her.

Olivia waited for some time, then continued responding to him. "So, you think you can come here with some fabricated story and expect me to buy it? What do you think I am? A fool?" she waved him off, signalling that he should leave but Stone was not going anywhere.

Stone looked at her intently and made a quick smile that quickly disappeared. He got up without saying a word and started walking. He walked into the Spar retail shop, bought a few things, and walked to his car. The moment he opened the door, Olivia entered the car, sat there without saying a word.

They drove into Stone's house in Stone Chart, his house was at number 9b, an upmarket apartment with swimming pool, gym, garden, gazebo, pool table among other things. The place was well kept.

In the house, Stone offered her a drink, she preferred strong drinks but Stone persuaded her to take wine. He made a charcoal-grilled bream sauce and served it with Nakonde rice. Simple meal yet it got to Olivia, perhaps the idea of seeing a man cooking for her made her feel important and she started having ideas about Stone.

They had drinks till Olivia was wasted and could barely walk. Stone took her and laid her on the bed in a separate room.

The following morning, he made breakfast in bed for her and when he entered the room she was up and upset with him.

"Stone, I didn't realise that you are a gentlemen," she commented while stepping into the bath.

"I can scrub your back if you need it, just call me if you need anything," Stone offered, a smirk on his face betrayed him.

Two minutes later, Olivia emerged from the bathroom with nothing but a towel she was holding an underwear and a bra that she had just washed. Stone was trying to figure out what was going on, but he was definitely beaten to it, she had made a move, and he was to respond to that. She came singing a hymn as if she was preparing for choir practice.

She almost passed him, then stopped and yelled.

"Stone, please come and scrub my back, keep your expectations low, and cage him well."

"To which Stone responded with a yes ma'am, duty calls on the morning shift."

Stone followed behind Olivia. He was tense, sweating all of a sudden and hands shaking as he was not sure what to do with this Olivia. Yet he was the one who had invited her.

Olivia was submerged in the giant bath tab with Radox form bath frothing to the top. Stone wore the scrubbing gloves in his hands he tried to reach out to Olivia but she moved to the centre of the tab. It became evident that she wanted him in the tab. He removed his clothes and stepped into the tub. At first, he was standing behind her till he was behind her. Opening his legs, he gently pulled her back close to him, it was a back and stomach contact. Stone started scrubbing her and when she raised her hand to signal that it was enough, Stone decided to massage her.

"You are such a woman, you know," Stone opined.

To which he go a flat, "Thanks. I was not aware that I was a woman."

Stone realised why she probably was not married and possibly not dating anyone.

"So what's your favourite colour?" Stone enquired.

Olivia turned her head managing to take a quick glance at Stone before responding to him, while her razor-sharp eyes were looking at him. "Really Stone, I am not a young girl that you should ask such questions. How about intelligent questions?."

"Very well then," Stone held his head down as if admitting defeat before he responded. "In avionics, why is it that the B2 Spirit Bomber Sratoforest will fly unnoticed by radar when flying in enemy territories carrying bombing or recognisance missions?"

Olivia was stunned and in the end she managed to say, "My favourite colour is pink."

Stone tickled Olivia, who initially did not want to laugh, she cried with anger, mixed with sincere happiness and these were surreptitiously turned into laughter. The scars of the past were not that easy to shake off.

Stone started making small circles on Olivia's back. She responded with ease and it was such a beautiful thing to watch. Stone had managed to tame the beast, the monster. He took some soap and applied on Olivia's breast, she twisted and breathed heavily. Stone moved his hands gently, making circles on the nipples. His hands were warm, soft and gentle. He was quiet, in the background was a distant philharmonic orchestra playing on the technics 16 piece suite, a rare jewel.

Olivia was burning with the sensation. The electric feeling released from Stone's hands, as she lifted her head in compliance with the commands of the feelings that came with the touch. Olivia wiggled with pleasure, she was feeling hot. She was burning with desire, she wanted a man inside her. She wanted him there and then. She had never been this vulnerable. Stone lifted Olivia from the tub, and took her to the nearest bedroom, but they almost failed to make it to the bed. Stone laid her on the bed skilfully and held her feet with a firm grip. He moved up the legs, holding her with a firm grip as he looked into her eyes. She was seething like an overflowing river. Stone held her by the thighs with both hands and pulled her close to him. She lifted her lower body to receive him but he had other plans. Stone pulled her closer, folding her legs, leaving the velvet happy place facing him.

He skilfully licked her, repeated the process till she was jumping with sensation, but his hands were holding her down. She screamed with pleasure and in an instant her screams were a mixture of pain and pleasure. Stone was inside her, stroking and pumping slowly. She made rhythmic sounds in unison with his movements. Looking down, Stone could not help but feel like a victor, he had done what no man had done. Taming the beast. It was there below him, tamed, helpless, and harmless. It was, ''his'' now and that thought made him erect more and more.

"We will be married in two weeks' time. I will bring people to arrange things here. I will pay for the renovations. Our wedding will be here," she commanded.

Stone realised that indeed Olivia was looking for a man to give her children but clearly he was going to be the ''mother'' of the house while Olivia was to be the ''father'. But Stone did not care, in the end he conceded himself lucky.

Olivia was now spending at least five hours with Stone. She found him irresistible, great company and intelligent yet she still resented how she was swept away but it did not matter at this point.

The following day, they met at Casamia DeCrux. Michael was there before them. When Stone and Olivia arrived, Michael was standing at the entrance, his gaze fixed on the horizon further away.

"Stone, meet my brother Michael and Michael please meet Stone," she stammered to say who he was to her but in the end, she managed to say, "My man".

Stone stepped forward and greeted Michael with a firm handshake, looking him straight in the eyes. The two men kept looking at each other in the eyes, while each tightening the handshake. It was a display of power and for Michael, it was a test of physical strength, one of the many tests that Stone was to go through. The handshake lasted for 30 seconds. Were it not for Olivia who cleared her throat, the two looked like they were determined to continue.

As they were sitting down, Michael looked at Olivia and then Stone trying to size and getting used to the new couple.

"So you are the lucky one, I see you have won my sister's heart?" Michael enquired brimming with confidence and excitement. Yet with a cloud of suspicion hovering over.

"I am lucky and Olivia is privileged to be with me. I am a man of many talents and there is nothing I can't do for her," Stone responded boldly.

Michael was beginning to see what Olivia had told her about Stone being a fearless, bold and arrogant yet gentle in his approach. His humility was unparalleled while his convictions were not negotiable.

"So what do you do Mr Stone?" Michael asked without putting a lot of emphasis on the matter, as if it was a negotiable matter which he had a choice to respond to or to ignore.

Stone looked at Olivia, who had asked the same question yet she was not sure if she understood what Stone was all about.

Stone took some time to answer as if he was making a memory note of all that he did and when he was done, he looked up before he spoke. "I move money from one jurisdiction to another. I work with a network of money movers and daily we move at least USD 5 million up to a USD 1 billion," Stone explained

Olivia cleared her throat and licked her lips in admiration while Michael was trapped in emotional conflict. He was not sure whether to rejoice or to be jealous, but he understood why Stone was a perfect fit in the family. His skills were needed in the family.

"I have USD 3 million I need moved from Zimbabwe to the UK without any paper trail," Michael finally spoke.

"Doing business with an in-law is a bad idea. I know people who can move the money for you, and they are actually cheaper than me," Stone responded almost immediately.

"Come on babe this is my brother. Let's do business among ourselves," Olivia responded trying to persuade Stone.

In a show of loyalty and demonstration of power, Stone agreed to do the transaction much to the amusement of Michael himself. Michael had used guys who had taken him weeks to send money across.

In three weeks the two had wedded and Michael paid for their honeymoon for a month. A year later, Tin and Bob were born, identical twins.

Chapter 27

A new business line had emerged. What started as a mere discussion during a game of pool between Michael and Timothy became a perfect idea. They met at St Agness Café, an upmarket coffee place in Borrowdale, off Peers Road. This is a leafy suburb near Samy Levy's village. Michael was the first to arrive and looked for bugs as he normally does.

Timothy arrived ten minutes later, followed by the criminal lawyer. Nathan Nzarayakura was dubbed a criminal lawyer not because of representing criminal cases but being a lawyer who happens to be a downright criminal himself.

He holds the title for defrauding clients, selling their property, doctoring the deceased will, sand theft of clients' unclaimed trust funds, among many other schemes. Michael could not have chosen a better partner to work with.

"Good afternoon gentlemen. We are pressed for time, we know each other, and I will ask my learned colleague Nzarayakura to lead the discussion," Michael started immediately after people were seated.

"Thank you Michael," Nathan remarked while adjusting his position to make himself comfortable. The smirk on his face betrayed the delight in his heart to discuss such multi-million dollar illicit businesses. He was born to do this. He was a master of the game even the Law and Legal Foundation of Zimbabwe failed to rein him in, as it always proved to be a futile exercise.

"We have an array of revenue streams that we can look at in order to maximise our revenues, and these are as follows," Michael continued.

1. Use an estate agent to manage properties for the diaspora clients. Create "legal battles," with tenants occupying the property. Collect rentals for up to one year, then influence the court to grant the eviction order. By that time the owner will be eager to have access to their property and nothing else. Thus income for 12 months will be ours.

2. The second will be looking for vacant stands. Get the position of the property at the deeds office, change the physical number on the stand, forge a deed and file it at the deeds office. Then after some time file for a lost deed and subsequently name change or sell at that point.

3. Forge deeds for vacant houses. Deploy people who monitor properties in the various upmarket stands. Forge deeds with the assistance of our inside man at the deeds office and sell the property. The idea is to target people who are not known, the unpopular in society.

4. The fourth and final one is open spaces and sports clubs, these are places where councils do not have proper lease registers and title deeds for land. The idea is to create deeds through our colleagues at the deeds office and subdivide them for residential and commercial stands.

After the presentation by Nathan, Michael had to admit that he was dealing with a hardcore criminal. The ease with which Nathan presented the fraudulent matters left everyone in awe. It was quite revealing and very scary. He was capable of stealing from Native Investments that was the first red flag that Michael observed. Secondly Michael did not like the systemic risk that Nathan brought to the team. Native Investments did not want to deal with someone with a tainted image, they needed men and women respected by society for their value. This was meant to keep giving Native Investments some form of credibility and the benefit of doubt.

"I must say that you are a great business partner with unparalleled business acumen. I can see great times ahead, and these are great opportunities." Timothy remarked.

After that, Michael asked to be excused. It was an agreed position that when Timothy commented first, then Michael would not pursue the deal further. Nathan was left with Timothy to finalise the transactions, but the truth of the matter was that the deal was off. Michael did not want businesses with too much paperwork and too many witnesses. Hence, the proposal was not suitable for his business and for his stature.

Nathan left the restaurant with a bounce in his step, beaming with confidence and thinking he had impressed but that was the last time he heard from Mike.

After the meeting, Michael went to visit the sick in hospitals as part of his ministry work. He prayed for the sick, gave blankets to the hospital and food stuffs. The session was captured, televised and posted on Facebook as well as on Native TV. A Christian-based 24-hour gospel channel where prayers, intercessions are done from time to time.

There was a hype and some of the sick claimed to have been healed and woke up from the bed, ready to be discharged. The television had a following of five million people globally, and the numbers had been increasing.

Michael had become a trusted Man of God, yet many who analysed his work simply labelled him a false teacher and a false prophet. But that did not deter many of his followers who did not care what the "pagans" thought of their "papa." To them Michael was God sent and he was their saviour. A man who was created and sent to redeem them and give them hope. Many in his congregation had experienced his grace and blessings.

The man had multiple personalities, and it took those who dwell in the spirit to see it .The man was on fire, and that was the agreement amongst the congregants. His church sold anointing oil for USD 50, wrist bands written WWJD for USD 5 each. Anointed pens for USD 15 for those seeking a breakthrough in their exams, and anointed perfumes and shoes, handbags at a thrice market price. The orders were always not adequate to fulfil the order book.

Chapter 28

Michael arrived in Marondera at 07:45 am. He waited till the council employees were all in. His meeting was with Engineer Mawadze, a well-known engineer. The news that Native Investments wanted to do business with the municipality had spread like veld-fire. With most of the 98 councils, town clerks are taking time to call the Marondera TC to express support and share tips on how to avoid being conned by Native Investments. Native Investments employed all sorts' tactics to get business, mostly dirty ones.

Three days before the meeting, the Engineer had a meeting with the Town Clerk and the Mayor.

"You have had a bad record in promoting investments in this town. All the investments that the department of business development has come up with have been shot down by you or your team. Clearly you are lacking foresight regarding development of this town," the Town Clerk laid out the charges.

The Mayor looked at Engineer Mawadze to see how he was processing things as they weighed in.

"We have been made aware that a well-known investor is coming to invest in our town. See to it that you give them the maximum support they need. We need businesses in this town, and your role is central. We are giving you a warning letter and this is a final warning regarding poor performance in this area."

The Town Clerk handed over the warning letter to the Engineer. He was in shock and was not sure what hit him.

Back home, all was not well as Brian Mawadze was in police custody after the police found him with marijuana in his school bag. The police were alerted by other students, and being an 18-year-old boy, he was locked in and was to appear in court within 48 hours.

As if that was not enough, the Engineer received news that three bulls had been stolen at his farm. He had purchased them at a cost of USD 25,000 each. He was breeding a good breed and was extracting semen for sell for artificial insemination to nearby farmers. A police report was made, and the Engineer was still to go and deal with the matter.

Some fifteen years back, the Engineer once ran over a drunkard, and the matter was concluded with all culpable homicide charges being dropped. The other reason was that no witnesses were found, the only witness who had agreed to testify decided not to. That afternoon fresh murder charges were laid against the Engineer. He was to appear in court in three weeks' time. A former girlfriend had framed the Engineer that he had raped her. The matter had been dismissed, but the Engineer was informed that he was to be notified of the court date to answer to charges of rape.

All these things happened in one week, and the Engineer was sure that someone was doing this to him.

When the date of the meeting came, the Engineer was flanked by his two junior engineers and one senior engineer. That day, he had used public transport after his two wheels, a car radio, and a battery were stolen overnight. Something that had not happened in the past ten years. The night before, the Engineer had been called by the bank to explain a mysterious transfer of USD 25 million from the Caribbean bank.

The Land Baron

In the meeting was Michael himself, Timothy, his right-hand man, and Stone his brother-in-law.

"So good to finally see you Engineer, we have heard great things about you." Michael remarked.

"You have come at a bad time, were it not for the bosses here, I would have taken time off to resolve a number of personal issues that I am going through." The Engineer responded.

"That's so selfless and considerate of you, Native Investment is indebted to you," Michael complimented.

"We have received your proposal, and it has gone through the committee. The proposal has two sections. The first part that relates to the construction of a service station and a business centre, I am afraid that one is on the road servitude, the area is reserved for future road and rail developments. The investment is greatly appreciated, and we are thinking of looking for another spot for the same development if you do not mind," explained the Engineer.

Michael was looking at him intently taking some notes. At some point, two beautiful girls walked into the meeting, their skirts were above the knees. They wore nude colour revealing that they were not wearing any underwear. The two girls were introduced as Tina and Tamara, secretary and administrator at Native Investments. They both sat opposite the Engineer and started taking notes.

The Engineer started repeating himself, failed to follow the discussion line, and in the end, he failed to concentrate as the girls in front of him seriously affected his thinking process.

The second part of the proposal was the development of low-income houses in Cherutombo Extention. This project needed to start as soon as possible, as President Kufahazvinei wanted to achieve it before seeking his next term in Office. The project needed to go to tender but Native Investments had gotten wind of it and submitted an unsolicited tender that closely met the requirements of the project. The Engineer was baffled, and in the meeting, it became clear that he was not dealing with ordinary men, or ordinary company, he was dealing with hardcore criminals.

"I have a counter proposal which I need to present to you. I need to have the tender proposal done, and you will respond to it with my guidance till the process is completed," the Engineer offered.

"There is little time Engineer, we are ready to commence this project. We believe that if you go for direct procurement, you will not be able to secure it," Timothy countered the proposal.

"My position is that all the terms of the contract will be discussed further and a response will be sent to your formally," the Engineer responded almost immediately.

As the Engineer was about to conclude the meeting, it became evident that the Engineer was not going to budge in. There was a call that came through with one of the technical staff.

"Engineer, here it's your wife on the call, she said it's urgent." In the background he could hear his wife crying."

"Our son was just sent to court, he was remanded in custody and will only appear in court in two months' time, do something."

When he cut the call, the Engineer was sad.

"What's the matter engineer?" Timothy enquired.

The Engineer looked at him, but could not speak, he was crushed. He was in pain, his well-behaved son had been found with marijuana in his bag at school, three kilograms of it. And now he was going to be in remand prison.

Michael stood up. "Engineer, why don't we postpone this meeting so you can deal with your personal matters at home, then we reschedule after three days or so. What do you say?" Michael suggested as if he cared so much about the streak of bad luck that had befallen him.

"Do you mind if I call a colleague to see how your son can be assisted?"

The Engineer did not respond, and Michael took the silence as consent. He made a few calls and was informed that the boy was wrongly charged. The case had no witnesses and the marijuana could have been planted by anyone. Michael agreed to pay for the lawyer who filed an urgent application to have the son released citing toxic environment that was more likely to damage him. At exactly 4:30 pm, Michael showed up at the Engineer's house with the boy. Later that night. the police managed to "recover" the stolen bulls at the farm after Michael had intervened.

The following day, the Engineer was at court for the culpable homicide case, but no one appeared. The case of rape was in the afternoon of the same day but no one showed up. In the end, he took some time to reflect and after being persuaded by his colleagues, he declined the proposal from Native Investments.

The next day, Engineer was travelling to work when a Toyota GD6 with an enhanced bumper followed closely and hit him from behind. His Toyota bubble veered off the road before it overturned.

While in the hospital, 13 bulls were found dead at the farm, two days after he was admitted. The trial for the rape case was resumed, but the Engineer's lawyer requested that his client be given time to recover. However, the state applied that the Engineer be chained to the bed and be monitored 24/7 by a prison warden as he was considered to be under remand in prison. The healing process took time, and while recovering, the Engineer had some reflections to do. Bridget, Engineer's wife of 16 years, brought him food daily, but on this particular visit, she did not bring food, she only came holding a phone.

"My love, have I wronged you in any way?" Bridget asked.

Engineer Mawadze was caught off guard and was not sure how to respond to it. "We have all wronged each other in one way or the other. We have been together for the past 16 years, and that's a long time," the Engineer responded.

"My love, why have you found it in good order to look for another woman? I have given you six children. What hurts is the lack of respect by your women. They have been calling on your phone and have been sending naked pictures. They have called me all sorts of names. Where did you get these kinds of people?" Bridget fumed with anger, had it not been for the HDU machines, she would have manhandled him, but she decided to control her temper.

"What are you talking about my dear? I have no idea what this is all about. I have no other woman in my life apart from you. You are the only one I love and cherish. I really love and cherish you," the Engineer pleaded.

"Did I hear cherish? You know, when this rape case emerged, I dismissed it and I vouched for you. I did not realise who you really are. You even have two children that you have been maintaining behind my back? You must be ashamed of yourself," Bridget was visibly angry and pacing up and down in the HDU.

"Calm down, babe girl, honestly I do not know what you are talking about. I think you are overreacting," the Engineer responded trying to wake up, but a sharp pain cut across his chest as if he was struck with a stick. He retreated back to bed and looked at Bridget making her perform.

Bridget moved to the bed, and at that time, the Engineer raised his hands to protect himself, Bridget stopped.

"Do you honestly think I have come to beat up a wounded man in the hospital? My own husband? Look at these images my love. You are really breaking my heart, these images show that you were in bed with this girl and here are the copies of birth certificates for your two children. What do you say about that?" Bridget cried and in the end she walked away and for three straight weeks she never returned to the hospital. She only sent the kids with notes of encouragement, she was heartbroken she could not understand what had happened to her.

The prison warden moved closer to the Engineer, glanced sideways to make sure no one was watching, then began to speak.

"You have serious balls to cross paths with the big boys in town. They control everything, they have access to everything, they see every message you write, and they can create any story and supporting evidence. You are playing with fire man." The warden's words were like a thousand knives at the back. He felt each incident that happened to him was linked to them. The death of his bulls, marijuana in his son's bag, the images in his phone, the accident and many more mishaps that happened to him. It was a turning point, the birth of a new man.

"Do you have access to these big boys?" the Engineer responded.

I don't, but for USD 100, I might remember. The warden responded, much to the surprise of the Engineer.

"Ok then then let's do it. I will pay you when my family come to see me," the Engineer pleaded.

"That's not how it works around here. Here we do cash transactions hey. And if you stay here too long, there are boys eager to claim every man as their girl. The weaker you are, the more interested they are, you'd better hurry up," the warden charged.

The Engineer managed to call home using the warden's phone a at USD 5 per minute. The call lasted for 10 minutes and when Bridget agreed to bring the money the total bill was USD 200, including permission to make calls from the prison.

The Engineer was given the number to call and when the phone went through, he went straight to the point.

"Timothy, I want us to make a deal," the Engineer demanded.

"Very well then, let's meet in the office tomorrow," Timothy responded.

In 20 minutes, the Engineer was dragged to court for a sit-down and the charges were dropped in a session that lasted for 20 minutes, he was a free man.

At the office, the Engineer was in the Town Clerk's office by 8 am.

"Engineer, it's great to have you back, as you know, we are out of time. We need to finalise the agreement with Native Investments," the Town Clerk explained the importance of the matter at hand.

"Thank you TC. I am ready to go, I am hoping to have the matter finalised this week."

In the meeting the Engineer requested to see Timothy alone in his office.

"I want USD 1.5 million for the two projects, and I have another project that I want to discuss with you. There is a farm under dispute, but there is a need for a person with muscle, and we can get the entire 750 hectares of land."

There was a moment of silence, and Timothy requested details of the new deal, and when he was satisfied he made a call outside for 30 minutes. When he came back, he agreed to the deal and demanded that the process be finalised the same week.

Two weeks later, graders started working on the ground, preparing for the subdivision of the stands in preparation for construction. The Engineer got a down payment of USD 1 million in cash, and the week that followed, he was to receive USD 3.5 million for the remaining deals, but the full council met and decided that the scandals that the Engineer had brought to the council were damaging the reputation of the municipality. He had his package negotiated and settled. After working for 20 years, the council awarded him benefits of USD 35,000 before tax.

The day after leaving office, 22 armed men arrived at the engineer's house and robbed them of USD 700,000.

Chapter 29

Michael had grown to become a force to be reckoned with. His evil deeds were sanitised by his capable British company that ran programs on national TV, which portrayed him as a giver. A compassionate businessman employing local people from underprivileged backgrounds.

It was 3:30 pm, and President Kufazvinei was waiting for a guest, a man who was popular in Zimbabwe. The President had not bothered to have a meeting with him, he believed in leaving people alone and letting them mind their business. Michael had worked with President Kufazvinei a long time ago.

A convoy of 8 Range Rovers entered the state house, and in between, there was a BMW bike. Instead of being in any of the top-range cars, he was the man rocking the 260 top-speed BMW bike to disguise and send mixed signals to his enemies since his last two assassination attempts.

"I see your military skills are still of use to you, it's a pity you did not last in the military. I would have promoted you to the rank of General by now. I need a person of your intelligence," President Kufazvinei remarked as he offered a firm handshake to Michael.

"Mr President it is a blessing to see you here at the state house. I consider myself privileged to come before you." Michael responded while kneeling before the president Kufazvinei.

"Today we bless the Lord for the blessing of meeting with you, and I proclaim blessings and long life to you. I proclaim victory for you in the upcoming general elections. You will overcome, I have seen that in a deal the Lord is showing me even right now, your kingdom is standing on firm ground, your people are happy with you," Michael continued.

The President directed Michael to the meeting room where he was joined by three state house officials, and Michael was joined by Timothy and two women.

State House protocol was initiated, introductions were done, and it came to the business of the day.

"Mr President, we have observed the great work you have been doing, and as citizens we have come to pay homage to you. I know you are a businessman and a farmer. We offer you three tractors, planters and two combine harvesters. We have brought you pocket money of USD 1, 5 million for use when you go on international trips," Michael offered the gifts as he praised the President who was happy with the talk.

"We have brought you cars to use, a Range Rover, Bullet Proof, with three side guns. It came with cameras and route recording, GPS RPG Launchers and two other Toyota VXV 8 cars," Michael continued.

"Thank you Michael for coming, it's a great thing that you have become a Christian. You could have been a hardcore criminal but the path you chose is great and I will support you on your projects that you need to undertake," the president responded.

"I have been informed that you have a program that you want to carry out in Mashonaland province. I have approved the development of Rural Land into orderly residential stands with proper services. The resident Governor and Ministry of Public Works will communicate this position formally," the president continued.

"I am grateful for the opportunity that you have afforded me, I will not disappoint you Mr. President., Michael could not hide his excitement.

The team went out for photos as is the custom at the State House and left.

The following morning there was a campaign for the sale of land in Mashonaland East. Word swelled in the UK and South Africa that Sabhuku deals were being facilitated by Native Investments. The stands were selling for USD 4.50 per square meter and they were selling like hot cakes. Native Investments worked with at least 15 Sabhukus and by end of first week, at least 50,000 square meters had been sold, generating USD 225,000 with 10% being given to the Sabhuku, with the remainder going to Native Investments.

It's the dream of every Zimbabwean in the diaspora to be able to own land and come stay here in Zimbabwe. However, this dream had eluded many, and in recent times, there has been an influx of Zimbabweans and other nationals flocking to the UK and other countries. This caused an oversupply, driving prices down. The offer for sabhuku deals by Native Investments could not have come at a better time, it was a great opportunity for many. The deal required no paperwork as it was against the law to sell rural land, the land belongs to the President, and Michael was aware of that. He wanted to make his money before the government started making noise about the whole situation.

The price has increased from USD 4.5 to 4.80 per square metre. The word of mouth created a certain element of deniability, there was no formal communication from Native Investments.

By the end of week 6, Native had sold over 369,000 square meters of land in the Sabhuku deals, racking in USD 1.6 million. The demand kept swelling and murmurings were beginning to emerge in the corridors of power. Native Investments started building a shopping complex made of farm bricks, employing local people, paying cash USD 2 per hour or USD 16 per day, this appeased the community.

The next was the construction of classroom blocks for preparatory, school and senior school. These were being constructed with face bricks from Harare. This created an impression that the company had people at heart. A private hospital was constructed to serve the people. It seemed a great plan. Soon the news reached other provinces who wanted similar progress in their communities.

In six months' time, some Sabhukus were running out of land and thus a total of 35 people had been double allocated, then it got to ceasing land for those who had purchased but were not living there. A total of 330 stands of varying sizes had been bought by people in the diaspora and they were not physically present. These became the target.

For those who were on the plots, Native Investments started requiring them to register with the resident association as their stands were considered peri-urban development plan. Each household was to pay USD 25 per month plus any amounts that would be required from time to time.

Native Investments was now averaging USD 1.5 million per month from the sale of stands in the sabhuku deals and USD 58,000 per month in subscription. For those who defaulted in the payment of subscriptions, their stands were repossessed after six consecutive months of non-payment.

A total of 165 stands were repossessed and resold at a total of USD 412,500 as the price had gone up to USD 10 per Square meter.

It was a Tuesday afternoon, and the parliament was in session when the lawmaker for UMP. He raised a question to the local government minister about the parceling of state land without government approval. The lawmaker for Chivhu Central East raised the same concern. The question required ministers of land and Local Government to respond.

"Mr Speaker Sir, we have witnessed the mushrooming of illegal structures in the rural areas such as Chikomba and UMP. A company called Native Investments has been selling land to the people working in cahoots with corrupt Sabhukus. We demand accountability and transparency in the sale of stands," the Member of Parliament for Greater Mwenezi fumed.

The Clerk of Parliament leaned to the left after an advisor came to whisper to him, and he nodded twice before he sat upright. At that moment, the lawmaker for the Rift Valley stood up,

"Mr. Speaker, we demand that the Native Investments be brought."

"Honourable member, please sit down, I did not recognise you, please sit down," the member continued, and this time he jumped on top of the table and was cursing in all sorts of vulgar language.

"Order, honourable member, order, please sit down! Honourable member you are about to be ejected!"

In the end, two sergeants-at-arms were called to expel him. The expulsion was swift and decisive, the men were strong and tough. It was a showdown that ended in a messy manhandling of the law maker. The scene, however, worried the other parliamentarians who expressed concern over what they called, "heavy-handed" approach. In the end, the session went on.

The Land Baron

The following day the President announced a commission of enquiry to investigate the claims that Native Investments was involved in the sale of land improperly.

The commission of inquiry had a thirteen-member team being chaired by Justice Joseph Mwanda, a seasoned judge of the high court with an impeccable record of delivering justice. There were two more lawyers, an accountant, a development study expert, and an engineer, among others. The commission had the following mission.

1. To establish if Native Investments was selling state land to the public without approval from the government;
2. To establish if the Sabhuku deals were indeed involving the Sabhukus and who were part of the team of Sabhukus involved;
2. To determine the actual number of people and extract the records for the people who were paid;
3. To determine the extent of the payments made and the number of people who have been prejudiced.

The team got to work and set the terms of reference as well as the investigation methodology. On the fourth day, the hotel they had booked announced an urgent need to fumigate, and alternative accommodation was needed. One member was involved in an accident and died on the spot, the colleague he had offered a lift had a fracture and needed to recover from the injury for at least three to five months.

The judge chairing the commission was called to Australia after his son was robbed at gunpoint and left at the car. He sustained injuries in the head and left leg. He was in the ICU, the judge had to monitor the progress, and hence requested leave to attend to his son.

The investigations stalled for six months, and names of replacements were put forward, but the president never got the time to appoint the new team. Subsequently, the people would have been reassigned or their circumstances changed significantly by the time they were offered the appointment.

Native Investments had people in high places. From the police senior officers, Department of Justice, the Defense, the Prisons etc. They had managed to create a racket of people who were close to the decision-making team, and in some cases, their team members were the actual decision makers. And thanks to the son-in-law who had managed to activate his international contacts. Olivia's husband, Stone, was the one responsible for reaching out to anyone financially.

In the end, the president managed to appoint a team to resume the investigations.

Native Investments Interview

Timothy was the one to handle the investigation, and Native Investments had hired a team of 16 lawyers. The team consisted of the three best lawyers in the UK and the USA. The first thing was to jointly charge the Ministry of Local Government and the Ministry of Lands for defamation of character. A claim of USD 17 million was being sought.

The interviews were being held at the Ministry of Justice boardroom.

The introductions were made, and the legal team for Native Investments was introduced.

"By now, you are aware of the reason we have called you?" the chairman one Mr Gare spoke while standing.

"Mr. Gare, my client needs a verbal explanation of the purpose of the interview to make an assess if they indeed have a case to answer," Dr Leonard Simpson remarked, his was firm and insistent in his posture and perhaps intimidating too.

"Very well then," responded Mr Gare.

There was a long silence in the room, and Mr. Gare looked like he was a defeated man, but those who knew him would not conclude that so soon. He adjusted his necktie as if the position of the tie had an effect on the subject matter at hand. In the end, he called for a break soon after starting. This gave the Native Investment a false sense of early victory, and indeed, they played into his hands.

At the end of the twenty-minutes break the session resumed. Gare was facing Timothy.

"What does Native Investments do?" asked Gare.

Timothy looked at him and realised that he was trying to build something up.

"Here is our profile with details of what we do. Should you need any more information after going through that, you may write formally to our company secretary she will be happy to respond to you," Timothy spoke while handing over a firm profile, it was scant and to the point, it may have been stripped of many details to make it less revealing and cut off too many questions.

"Timothy ,I am required to ask you questions and have you respond directly to me verbally," Mr. Gare charged in, showing visible signs of exasperation and irritation. This was part of the plan. To make the team angry and make them lose objectivity in the process.

Timothy looked at Mr Gare peeping over his glasses. He looked at him from top to bottom as if he were assessing his fitness for military training or some kind of special vetting. After that, he remained silent and started making some notes.

"I am here. Speak to me, but do not ask me things that I have already given you, it will only waste our time," Timothy finally responded.

"You see, if you do not want to cooperate with the investigation you will only make it longer than it should be, and it will only waste your time," Mr Gare responded.

"Confirm what your company does and the address," Mr Gare enquired.

"Real Estate business at 13 Magnum Close Gunhill," Timothy responded.

"Have you been involved with Sabhuku deals before?" M. Gare pressed further.

"What is that sir? What's the meaning of that? Can you explain what that means," Timothy responded with a calm and firm voice.

Mr Gare did not see that one coming. He was not given a task to explain the meaning of a transaction in which Native was involved and was not willing to admit, so it was, everything started where it's supposed to, the definition.

"Sabhuku deals are deals for the sale of land to customers seeking land in the rural areas." M. Gare explained.

Timothy jumped to respond almost immediately. "Wait, and you have information that we are selling land to customers in the rural areas? Please put a receipt or an offer letter given to any of the customers who bought from our company. Please go ahead and do that. Show us proof of payment, then, or at least a customer who has dealt with any of our employees, then we will talk."

Mr Gore did not see that one coming. He was sure there was something wrong with the whole deal. There was more to it and yet there were no records, zero records. It was a dead end. How were they supposed to start the process?

They thought of a weak spot, someone the government was able to beat into submission. The sabhukus themselves.

The following week, the suspected sabhukus were rounded up, their chiefs and headmen were present. They were each told to inform the government of the company that was selling the stands, but Native Investments name was never there. There was no company name. It was an individual who was introducing people to them, and in return, the settled families would pay a token of appreciation. It was a USD 20 appreciation fee.

The lack of agreement or receipts was worrying. It became clear that it was a well-coordinated transaction where there was no paper trail, no witnesses, and hence no evidence.

In the end, the president was frustrated by the lack of progress and relieved the commission before it could write a report.

Chapter 30

It was on a Thursday afternoon and the met department's radar had missed the weather changes that were building up. Even the US met department, with its sophisticated equipment had failed to pick the changing weather. A hurricane of legal battles that would be remembered for years to come was brewing, and history books were to be written and various versions of the story were coming.

Michael was at Native Investments when the Anti-Corruption Unit arrived at the offices.

"Good afternoon ma'am," the head of the Anti-Corruption Unit leading the various illegal land acquisition and fraudulent parceling of land remarked. He was tall and handsome, but today none of that was important.

"Good afternoon Sir, how can we help you this afternoon?" Rejoice responded with a wide smile enough to charm the investigation team but not today.

"We are here to see DR Michael Paradzai, Is he in the office?" replied Noel Mavima, the head of the Anti-Corruption Unit.

"Do you have an appointment with him, and what is it in connection with?" Rejoice responded again, typing something on her laptop.

At that moment, the Anti-Corruption team realised that there could have been communication between Michael and Rejoice, the team wanted to apprehend Michael before he escaped. They were sure a person like Michael would have some plan of some sort. They needed to determine what that plan would look like for him.

Michael had seen their car approaching the gate and suspected that they were up to something nefarious. The government plates and the mannerisms they portrayed gave him a warning that all was not well. He was watching all the activities from his office CCTV and heard everything they said. Michael bolted from a private entrance.

It had started raining- the shit storm was finally here. But this wasn't for the entire city, it was for Native Investments. Not for the fields, but for criminals, not just any type of criminal but the land barons in particular.

Michael hired an inDrive, which took him to the airport. He asked airline by airline and found a seat on Sahara Africa Airlines.

"Good Afternoon Dr Michael, well come back to Sahara Africa Airlines. Do you have any luggage to check in today?" the check-in counter lady asked, but Michael was deep in thought. He saw some people running to him in his direction, and he was ready to run away, but these were economy passengers trying to beat the time before the ticket closing call. He breathed a sigh of relief and was handed over his passport and a boarding pass. Boarding was at gate number 19. Michael called his identical twin to come to the airport. When they tracked the call was closed, there was confirmation from the airport Central Intelligence Organisation stationed at the airport that the cargo manifest indeed had a Dr Michael Paradzai.

All security units were placed on high alert. Michael walked to the domestic Terminal as he was booked to fly to Victoria Falls. The plane took off 2 hours before the Sahara Africa airline took off to South Africa. The airline was further delayed by 30 minutes as the aircraft arrived late and was further delayed by 15 minutes as the pilot was asked to circle around the air to allow the VIP protocols.

Back at the office, Rejoice had told the Anti-Corruption Unit that Michael was not in his office. The team went away without a word but came back with a search warrant. They collected laptops, computers, servers and files. Michael's office was locked, and a 9mm-stainless steel was used to secure his office.

An intercom rang at the gate, and no one answered. The Anti-Corruption decided to break in but immediately before they could do that there was a phone call that the team should stand down and so it was. The Anti-Corruption team left Michael's residence.

It was boarding time for the Victoria Falls AirSky plane. Michael was the first to present his ID and boarding pass for check-in, his boarding pass showed that he was seated at number 8 of the Mitsubishi-made 50-seat plane.

"Ground floor staff, please leave the aircraft," a voice came from the onboard communication system.

After that, the airhostess came with announcements about safety seat belts and in the 1 hour that followed, the plane landed at the Victoria Falls International Airport.

Back at the Robert Gabriel Mugabe International Airport, the police, Anti-Corruption and the CIO staff were positioning themselves to arrest Michael, they had seen him on CCTV and he had checked in and the CCTV footage showed that he was seated in the lounge closer to Gate 1.

Boarding time came, and there was an announcement for priority boarding call for Sahara Africa Airlines. The security team started looking for Michael frantically.

There was a beep followed by, "Good afternoon ladies and gentlemen, may passenger Michael Paradzai report to the security checkpoint immediately, thank you."

The head of the Anti-Corruption looked at the ZRP colleagues.

"He is not here. That's not how such criminals work. He is a step ahead of us. Those people have a strong intuition. They plan through scenario analysis, and these are not your usual criminals," the head of the Anti-Corruption team remarked.

The ZRP member sitting next to him looked at him with disbelief. "Sir this is not some murderer, this is an office person with very limited thinking capacity, they do not think like thieves," the ZRP member responded beaming with confidence and pride.

In the end, the police in plain clothes went onto the plane and announcements were made. "May passenger Michael please identify himself to the cabin crew?"

"This is laughable to say the least. So you think that Michael has cornered himself here and we now commit the talk of arresting him to some fucken air hostess." The Chief of Anti-Corruption said angrily.

The CIO ran CCTV footage and saw that Michael boarded a plane about 30 minutes earlier through the gate. However, the man resembling Michael went by the name Mathias Matunhuru. This name was his grandfather's name, and when he was born, the Paradzai name could not fit. It was a nickname, not a formal name, and Mathias was the only Paradzai who used his grandfather's nickname as his surname.

Communications were established to arrest and fly him back, but when a lawsuit was raised against Anti-Corruption, Foreign Affairs the whole matter was dropped, and Mathias went about his business in South Africa.

Michael was having dinner in a boat at Long Ireland in Victoria Falls. He had rented a boat, and Lizzy was waiting for her there. Five muscular men were on the upper deck to offer protection to him and his girl Lizzy.

Lizzy had visible dimples on her face. She was a beautiful girl whom Michael had resisted for a long but the more he resisted, the more he found her appealing. She was a handy many during crisis times.

Lizzy was in one of the three bedrooms on the bottom deck. She had left Michael to make communications and get updates concerning the state of things. It was a tough time for him, and when he was done, he went to bed thinking he was just going to rest.

Michael opened the door, and Lizzy was there in red lingerie smelling perfect, her body spotless. Michael looked at her, and he had to admit that it had taken him being a fugitive to realise how beautiful she was.

Lizzy's breasts were erect and with each step that Michael took walking closer to her, she was filled with a thrill that she had never experienced before. Michael touched her from the neck, his hand magically going down her chest. His touch increased in intensity. Lizzy was moving her upper body as Michael touched her. She moaned and groaned. Michael kissed her on the forehead, and his warm breath sent her wild. In a snap, Michael removed her bra and there it was, an open treasure chest for the treasure hunter to enjoy. The breasts were so fine, a pure bliss in front of him, Michael was holding the entire breasts, releasing them slowly and in the end holding the black part and circling the nipples while kissing her on the neck. He moved to the ears and she screamed with pleasure, electricity went down her spine, and she was in another place.

Lizzy moved her hands, hesitantly, but finally grabbed Michael's dick. It was big and firm, the warmth of her hands caused it to swell. As she looked at it, she began to shake helplessly, she wanted it and she wanted here and now. She ripped Michael's trousers together with his underwear.

Michael lifted Lizzy up, legs on his shoulders and started licking her hard while holding her suspending her in front of him. It seemed as if Michael was offloading all his energy and frustration on her. It went on and on, and Lizzy was literally screaming with pleasure. She squirted much to Michael's pleasure.

Michael lowered her to the bed and barely before touching the bed Michael was inside her, he stroked her breast as he pumped into her, and each time the pumping was complemented by the loud cries of joy from Lizzy.

Michael turned her skillfully, and with care, gave it to her from the back. There were loud cries, cries of joy, and also cries of victory. She had been looking forward to this, and all she needed was for him to taste. And that was the beginning of a long-term relationship, ride or die. It was secretive initially till Michael was tired of sneaking around.

The following morning, Michael was arrested, the ZRP marine acting on a tip off from airport staff and a fisherman along the Zambezi River.

Chikurubi remand prison was the place for Michael.

1. Native Investments was facing sixteen counts of fraud involving land in councils and one for rural land;
2. Attempted murder two, counts ;
3. Theft;
4. Corruption;
5. Abuse of office;
6. Dragging the name of the President into disrepute.

Chapter 31

A green Bedford with tiny windows, wielded with steel, loomed in the Horizon, the windows were small but big enough to see the scores of people who had gathered at the Rotten Row Magistrate Courts. Rumours had swelled that Michael Paradzai was arrested, facing a number of cases.

As the prison services vehicle turned to approach the courts, it was clear that the matter had become high profile. Reporters from CNN, BBC, SABC and ZBC as well as private reporters were lining up to catch a glimpse of Michael.

Michael was disembarking when he saw the people taking photos, his gut twisted, he missed a step and was almost falling, managing to lean on the fellow remand prisoner nearby.

Michael's wife's unmistakable voice was shouting, "You will get over this Michael, we are with you." That might have been true but there were many cases. Today's case was a lengthy one that was most likely to drag on for a long.

"All rise, her majesty Gertrude Mwaka." The Magistrate was holding some files in her hand, and the first on the list was Native Investments' CEO Michael vs. Marondera City Council.

The defendant was called to the stand and was asked to swear that he was to tell the truth and nothing but the truth. After the process, thirteen lawyers swarmed the court, and these were big names.

Before the trial could commence, the defense council requested to engage the Magistrate on account of a technical matter that required immediate action.

"You're Majesty." Councilor Lewis for the defiance council started. "This court has and will continue to be one of many administering justice, For that we as attorneys are pleased with the work you are doing and being done in this noble court. However, we would like to bring to your attention that the matter between Native Investments being represented by Michael Paradzai vs. the City of Marondera is worth USD 10.6 million. An amount that is way higher than the mandated capacity of this court of USD 10,000. We therefore seek that our client be removed from remand and ask the case to be submitted to the right court."

The Magistrate looked at the papers and the claim that was being made against the Native Investments. In the end the plaintiff was advised to approach the High Court. But Michael could not be released just yet as he had other cases to answer.

The days that followed saw Michael going to court daily to defend the various cases. What looked like a simple matter to Michael had minutes turning into hours, hours into days, and days into weeks, weeks into months.

Michael's empire was collapsing right before him.

#

It was on a Monday afternoon, Michael was brought to the Magistrate's court for sentencing on the matter regarding abusing the name of the president. Dragging the name of the president into disrepute through name-dropping and intimidation of council officials using the name of the president. While not proven, Native Investments was judged to have had links in the sale of the stands in the Sabhuku Deals. The court heard that there is no written evidence that Native profited from the sale of stands. It was upheld that Michael had made several discussions with the village headman (Sabhuku) where he indicated that the President had asked him to work closely with the headman and assist them to settle people.

In finding him guilty, the Magistrate took note of the nature of the offence. He noted that Michael had misused his access to the president and the hospitality of the president in welcoming all Zimbabwean citizens. It was further noted that Michael, while facing charges of dragging the president's name into disrepute, the court also found that he had exhibited criminal mind and a mind that could easily commit fraud. In the end, Michael was found guilty and was asked to make a payment of USD 3900 or serve a jail term not less than 2 years.

The defense argued that their client had spent one year in the remand prison already, hence there was a need to waive the entire penalty. However, the Magistrate required that the money be paid or a jail term kicks in. In arriving at his position, he indicated that Michael Paradzai was not in the remand prison for this particular charge, but many others that were far more complex hence this matter had to stand alone.

That week President Kufazvinei addressed the nation and made a specific reference to the ravaging impact of the land barons who were hoarding state land in towns and rural land. The President was visibly angry and was not going to let the land barons get away with it.

Chapter 32

After battling trials for two straight years Michael tasted the sweetness of freedom. It was on a Monday morning at 10 am, and at the stroke of 9 am that day marked one year in remand prison. His cases fell apart one after the other, and evidence would disappear, key investigating officers would be posted on foreign operations, while key witnesses would either disappear or decide not to cooperate in the process. There were three witnesses who died mysteriously, each dying a day before they had committed to a state witness.

"Well, come back home, my brother. I have paid for your holiday in the Bahamas. I need you to rest and collect your thoughts before you start working." Olivia remarked. Michael's wife ran to him with arms wide open but Michael had his eyes set on Lizzy, his girlfriend, who was running things with Timothy. Lizzy was dressed casually and decided to downplay her emotions for the sake of maintaining peace and tranquility.

"Thank you so much my sister," Michael managed to respond over his wife's shoulders.

Timothy was waiting for his chance and when he got his chance he managed to say, "Welcome back home boss."

Rejoice was a darling, she was an excellent administrator and assistant to Michael. She had gone to see Michael every day in the morning and gave him updates of what was happening at the office and with the business in general. Native had made USD 22.5

million in losses and was making good on developments that were ordered by the court for various housing schemes.

Rejoice greeted Michael with the usual African style of bending one knee, showing respect and honour, and Michael was obsessed with the way Rejoice greeted him. Each time he wanted someone to massage his ego he would ordinarily work with Rejoice side by side, and that gave him a lot of boasts.

Michael proceeded straight to the Mahogany meeting. Rejoice had informed Michael that he was to stop over at Quick and Easy Hotel on his way to the meeting. There was exactly one hour of leg time between whatever Michael was to do at the Quick and Easy and the Mahogany meeting.

Michael entered room number 109, which was a room overlooking the entire city, where one would see the entire Harare city.

Lizzy was there waiting for Michael. She was beautiful and her body much purer than before. Lizzy was radiant like a sunrise, she did not speak, Michael did not speak ,he walked straight to her and without preamble he grabbed her throat as if he was about to choke her, his right hand slapped her ass and moved front to touch her labia minora and rubbing her and making repeated movements to the G spot. Michael tore the bra and the pants in one motion each, and without saying much, he was inside her. He was passionate and sent Lizzy screaming wildly while Michael pumped repeatedly. Lizzy screamed for him to stop but there was no stopping. He lifted her up, facing her while holding her in his hands pumping continuously looked her in the eyes.

"Michael, you are killing me it's so sweet please don't stop, I have missed you please don't stop, don't you ever stop Michael, if you stop I will kill you," Lizzy shouted at the top of her voice.

Michael turned her and gave her from the back and Lizzy was delighted and Michael released all that the reservoirs were holding for two straight years.

After that, they both showed.

"So, what was that about screaming like a demon?" Lizzy teased Michael

"They did not allow pussy in the prison, but only paid for bitches that were expensive going for USD 300 per shot. I did not have that kind of money hey," Michael retorted.

They both wore new clothes, and just as they were walking to the door, Michael looked at Lizzy and he was erect as hard as a dry stick. He grabbed Lizzy by the waist, bringing her to him in one motion. He kissed her and moved his hands skillfully inside her garments, Lizzy was stiff initially, but the warmth of Michael's hands rubbing against her breast created a spark that rapidly grew to engulf the entire forest. There was no putting out the fire now it had gone out of control, out of hand, and Michael kissed her slowly and she responded like a bar of chocolate melting in slow heat. She was flexible, and he followed the rhythm. They walked to the bed Michael started undoing the buttons while Lizzy was quick to unzip Michael. This time, Michael removed Lizzy's lingerie skillfully and gently. They made love to each other, and at the climax, Michael started a conversation.

"Lizzy, did you betray me to the police the night we made love in the Zambezi River Champions Boat? Did you call the police? Were you the link because the fishermen who were there that night were interviewed never confessed to seeing anything?" Michel asked as he continued making love to her while his eyes locked onto hers.

"Michael, I do not know what you are talking about. I made arrangements for your safety and gave you food to eat, and made love to you. I soothed your spirit and your soul." Lizzy responded that Mike was making love to her slowly before he cut her off.

"And you also handed me over to the police, right?" Michael responded.

In the end, they were all totally spent and took a shower. Michael looked at Lizzy. "Don't you ever do that again, don't you ever betray me again, I will kill you. It's a pity you are a beautiful woman and the best I have been with so far, but if you fuck with me, I will kill you," Michael warned Lizzy.

Lizzy looked at him, then started. Michael, I would never do such a thing. I was blackmailed, I was put there, and the police has all evidence that could send me to jail any day. They have been using me to do such high risk assignment. I need your protection.

The following day, all the files with incriminating evidence against Lizzy were destroyed. A state-assisted burial was offered to 7 officers who had intimate details of Lizzy.

Lizzy finally was the inside police with high-level access to information destroying evidence and any matter where Michael's Native Investments was involved.

Chapter 33

Michael had 32 missed calls, he had slept at the Quick and Easy and woke up three hours after the meeting time for the Mahogany meeting. Lizzy was released to go back to "police work',' while Michael arrived alone at the meeting. Rejoice was the first to meet him in the corridor.

"Boss where have you been? You need this if you have passed anywhere, you need to show no sign of weakness. Your wife has been calling you she has called me, she thinks you were with a woman. She thinks you were with Lizzy."

"It's not your place to ask me where I have been and who I should not be with. The details of my family are off limits." Michael responded with a voice firm and final."

"Not when your reputation and that of the company are at stake sir. I will do anything to protect this company, with or without your approval. I have been at this organisation for two straight years .I have answered questions from the police, Anti-Corruption, now you come here and tell me what to do? This is my company too, and I have the right to be treated with respect. Take Lizzy and make her your administrator if that's what you want." Rejoice responded angrily

Michael had never seen Rejoice that mad and upset. He had to admit that the girl was an asset to the Native Investments, but he did not want the idea of an employee who would stand up to the employer and specifically stand up to him.

"You are fired." Leave this place and go," Michael demanded.

Rejoice went down on her knees to beg for mercy but Michael walked on into the meeting.

Timothy was chairing the meeting and there was an unwanted guest. Olivia was in the meeting, and that did not go down well with Michael but he wanted to get to the bottom of the story before he reacted.

"Mr Chairman we welcome you to the Native Investments' first meeting with you after two years. I open the floor for you if you have any words to say before we commence," Timothy started.

Michael waved to signal that he was not ready to speak, he wanted to understand what had been going on. Proposals were discussed as follows.

Real Estate Investment South Africa, UK

Ladies and gentlemen, we have made great progress in securing investment opportunities in safe havens. We have conducted due diligence for South Africa and United Kingdom investments. South Africa we have 35 properties in at the Beach front where we are required to deposit only 40% of the cost and the balance will be paid off by the rental income. Native Investments will get the remainder of the profit. We project that USD 2.7 million will be needed for the full purchase price but we will only pay 40% of its which comes to USD 1.1 million, and the balance will be paid for by the installments.

"Michael raised his hand as if he needed permission to speak. He cleared his throat then started. "This is a great deal, please commit USD 5 million as the 40% down payment, How much will that give us in number of properties, and what is our net profit per month per property and for the entire holding." Michael asked frantically.

"That will give us 79 properties, as we stand to purchase the properties at ZAR 1, 2 million if we purchase more than 50 Units," Timothy responded beaming with confidence and a sense of keenness. "Regarding the profit per unit we project that holding interest rates and inflation constant, we will get plus or minus ZAR 7, 5000 per unit which translates to USD 395 per property at the rate of 19 USD to ZAR. This will give us a total profit of USD 31,205 per month and USD 374k per month. We might get a 7.5% discount on cleaning and related costs making a case for higher profit. The profit will increase as we go and based on the recent economic projections, we foresee a 5.5% increase in profit," Timothy continued.

Michael was amazed and the time spent in jail had changed him but no one could pinpoint it yet it was clear as day and as loud as fuck.

"So let's invest immediately, you have my go-ahead." Michael responded sitting on the edge betraying his fascination and appreciation."

Timothy, emboldened by Michael's proceeded. "For the United Kingdom investments we have a similar structure where 40% will be required plus 10% of the property value for conveyancing services. The properties are going for GBP 90,000 for basic two-bedroom apartments. The 40% will come to GBP 36,000 and GBP 9,000 for conveyancing services making the total of GBP 45,000. We had intended to purchase 267 units by investing GBP 12 million, which is 40% of the property value. We stand to get a discount of the conveyancing and legal services to GBP 7.5k, making a compelling case for investment. The Bank of England has forecast an interest rates drop and inflation to be within the target of 3.6%. We expect to get a profit of GBP 1 million out of the properties invested in," Timothy explained to the loud applause, again a new culture that Michael had to get used to. Those ideas come from anywhere.

Again, Michael was looking at the power point and he had to admit that while he had done things the hard-core way, he had missed on the smart earnings. But who cares even international leading banks were bankrolled by profits from the slave trade.

Michael raised his hand. "I understand that the property market in the UK does not allow the purchase of the underlying land. Rather allows one to purchase use of the land for a certain period under a leasehold arrangement. What is our consideration of this matter?" Michael demanded to know, he was somehow thinking that team had overlooked the idea.

Timothy raised his hand and looked sideways as if looking for a clue. It was a trick that he had learnt, that when a question is asked by the boss, you give it weight by asking for time to research more, or you wait and ponder before answering and gosh he was good at it.

"Ladies and gents, allow me to conclude this session. Mr. Chairman, regarding the ownership status of the UK proposed investments a 999 lease is granted meaning up to the 4th generation will benefit from this before we eventually hand over the land in a thousand years. However there will be a regenerative effort in that after three years each property value will have increased resulting in significant value. Each property will have the increased capital gain remortgaged to deposit another 40% for another property and a new stream of income and deposit of properties will emerge. Additionally our investments are in new properties in London, Birmingham where the student accommodation is expected to soar alike and rental increasing as well," Timothy responded to Michael showing a clear understanding of the subject matter and making it clear he had researched well.

Michael raised his hand again. "What are the tax implications of the capital gains that we intend to remortgage?" Michael asked casually as if it was an unimportant matter. But Timothy was aware of the person he was dealing with. Michael was fully aware of the whole process.

"Mr. chairman, the capital gains are exempt from tax as they are considered rolled over in purchasing a qualifying asset under the Income Tax Act," Timothy responded looking intently at Michael to see if he was satisfied with his answer. But Michael was not the one to give away his mood he liked to keep people guessing and on their toes.

There was a 30-minute break, Rejoice was called to have a discussion with Michael. She had stayed out of the meeting all along, and she had worked so hard to make the meeting happen. She is the one who had brought the business ideas as a lasting solution to the deal, creating a clean income without controversy.

The meeting resumed, and Michael had asked Timothy to respond to how they were to invest GBP 12 million without raising eyebrows. Timothy called Michael's brother-in-law, Stone. Stone was a man of few words. When he started talking he was straight to the point. "Ladies and gentlemen our income will come from a recent tender that we won from the government of the UK. The income is properly taxed and considered the cleanest money on God's earth. Are there any questions?

Everyone was stunned, and not even Michael had questions. The government of the UK had wanted a certain number of farms protected, and Stone had managed to make that happen. These farms belonged to whites who were of British origin and held export permits to supply several special produce that were used by the elite as well as the Monarchy. In exchange, a contract for special services was granted to allow payment for such services.

This marked the beginning of the transition into clean money, but there were programs were still running, and significant money was being made in kidnapping and sexual slavery.

Finally, I want to introduce investments in Dubai, specifically in the hotel business. We are not going to buy the entire hotel, but rooms, each room in a seven-star hotel going for USD 300,000, we propose to invest USD 82 million into this project. We can take our money there without questions asked. It's the safest place to invest our stock of cash. We intend to invest in 273 rooms in different seven-star hotels as these give us a cash out of USD 300 per day for 365 days in a year, giving us a net profit of USD 109,500 per month translating to USD 29.9 million per year. Timothy explained with great enthusiasm and confidence.

"Last but not least, we have managed to make a deal with high-ranking officials in Ghana. We intend to invest USD 5 million into the Nova Ridge gated community spanning 780 hectares. It has its own security system, sewer and water reticulation system, as well as refuse collection. We have managed to allocate USD 1.9 million in Zambia, where an upmarket private school will be built. It will have from preparatory, High school and up to University. Complete with student accommodation and transport system," Timothy completed his explanations.

Michael stood up and ordered all the investments to be initiated at once. He created a project steering committee that he was to chair, and he needed reports daily concerning all the proposed investments.

1. Michael travelled to the USA, where he had meetings with the who's who. The first meeting was held at Trump Towers in New York in a room going for USD 3,900 for bed and breakfast. He was impressed by the sheer size of the hotel, the design, and the staff's professionalism. While there, he

managed to clinch a deal with a local contractor, Age Rea Estate contractors who sold him an up market hotel for USD 155 million which he purchased through Bitcoin managing to evade the money laundering challenge.

2. A meeting was held with Avita Investment managers, Timothy had arranged the meeting and Rejoice was in attendance. There was no formal discussion on whether she had been forgiven by Michael, she was just informed that she would be one of the people traveling to the USA.

The meeting took place on the third floor of the 115-story building. It was a marvel of architecture. Norman Avita was the Senior Partner and Chief Investment Officer (CIO) at Avita. He had started as a clerk at Goldman Capital rising to Partner before one client in the telecommunications industry approached him to manage a fund for them. That was the beginning of greater things. He had invested in so many instruments, stocks, bonds, junk bonds, emerging markets, and alternative investments. Cryptocurrency as well as the Bricks.

Norman had been informed of the need to invest USD 135 million.

"It's such a pleasure to meet you in person. I will be the one managing your portfolio personally. We have looked at your Investment Policy Statement that you have been assisted to craft by my competent team and based on that we have the following allocations:

35% allocation to Tech Stocks, these have outperformed average stocks by more than 20%;

1. 20% will be allocated to pharmaceuticals, due to increased demand for medicines and vaccines and increased instances of diseases. We see this as a stable and secure investment offering steady growth;

2. 15% will be invested in War Stocks, we see the geopolitical and increased spending by the EU as a growth point for stocks such as General Dynamics, Boeing, and Lockheed Martin etc. The demand for arms, fighter jets, drone technology and laser tech in the warfare primes this area as a key focus point;
3. 10% will be invested in Clean Energy;
4. 10% in Gold;
5. 10% will be invested in cryptocurrency."

There were no questions. The proposed investment had been sent to Michael and he had recommended that it be changed to what it is after consulting his Investment Banker friend based in the USA. And so it was. Michael a man who had been labeled as a hardcore criminal, was now transforming into an international business mogul.

Chapter 34

Michael was in his office, he was reviewing the latest numbers in the prostitution business service. They had put a stop to the kidnapping and trafficking after it became too risky and Interpol and AFRIPOL was closing in on them. A case was pending of kidnapped girls and Michael had been tipped by Lizzy that the police were close to apprehending him. He thus remained with the premium brothels that he operated on willing girls and agreed rates. He managed to make this business very profitable.

Michael realised that he needed men on the streets for his drugs. The constant meddling from the Medicine Control Authority made it difficult to sell drugs through pharmacies. Hence a bloody war was on the horizon. A war to take up space in the drug distribution. Michael did not like the simple idea that money was working for him while he was seated. He had realised that there was more money to be made out there but he needed a source, a real source of raising the funds. Zimbabwe was his place of raising the money and investing it into other markets.

And so it was, a turf war had started, it had begun.

Chapter 35

Timothy paced in front of the window, sweaty fingers twitching. Michael's portraits were covered in dust. He had fired the previous cleaners, accusing them of spying on him. Since his return, he'd been harder to please, quicker to snap and slower to trust. His moods shifted without warning. One moment calm, the next explosive. Even Rejoice had started applying for other jobs out of town and in South Africa. Any day could be her last. Michael's unpredictable temperament made his wife and Timothy jittery too. She flinched when he raised his voice even when she wasn't at fault. Sometimes, she wished he had remained locked up. As for Timothy, he spoke in short sentences. Anything more than five words felt risky.

At last, Michael sauntered into the office, sipping his chai latte. This was the next best drink after whisky, as he liked to say. He didn't offer a reason for being late. He didn't need to. Timothy stood at attention and wiped his sweaty palms. He forced a smile and nodded at Michael. They went straight to the business of the day. They agreed that a man on the streets was essential for smooth operations. Control started at street level. Without a man on the ground, nothing moved. Harare was phase one. The rest of the towns would be set up soon after. Of the five suggested high-density suburbs, they would visit Mufakose together. Michael dismissed the idea at first, and Timothy resisted the urge to push back. He knew that with his boss, you had to walk on eggshells. Yet, he knew they needed to go together. After a moment's hesitation, Michael gave in to Timothy's second push, as if nudged by an invisible hand.

"Desperation makes people useful. But it also makes them dangerous." Olivia budged into the office, the door already ajar. She shuffled in and pushed the door shut with the heel of her foot. Her voice had come a second before her full appearance. Michael frowned, but a short giggle slipped out before he could suppress it. Olivia rolled her eyes at him, then continued to voice her opinion.

When she finished, Michael gave a tight smile and a single clap. "Great points," he said, "But this is a closed-door meeting. How did Rejoice let you pass? No, you don't do that."

"I'm your sister. Should I remind you now?"

A heated exchange followed, with Michael fuming and bellowing at his sister. Timothy stood to excuse himself, but Michael grabbed his wrist mid-motion and ordered him to sit.

Michael hurled insults at his sister with the same coldness their aunt had used all those years ago. His words hurt more. This wasn't an argument anymore. The air suffocated Olivia. Her hair prickled at the nape of her neck, and a shiver trailed down her spine, leaving her with goose bumps. She had seen enough signs. This one was clear. A bad omen, and the third one since morning. The first had been the dog that peed on her during her morning jog. Then, the encounter with a City Park officer who clamped her car for encroaching the white line by a centimetre. Olivia stepped back, head bowed and murmured an apology. She grabbed her handbag and left, Michael avoiding her gaze.

He exhaled through his nose, his jaw tightening. "Timothy," he said, already moving, "we're going to Mufakose. Now."

#

Michael hated this part of town. He didn't grow up here, but something about the place stirred memories he'd worked hard to forget. It was as though the streets of Mufakose held a story he never wanted to hear again. The streets swarmed with people. Crowds. Noise. Laughter. Some huddled in corners, whispering. Others sat by the drains, smoking and watching whoever walked by, mostly girls. It appeared everyone was watching someone. Michael and Timothy often donated to the suburbs but rarely set foot in them.

The streets of Mufakose were famed for raising the most notorious robbers of the 90s, and also the greatest sportsmen, actors, and musicians to ever grace Zimbabwe. The suburb had seen it all, stories of struggle, fortune, loss and triumph. As one of the oldest townships in Harare, it had an eclectic mix of houses. Some houses sat behind crooked fences, their old asbestos roofs covered in moss and lichen, faded with patches of orange and green. Others were newly built or renovated, sleek with modern designs. There was no uniformity; old and new stood side by side, like strangers forced to share a bench.

The once numerous recreational spaces had been converted by land barons into churches. Even the infill spaces had been built up. The mushrooming of wellness centres and churches on open land sparked mixed feelings, some residents resented the changes, while others welcomed them. For those who had once grown crops like maize, the transformation felt like theft with their self-given fields taken away. Meanwhile, the land barons who had claimed ownership reveled in the profits. On the other hand, the maize fields had long been infamous for robberies, muggings, and assaults. These were rife during the December and January months when the tall, dark maize provided perfect hiding spots for thieves. Even the council slashed those crops just as the cobs neared harvest, much to the dismay of the field owners. Of course, those who had never been victims of assault in the fields would never support this move by the council. As such, the creation of those spaces served as a buffer, a safe haven. Back then, the youth and older men played social soccer, gathered for community events, and held church crusades in those areas, but not anymore. Now, there are alternative forms of entertainment, some as dangerous as wasting away on drugs.

Michael sat in the car, his eyes scanning the street through the rearview mirror without turning his head. Timothy went inside the house to call their contact after they'd attempted to reach him, but the phone went unanswered. A few kids scurried near their car as a drunkard staggered by, shouting at no one in particular. Michael was surprised to find that one of the quietest streets lay hidden behind a beer hall and a busy shopping centre, the irony of life. Much like himself, living a double life, playing both the hero and the villain. Was this the life he wanted?

After what felt like a decade, Timothy finally returned to the car, a middle-aged woman in a loose kaftan at his side. A teenage boy followed close behind. Timothy nodded toward him and introduced him as her second-in-command (2IC). The woman, known as Aunty Jo, owned that recently renovated house, its gate pushed forward, intruding on the pedestrian walkway like she owned the street too. She ran her business empire like a general on a battlefield. Commanding every move with ruthless precision. Her husband had long since retreated to the terraces, grateful to be alive and healthy. They called him as good as a man on a toilet sign, a mere symbol, not a real man at all. She never listened to his advice, warnings or attempts to rein her in. Aunty Jo was the boss. Some neighbours claimed she had placed her husband under a love potion to disarm him, since he was too soft with her and powerless. Aunty Jo also operated a fleet of commuter omnibuses plying several suburbs across Harare and Mutare. In addition, she controlled a fleet of haulage trucks operating along the Beira Corridor, particularly the Beira–Lusaka route. It was one of the shortest and most cost-effective links to the sea for Zambia and its landlocked neighbors. These trucks also made it easier for her to facilitate her drug smuggling operations. Meanwhile, she drilled boreholes for her local ward, to address the clean water shortages plaguing most of Harare. Every six months, she donated basic groceries to widows and orphans in her local ward. They loved her for that but despised her drug shenanigans, which were ruining the youth. Some even preferred her *kachasu* (traditional distilled alcoholic beverage) to the drugs, though it was equally destructive. Her *kachasu* business was her flagship operation. After introductions, they all went into the house for a tour. Dealing with Michael would expand her reach in a win-win deal.

Three men stumbled away in a daze, while another one lay passed out under a tree. On the verandah, a group of men crowded around a pool table, waiting for their turn. Some had money, most didn't. It didn't matter. They all needed it. Cheap and strong, the drink was the only escape for many from the harsh reality of life. At the back of the house, a thick, heavy and musty aroma of fermented grain filled the air. It clung to everything, sinking deep into your clothes and your skin. Two men tending to the brewing in the backyard laughed at something on their phones, while another swayed to the music blasting through his earphones. Timothy stood with a subtle smile tugging at his lips. Beside him, Michael's eyes darted across the backyard, settling on a large bubbling pot over an open flame in the corner. Around it stood rusted drums and containers filled with fermenting maize, sugar, and other unmentionable materials. He kept a straight face, though his senses stayed sharp and alert. It wasn't the place that bothered him. It was what bothered him at all. Damn, Timothy is dragging him here.

Aunty Jo and her 2IC smiled at their special guests. It was their territory, and they moved through it with practiced indifference. To them, it was another part of the business, nothing more than a means to an end. And in their world, if it sold, it stayed. Neither of them drank *kachasu,* they never did. To them, it was simply a product, another commodity to be sold and discarded. They cared about their customers, cared that they came back and bought more. But beyond that, their well-being didn't matter. Only the profit mattered. In the current economy, survival meant taking whatever you could. And if that meant selling poison to survive, so be it.

"You don't drink it, huh?" Michael asked, watching Aunty Jo stir the concoction. Her hands were steady, moving with the ease of muscle memory, like a violist syncing bow and finger without thinking.

She kept her eyes on the fire. "Of course not. I don't mix pleasure with business," Michael gave a slight nod. He respected that. You had to stay sober in business. You couldn't sell that kind of stuff and drink it too.

Aunty Jo handed back the cooking stick to one of the two men. He wiped his brow with the back of his hand, pushing aside the thick steam rising from the pot. He knew what to do, so Aunty Jo left him to it. She then led her guests inside the house. A soft ambiance welcomed them, a sharp contrast to the scene outside. They discussed their partnership and agreed on fair share percentages. *Kachasu* had been sanitised, and the police never bothered her. And she silenced those who pestered her with a few dollars. This gave her a competitive edge. She could sell anything else and whatever Michael wanted. The constant traffic made drug peddling easier and less suspicious. Even though Aunty Jo operated freight trucks, Timothy suggested they bring in Olivia's Famba logistics company. Michael dismissed the idea right away.

Chapter 36

Meanwhile, Olivia sat in her office, the faint scent of lavender lingering in the air, doing nothing to calm the tightness in her chest. Oblivious to the trickle of the fountain or the soft music playing through the spa, she stared at the computer screen. Her fingers hovered over the keyboard, but the screen stayed blank. She tried hard to focus. Michael's outburst earlier had shaken her more than she wanted to admit. That struck her as strange and new. Michael knew how to maintain his composure even when angered. Then again, there wasn't anything to be angry about in the first place. He overreacted. It's often said that when siblings argue, the younger one is to blame. But that's not always true.

She stared at the framed photo on her desk, Michael with their parents, all of them smiling. Today, she saw a horrendous Michael. Her throat tightened. A cold, creeping dread moved through her body, the kind that made her stomach churn. A feeling that made her glance at her phone every few seconds, expecting it to ring. It was the kind of feeling that crawls in before bad news arrives. Death. Disaster. Tragedy. She grew up an orphan, facing adversity every day. But what could be worse? Losing everything she'd worked so hard to build? What if it was her husband? Or her brother? The weird rough events of the morning, combined with Michael's fury, seemed to point to one thing: impending doom.

Her hand moved to her phone, but she didn't unlock it. Olivia grabbed her car keys from the mahogany desk. But she fumbled with them and they slipped from her fingers, hitting the floor with a soft clink. She stared at them for a moment, then reached down slowly, her hand trembling. With the keys in her hand, she stood and shuffled towards the door. Then she stopped. Her other hand hovered near the knob, fingers twitching. She turned back to her desk, sat for a few seconds, then got up once more. Her jaw tightened as something twisted deep in her gut. She pressed the heel of her hand against her stomach, as if she could push the feeling away. It only grew stronger. The dread crawled up her spine, slow and suffocating. She clenched her fist so hard that her stiletto nails dug into her palm. Almost painful.

Olivia reached for her phone and called her husband, Stone. It rang for thirty seconds. No answer. She stared at the screen. Of course, he was in a meeting with their international business partners. She had reminded him about it that morning. But with everything going on, it had slipped her mind. She kept staring at the screen, her thumb hovering. Then she typed out a message with stiff fingers: "Please come get me? I don't feel too good." She hit send and put the phone down with a bang. Her heart thudded, as if it was waiting for something she couldn't name.

Stone sat in the middle of his online meeting, eyes fixed on the screen as the discussion progressed. His phone flashed, but he ignored it, focusing instead on the negotiations with their esteemed international partners.

Then a buzz. He looked at the screen. His wife. What did she want? Olivia could be too needy sometimes. Was she sexting him, teasing him again like she sometimes did? His brow furrowed. A missed call plus a message. That wasn't like her, especially knowing he was in a high-level meeting. His jaw tightened. He stared at the pop-up notification, his fingers lingering on the screen for a moment, unsure of what to do. The office blurred as the final words of the meeting faded into the background. With a quick press, he dialled her number. By the time he called her back, five minutes had passed since her missed call. She explained she was feeling woozy and somewhat paranoid. His heart rate quickened as he listened, but his voice remained even as he reassured her. She trusted him. Besides her brother, he was her pillar, a man she could count on, especially in times like this.

On the drive home, she told him everything in a flat voice. She kept staring out the window like someone trying to locate something. He drove in silence, but now and again his hand reached out to squeeze hers. Once in the house, she headed straight for the kitchen and gulped down a bottle of water. Stone offered to run her a lavender bath, something to soothe her. But she shook her head, her eyes distant. Instead, she slouched into her recliner, pulling a fleece throw tighter around herself. He fought the urge to insist, then sank down besides her, wrapping his arms around her. She didn't pull away, letting him hold her, her head resting against his chest as he placed two kisses on her forehead.

Then her phone rang.

She answered and stayed quiet, listening. When she hung up, her face went blank. "It's my aunt," she said, rolling her eyes. She shrugged, looked away, and fixed her eyes on the TV, avoiding eye contact. "She's in critical condition at West General Hospital." The syllables dragged as if heavy on her tongue.

Whatever had been gnawing at her all day, she understood now. None of it was random. It all foreshadowed this moment. Screw Michael. His fit of rage was the omen that hit her hardest. Olivia called herself a modern woman but still clung to her superstitions. It annoyed Stone whenever she brought up her superstitious beliefs, dismissing them outright. But now, she had proved him wrong.

He pulled back a bit, raising an eyebrow. Then he hugged her again. "Should I phone Michael?"

She stared at him, then looked away, and whispered, "No."

He drew in a deep breath and held both her hands, telling her he was there for her, no matter what she decided. She paused for a split second as her fingers trembled in his grip. Her eyes shifted between him and the marble floor. Stone waited, giving her the space she needed. He kissed her on the forehead while his thumb brushed over her hand.

She murmured, "I'm sad. I'm not sad. I don't know," followed by a soft, shaky chuckle.

"It's okay babe. "Do you want to see her?"

She snapped her head around, narrowing her eyes in disbelief, staring like he'd lost his mind. Such absurdity. After what felt like an eternity staring at him, she spoke at last. Her voice began soft, rising to a crescendo as she finished. "I don't know. Why should I? To finish her off? Or to beg for forgiveness for running away? Who needs absolution? Bullshit!"

Chapter 37

The air had that hospital smell, disinfectant trying to be sterile, but overpowered by an unsettling stale odor. The smell didn't exactly stink, but it was off-putting enough to make Olivia feel nauseated. She was used to the gentle, airy scents of her spa. She spent most of her time there, after all. Her husband, did most of the talking, enquiring at reception and making some phone calls. He also phoned Michael but she refused to speak to him. The continuous hum of machines broke the tension and kept her distracted. But the hospital didn't feel like a place of healing. Perhaps a place of hearing, but only for today. A few visitors huddled on worn-out metal benches, their quiet murmurs blending with the beeping of machines. A man in a pink high-visibility jacket weaved through the crowd, balancing a tray of snacks and bottles of water. He disappeared now and then, dodging the security officers in a quiet game of cat and mouse. The bright pink jacket didn't make it any easier for him to stay hidden, but he needed it so customers could spot him quickly. Every businessman faces trade-off dilemmas, you have to know when and how to strike the balance. Even in everyday life, the same rule applies. A few young boys gathered in a corner near the Wi-Fi router heads bent over their phones. With the recent surge in mobile data bundle charges, this has become a necessary move. Making use of every free Wi-Fi opportunity, the security risks of public connections weren't a priority for most youth. They needed to stay connected to their socials. While the boys stayed absorbed in their phones, others kept glancing at their watches or fidgeting with their bum bags. On an early sunset like this, the hospital was growing busier. More people trickled in, some wailing, others walking with hurried steps for the visiting hour.

Olivia and Stone were headed for the stairs when the hospital doors slammed open, and a group of four men rushed in. They dragged another writhing, howling man inside. One man's arm was wrapped around the man's chest, the other struggling to lift his legs. They stumbled as they pulled him inside. His weight made it harder for them to move. His limp body hung between them like a log. He bellowed like a cow, louder as his tongue hung out. It was an unmistakable bright blue, typical of a prescription drug used by young people to get high. The most common mix nicknamed *mangemba* consisted of water laced with chlorpromazine, diazepam, and other drugs meant for the mentally ill. There was a blue and pink variation, blue being the most popular. The liquid was a distinct bright blue, commonly used for its sedative effects. An alarming number of youth drank it to feel drunk for days. A constant stupor. Drinking water made the effects stronger, and even being rained on had the same effect. Cheap and rampant on the streets, this concoction plagued the high-density suburbs. Olivia sighed as she watched knowing she had no part in the distribution of illicit drugs. But her brother...the life choices we make for money.

A girl, no older than 18, stood by the entrance. Her uncombed cropped hair had bits of grass, sand and blanket fluff. She leaned against a pillar, hands shaking at her sides as she watched the men drag him in. She wore an oversized black hoodie, its front soiled with what looked like dry vomit, gravy, rice grains, handprints and more. She struggled to stand straight, bending as if her head was loose. One of the men motioned for her to sit on the bench. They tossed the man onto it, one of the men grunting as he let go and stepped back to catch his breath. The men introduced her to the nurses as the patient's wife. She stood there, dazed and frozen, staring at her husband's body like she was seeing him for the first time. Olivia studied her for a moment, then felt Stone nudge her elbow. "Let's go," he whispered. Together, they shuffled towards their visit.

Olivia stood by the ward door, watching the figure hidden under a heap of blankets. She was sunk into the bed, the one who had once held her life at ransom, now ransomed by life itself. She was young, innocent and helpless back then. Now she owned a successful business empire. The woman who made her life unbearable, now lay barely able to breathe without mechanical assistance. Life is a wheel. What goes up, comes down. There she was, only the faint rise and fall of her chest and the beeping machines showing any sign of life. Pale and frail, her once stern face was now softened by age and illness. The great aunt, now a grey shadow of her former self, lay there at the mercy of nurses and time. Her vibrant vitality gone, a mere distant memory. No single trace of it. Erased by time itself.

"I didn't think you'd come," her aunt said in a raspy, weak voice. She strained to lift her head, but it dropped back down.

Olivia paused for a moment, torn between sobbing and staying indifferent. Instead, she studied her relative, the woman who had once held so much power over her. At least oxygen was still free, otherwise, she might have found a way to ration that too, just like everything else. Now, she relied on rationed oxygen from tanks just to survive. The irony of life. This frail woman had orchestrated untold suffering for her. She turned her childhood into a series of lessons in survival. A catalogue of disasters. A series of unfortunate events. A living nightmare. The woman who had berated her and isolated her, instead of being caring and nurturing. She cared more about her pets than Olivia.

"Someone had to," Olivia answered without much thought, cold and flat. She didn't owe her an explanation. Being there was enough. The truth was, she hadn't been forced to visit. But she had been told. Told by the uncles who failed to intervene when she lived a horrible life with them. "They said I should come. The Charakupas, your uncles."

A long pause followed, making Stone fidget uncomfortably while Olivia swallowed hard. She could hear the shallow breaths of the sick woman, the soft whirr of the ventilator by her side. The room felt almost too quiet. Her husband asked if he should excuse them. She shook her head and clutched his hand.

She looked at the monitor, then back at her aunt. "Are you sorry?" she asked, more out of curiosity than anything. She wasn't sure if she even wanted to hear the answer. Aunt sheltered her, and food depending on her mood. There were days when Olivia wondered if she'd have been better off if she'd grown up on the streets. At least the streets welcomed everyone. You had to fight to survive, that's all.

The old aunt's eyes barely blinked, her lips parting as if to speak, but no sound came. She hadn't changed much, still as incapable of real emotion as she had been all those years ago. She had never learnt how to love or show kindness. Now, she was nothing more than an empty shell of the person who had once dominated her life. Only now did Olivia understand why her estranged husband may have left. She had treated him like nobody, as if he were a doormat. She had more money than him. Power dynamics. Life. Would he visit her?

Olivia took one last look at her ailing aunt, indifferent. "I don't need an apology. I'm not here for that. Get well soon, aunt."

She turned to leave with her husband, but at the door, she paused, then made a sharp turn back. She wasn't angry. She wasn't sad. She had forgiven her, for the sake of her sanity. She had let go of the anger long ago, simply because it no longer mattered. She had never been one to wallow in her situation. She had made tonnes of lemonade out of life's lemons. When she ran away those years ago,she went to one of the uncles from the Charakupa family, who had shown compassion whenever they visited her aunt. They were discreet about it, though, for fear of putting her in a more precarious position. They knew aunt pretended to love her like her own child, but they could not take her away because of the legalities. But when Olivia sought refuge with them, they protected her at all costs. She felt indebted to them for life. What had happened, had happened. She wasn't there to make peace. She visited her because she was told to. Even Michael apologised for lashing out at her earlier and encouraged her to visit their aunt, for old times' sake. He would also go to see her later.

When Olivia ran away at 16, she stole Buju's leash, the one with the diamond pendant that had her aunt and uncle's initials engraved on it. Buju had been a wedding anniversary gift from her uncle to his wife, perhaps that's why their initials were on it. When Olivia saw the engraved pendant, she had an inkling that it wouldn't end well. Time proved her right. Sadly, her aunt's affection for her husband had shifted to Buju. He became invisible to her as she grew distant and cold towards him.

Olivia forced her aunt's right palm open and slid the pendant into her hand. "You may want to keep this," she said, leaving before her aunt's trembling mouth could form a reply.

Chapter 38

After their aunt's hospital admission and the nasty squabble with Olivia, Michael flew to Cape Town. He visited aquariums when life got too noisy. Usually once a year, but only at three specific ones. He would pay for the entire day, even though he would only show up for five minutes, maybe an hour. Sometimes it was once in two years, sometimes more, sometimes not at all. He never told anyone his expected arrival time. Security and serenity mattered. The staff knew to be ready whenever he showed up. That is how he liked it.

He had booked the Glamis Atlantis Aquarium for an exclusive day. Security and serenity. He showed up at any hour during that day. The lighting painted the water and walls in shifting shades of blue, green, and yellow. It cast a mesmerising glow throughout the aquarium. Dressed in a Bottega Veneta tailored suit in signature cobalt blue, Michael stood before the giant tank, his hands clasped behind his back. He admired the Common Octopus *(Octopus vulgaris)* floating by with its limbs trailing like ribbons. He stood motionless, staring at the graceful creature with an uncanny fixation. Its slow, fluid movement mirrored his own life, all those tentacles, all the different aspects of his life that worked in perfect unison and often in the shadows. The octopus paused, as if looking at him. Three hearts, one to feel, one to fight, and one to survive. Just like him. He watched the octopus with quiet intensity, arms folded, and eyes narrowed. Lizzy and Timothy fidgeted beside him, he caught it in the corner of his eye and murmured something under his breath. That unsettled Lizzy and Timothy, who exchanged a glance but stayed quiet. Even the aquarium staff found it a little eerie, but they smiled, pretending not to notice. That was how it should be. Always keep the customer happy and Michael was the kind of customer you didn't dare disappoint. Most people became nervous when he focused like that.

"Three hearts," he said to Liza and Timothy. "It takes great stamina to survive with three hearts. One stop beating when they swim, you know. Makes you wonder, doesn't it? What keeps the other two going?"

The two exchanged puzzled looks again. Lizzy nodded while Timothy cleared his throat. They both knew better than to interrupt moments like these. Michael continued, his voice quiet but sharp like a blade. His eyes remained fixated on the octopus, cold and calculating. For a moment, it felt as if they shared a secret.

"They run on copper, not iron. That's why their blood is blue. Built for the deep sea, but not for surface life. It's all about adaptation."

He continued to follow the octopus's movement. "They don't belong anywhere except their world. The deep isn't kind, but they survive all the same."

The octopus's blood reminded him of how he'd endured scarcity growing up. He had conquered it and risen beyond even his expectations. Adaptation.

"They breathe in the deep. I breathe up here," Michael muttered and raised his chin as if exhaling a cigar.

Michael savoured that moment in silence. Then the octopus moved, like ShowTime was over. Same rules. Two different worlds. Always survival of the fittest and fittest. It seemed to pause, as if aware of the eyes watching. Its body pulsed, changing from a dark to a light color.

"They're escape artists too," Michael said, turning to look at Timothy. "No tank can hold them if they decide to leave. They find every weakness, every crack. And once they are out, they are not only escaping, but they are hunting too. Remind you of anyone?"

Timothy nodded, smiling at his boss and showering him with praises that felt a little forced. Michael's lips curled into a slight smirk before turning back to the tank. The octopus darted between coral structures, and Michael waved his hand. When you think of our business," he said in a low voice, "think like an octopus. No wasted movement. Always adaptable. And never trapped," Michael smiled so broadly it reflected on the glass tank. The muffled sound of water sloshing against the tank seemed to acknowledge his speech. It was the aquarium's serene ambiance that he liked, especially when he had it all to himself. He looked back at the octopus, now wrapping its tentacles around a chunk of coral. His lips twitched as it squeezed like a jealous lover.

"They can be down, but never out," Michael said.

Timothy's phone buzzed, a discreet message from their team outside. Three quick vibrations signal a warning of unwanted visitors outside. In an instant, Timothy was on the phone. Michael turned to him, his voice dropping to a low growl. "How many?"

"Two. Armed and moving through the front entrance."

Michael remained calm, like still water. "They'll try to corner us near the shark tank," he said, already five steps ahead of the game plan. "Take the front. We'll cover the back."

Timothy hesitated, "You sure, boss?"

Michael paused, throwing one last look at the octopus. "There's always a way out," he said in a cold tone. "Know where to squeeze, that's all."

Chapter 39

Timothy's forearm slammed into the first gunman's throat before he could raise his weapon. A perfect choke slam. His pistol clattered to the tiles, skidding beneath a display of jellyfish.

Michael and Lizzy watched the shark glide past, its shadow sweeping the tank wall like a blade. They saw the second man approach and waited for him to get close. The reflection in the glass gave him away. Tiptoeing and hunched like that, he looked like a cartoon burglar. Lizzy fought hard to muffle a chuckle, while Michael shook his head. Amateurs. He could smell a novice from a mile off. Sickening inexperience. You could see it in every clumsy step. Lizzy grabbed the second man's arm as he stepped out from behind the metal stairs, half-shadowed by the glow of tanks. Before he could react, she twisted it hard and drove him sideways into the filtration unit. His gun clattered to the floor, sliding out of his reach. The intruder lay there bewildered for a moment, eyes wide and chest heaving like he had been running from the cops. He looked way out of shape for such shenanigans. He could do better in an eating contest than in a fight. Better still, he could land a gig as Santa Claus with that beer belly. Meanwhile, Lizzy's taekwondo and self-defense skills had kicked in on instinct. No time for finesse. No shots. No shouts. Michael cracked his knuckles and stepped over the man, picked up the gun, and stuffed it into his coat. He always knew where to squeeze, like an octopus.

In the control room above the exhibits, the shift supervisor locked the main gate camera feed and switched to interior communications protocol. The front doors locked automatically, and emergency lights illuminated throughout the building. He knew Michael's visit meant heightened security. But no one had ever needed to use those procedures. Until now. And everyone knew one thing for sure: mess with Michael, and you might lose your whole life.

Michael grabbed the man from the floor, forcing him up to his knees while pressing his forearm into the back of his neck to keep him pinned.

"Who sent you?"

The man ignored Michael. He curled his lip into a sneer and stared at Michael without a hint of fear. Lizzy crouched beside him, searching his pockets. Michael checked his watch. He figured reinforcements weren't on their way. If backup was coming, it'd have shown up already. No, this was a small job for amateurs, and on purpose. A message. And he had received it loud and clear. But he knew that the quiet after the storm never lasted.

By then, Timothy had dragged the other man to where Michael and Lizzy stood. The shark circled behind the glass like a beast pacing its cage. Timothy pushed the first man into the same position as his partner, knees down, neck pinned. He drove his knee into the man's back until he gasped.

"Who sent you?" Timothy hissed.

Both men grimaced but kept quiet. Lizzy also dug through his pockets: a phone, a pocketknife, and a box of condoms. No ID. She paused, held the box up and gave a dry laugh. Timothy gave a low whistle. Michael glanced at the box, then back at him and muttered, "Ribbed strawberry flavor. Seriously? Brains full of hormones."

"Make him talk," bellowed Michael. Timothy's grip tightened, fingers digging into the man's neck. Lizzy knelt in front of them again, her tone soft. "You won't talk? If you behave, we'll let you go. If not, that shark is hungry."

Both men looked up as if mesmerised by her gentle voice. The second man spoke. Then his phone rang. Lizzy handed it to Timothy.

"It's Charles, boss! He sent them."

The name sent a chill through Michael. Charles was supposed to be dead, a fossil by now. At least, that's what everyone believed. Michael ordered Timothy to find out how he was still alive, who he was working with, and where he was. What Timothy didn't tell Michael was that Charles had asked him why his wife had an octopus tattoo on her thigh, and why Michael liked octopuses.

Chapter 40

Lisa went to her village in Chiweshe against her husband's wishes. She realised that being a wife also meant she sometimes had to be defiant, not always submissive. In-laws would step on your toes, as would relatives, workmates, and even neighbors. And yes, even the neighborhood dogs. Lisa, "the good wife" was a title she now felt ready to toss away, like over-chewed gum, long past its flavor. It could resurface. Who knows? Who cares anymore? Her in-laws always complained and trampled over her, saying their nephew stopped sending them money once they got married. They even blamed her for his infrequent visits to the village. For two years, her chicken project had flourished until her sister-in-law hijacked it. Frustrated and powerless, Lisa had to abandon it. Her infamous sister-in-law lived down the road, with enough manpower to take full charge of the chicken runs. This year, though, Lisa had had enough.

Lisa travelled to Nzvimbo, a communal area in Chiweshe under the jurisdiction of Chief Nzvimbo and his several headmen *(masabhuku)*. She struck a deal with Sabhuku Gore. Sabhuku deals were common, and Lisa saw nothing wrong with selling one or two herself. She knew her husband would never approve, especially with him being a detective. The police were hunting down Sabhuku deal culprits, but the law was hard to enforce due to lack of sufficient paperwork. Lisa wanted her land to run a massive poultry, piggery, and market gardening project. This would be entirely her project, one that her sister-in-law couldn't snatch from her. Here, her in-laws would have no stake in her venture. They had no basis.

Lisa arrived early, as the herd boys were leading the cattle out to graze. Dew still covered the ground as a fresh morning breeze blew through her weave, carrying the faint clatter of hooves on dry ground. The fresh air made her nose tingle, nothing like the polluted air in Harare.

Her husband was out of town on duty, chasing a narcotics case. He didn't need to know she had gone to Chiweshe. Each partner deserves a bit of independence. She had left her mum with the kids. Chiweshe being less than a 2-hour trip from her house, knew she would be back before her husband returned home.

Upon arrival, Lisa followed all the traditional protocols of respecting Sabhuku Gore. He greeted her with a broad smile, his eyes lingering on her for a moment too long. She found it odd but brushed it off. The headman's wife had run off with her high school sweetheart the moment he came back from the diaspora. She had left without a second thought. Since then, the headman had become one of the most eligible bachelors in Nzvimbo. He had a title, cattle, and a monthly allowance from the government. Many women dreamed of a life like that. Those who eyed him tried in every way to seduce him, but he chose to remain single. He still hoped his wife would come back one day.

Sabhuku Gore showed Lisa two plots of fertile land, ideal for her planned projects. He refused to price the plots, saying business deals were best discussed behind closed doors. Lisa understood. She had worked in the corporate world for a long time. After the tour, the headman dismissed his security detail and invited Lisa inside his house to continue the conversation and finalise things away from prying eyes and ears. He went inside first, and by the time Lisa stepped in, he had already taken off his track pants.

Sabhuku Gore stood there wearing only a floral viscose shirt, his massive weapon dangling but firm. Lisa's eyes widened, though she quickly masked her surprise. In the blink of an eye, the weapon sprang to attention, ready for battle. Lisa froze. She tried to scream but choked, managing only a gasp. She clutched her temples, too frozen to move or run outside. A strange mix of amusement and disgust rose in her throat. The nerve. How could he even think of that? Gross. Even in the modern dating scene, no one wants to receive an unsolicited dick pic, though, of course, there are outliers. Lisa knew right away she couldn't report the headman, after all, *ex turpi causa non oritur actio* (no action arises from a dishonourable cause). She was part of the same illegal deal. Above all, she knew she would never tell her husband, the detective.

With that, Lisa stormed out and drove back to Harare, struggling to unsee the disturbing image of Sabhuku Gore's manhood. Someone needed to create an app to help unsee things. Some things are just too hard to unsee.

Chapter 41

Standing tall, donning cargo pants, legs spread and arms folded and chin raised stubbornly mimicking a crocodile male submitting to the boss. Aunty Jo was crazy, steady, slim, sleek, slender and swift. There was an irresistible air of graciousness around her and she had a pleasant personality that she displayed whenever she chose to but when you cross her path you needed to be careful.

Back in the day, she had joined Karate as a sport in school, but when there was an increase in bullying from boys and other bigger girls, she took the sport seriously. She went all the way till she was a Black Belt Shotokan. However, with all that she chose a quiet life. Each morning, she would wake up at 4 am and exercise for an hour, then perform Karate Katas. Not many people dared to challenge her. Nobody was aware of her achievements, yet many kept their distance, there were danger signals written all over her, yet nobody had been harmed in any way.

"Timothy don't be a pussy, I need you to be in your best mood right, what you are thinking, we agreed that you were to look for contact people and establish a market to increase the uptake," Aunty Jo warned, fists clenched unmistakably pointed at Timothy.

Timothy moved close to Aunty Jo and he had decided that he was to put this meddling big-mouthed granny into her place. He raised his hand in an attempt to slap her, but she saw it coming, she grabbed his hand twisting it at once, while her right leg sent him to the ground.

Michael had always suspected that Aunty Jo was a tough bitch, and he knew it was a matter of time before they crossed paths with Timothy.

"What a rare pleasure," Michael said, he thought he was whispering but everyone heard him.

Timothy took forever to rise. Forget the physical wound, there was something bigger, and his ego was bleeding profusely. He was never going to recover from this incident. Michael's right-hand man, the henchman was "woman handled" by a granny. Olivia was missing out on a lot of time. Timothy knew that Michael was going to tell Olivia, and he decided to play cool and take revenge in a big way to turn the tables.

I have managed to set up a market in the following areas. Kuwadzana, we have maps as our man, Nancy Blue, the baddest bitch in town, has agreed to set us up as a consultant for three months covering Central town and Avenues, but she will train our boys and let them gain experience under her watch. We have Bra Eddy taking care of the Chitungwiza town, Luci is taking care of Mbare and Glen Norah. We need products. We must move fast, adverts have gone into the market already and I want my numbers up.

Michael was impressed, he approved the deal and on second thought looked at Timothy and asked what he thought and Timothy nodded in an instant showing his support. Timothy jumped to attack Aunty Jo but she kicked him in the gut in midair. A second defeat and a big lesson, fracturing what's left of the ego. Meanwhile Michael received a call, it was Olivia, and the aunt who raised her, the one they had visited a few days ago had passed on.

Olivia spent the day and the night that followed thinking deeply about her upbringing. Her relationship with her aunt was terrible, and she had endured abuse in the hands of her father's sister. Olivia had mixed feelings about her aunt. She was aware that life could have been so tough if she had not found anyone looking after her and she longed to have a father and mother figure.

Arriving at the funeral hour, the exact place she grew up, starting from the gate, Olivia started having visions, images of the cruelty that she had suffered in the hands of her aunt, who now lay in the coffin.

"Michael, this is a difficult funeral for me, I longed to have a great relationship with my aunt, but each time I reached out to her, she snubbed me. Olivia remarked.

"It's a tough one my dear, I believe we may need to remember her as someone who offered us shelter and food as well as hard training, if you had been taken in by a poor Aunt in the rural areas you could have been a wife to an Agriculture Extension officer attending filed days and always huddled at the back of a motor bike from time to time. Michael responded.

"Michael, you know this is not an easy thing, it's a complex legacy that my aunt left, and it will always be difficult to remember her. Olivia responded.

"I hear you, but the question is would you have looked after someone and do a better job?" Michael responded.

"Michael, I don't know if I have done a better job looking after someone's child," Olivia responded, tears flowing. The tears were tears of regret that perhaps she would have tried to reach out to her aunt when she was independent. She allowed her childhood upbringing to take a center stage and that precluded her from expressing gratitude all this time. But it was too late, the aunt had died.

At the funeral, there was a letter that the aunt had asked to be read to everyone.

"To Olivia, I knew that you were an orphan, and I raised you as such. I needed to raise a self-sufficient, self-reliant person who can stand on their own. As an orphan you needed to be put through some of the most rigorous training, and I purposefully denied you luxuries. I created in you a strong and self-reliant person and even in the grave I will never regret raising you and showing you how rough the world is. You were too young to get it. I hope you will be able to understand someday. I also have a challenge for you. I need you to take an orphan and look after them and do a great job.

"I know you will do a better job. To stone, I want to say please look after Olivia, my child, she is the only baby I know who can look after my things. For that reason I express my wish and desire that Olivia be the administrator of my estate, this is not negotiable. I registered a trust a long time ago and you signed the papers when you were young. I knew I could count on you.

Goodbye."

Listening to the letter being read, each word was like a knife stabbing on her heart, she broke into a loud cry. Stone was by her side to comfort her and tell her that all would be well.

Chapter 43

They say newspapers sell headlines, and indeed, some headlines are difficult to ignore. The Southern Eye had a headline, "Michael Paradzai on a free fall as empire crumbles, Farm burnt USD 2.5 million loss," Michael sent people to buy the newspaper in bulk from every street corner, kiosk and all supermarkets. By 9 am, many people had heard about it, and again he sent people offering USD 10 per copy to anyone who had that paper. The website that had carried the story was hacked, and for a week, it could not display anything. The internet was slowed down to a level where one could not send documents.

Michael sent people with money and groceries in Mbare, Mufakose and Kuwadzana, he left the goods in the care of vendors to distribute. The chaos that followed was unprecedented. Riot police in full combat gear were dispatched to all the local and international media houses that covered the story. In Kuwadzana 3 and 4 people were seriously injured as there was a tug of war as residents tried to benefit from the money and the food that was just dumped.

There was drama in Mufakose as a man was axed after refusing to give up some of the loot that he had acquired during the scuffle. Meanwhile the military had to be called in to quell the violence that occurred in Mbare and Mabvuku. Political rivals took the opportunity with each claiming that the money and goods were from their political party. In the end Native Investments issue was drowned by the numerous reports on social media and news bulletins.

By 4 pm, Native Investments was on the news, donating assistance to pay for medical bills for the injured and providing assistance.

Michael instructed an international Harley Reid Advisory Services to submit an offer to purchase all the private newspapers without revealing the ultimate beneficiary. The deals were handled by an international fund management firm in the US. Native Investments offloaded some of its investments in the US to purchase the local newspaper firms. The deals were done overnight with valuation reports done in four hours and a total of USD 10 million was required to purchase the 4fournews paper firms. Given the poor liquidity and limited growth opportunities, many owners saw this as an opportunity to exit with something. Michael was cursing himself why he had allowed these papers to write shit about him all along. He could have purchased the papers a long time ago and enjoyed the favor of telling his side of the story, but that was in the past. *Zvamanje manje ndini ndine chimuti* (Right now I am the one in charge.)

The following day, all the papers wrote heroic stories about Native Investments, portraying Michael as a responsible citizen. *"Michael is a philanthropist par excellence, a son of the soil with a heart of liquid gold,"* one of the newspapers wrote.

Michael was at the site of his burnt down-house. Several people came to see him and encouraged him. A team from a UK construction company was on site to redesign the house, while a South African company team was compiling the materials that were needed to rebuild the house.

Chapter 42

Simbarashe Makoni was a farm manager at Native Agri-business. A business that Michael Paradazai had started as a hobby. The farm itself was situated 40 km east of Harare. A river meandered across the 10,000 hectares farm with three dams having been constructed by the former white farmer who had used the farm for more than 50 years. The land was taken over by the government and was earmarked for expansion of the City of Harare. There were confidential documents which Michael was able to gain access to and after that, he saw an opportunity to make money. He was playing a long game on this one.

According to the future town planning, the farm was to be used for low-income housing on its north end while a commercial center was to be constructed on the central part of it. An airport was to be constructed in the south part, this was to be a mini extension to the City of Harare. Michael Paradzai had an eye for real estate. He was able to distinguish a good deal from a bad deal, yet all his deals were illegal but highly profitable.

Simbarashe Makoni was an experienced farm manager having graduated from Blackfordby College of Agriculture. He moved to South Africa, where he was a manager for a farm measuring 1800 hectares for ten years. Later he managed a farm measuring 20 000 hectares in Australia for 15 years. The farm had dairy cattle, and two wings where wheat was mass-produced. Australia produces between 3-4% of world's total wheat production. He had a short stint in the US in the state of Texas, where he managed a farm that was so big measuring 20 square kilometers. It was at that farm as well as years spent in Australia that he became a commercial farmer of note. Simbarashe received three Honours from the Prime Minister of Australia, a recognition of his outstanding contribution to agribusiness.

At the time of his return to Zimbabwe, he was sitting on a number of special purpose committees of the World Bank Food Program. He consulted CYMMATY, Syngenta, and a number of other global brands of note.

Simbarashe had been promised a 10% share of the profits among other benefits he was entitled to.

As pressure for Michael from his other illegal activities mounted, he began to spend more time at the farm. On that particular week he had come to the farm on Friday evening, something he had never done in a long time.

The farm had over 2000 hectares of wheat that was almost ready for harvest. There were 1000-hectares fields of winter maize that were ripe, and a combine harvester had been brought to commence the harvesting. On the other side of the farms were dairy farming operations where 100 Daisy cattle were being reared, producing 12 liters of milk per day giving a total of 1200 liters per day. 36,000 liters per month and an average of 432,000 liters per year. The manager had bought cheese making machine and managed to make lacto that was used as an accompaniment for *Nshima* (*Sadza*) a local staple food. Everything was falling into place. The manure collected were used in the 500 hectares of organic food production.

There were 35 rotating security guards with trained German Shepherd dogs trained to guard at night.

At 3 am on a Tuesday in the month of October 2024, the dogs started barking continuously, then went quiet one by one.

"What is the matter babe? Why don't you team up with the staff and check it out?" Charlotte, the farm manager's wife, urged the sleepy manager.

"Don't worry babe dogs are like that, if there are no distress calls from the security team, we will let it be," the farm manager responded.

"If you say so, babe you know the harvest is almost ready we don't want thieves breaking in and start harvesting our labour. Anyway I trust your decisions. I trust your judgment," Charlotte responded while moving closer to Simbarashe and resting on his chest, a place she desired all the time, and she went back to sleep immediately.

At 03:45 am, the alarm went off, and all the servants stirred awake, disoriented and half-dressed.

A fire broke out in the wheat fields. The balls of fire started from various corners. At first it was thought that one of the security guards had dropped a cigarette stub but the pattern was rather unusual. The blaze came from all angles. The foreman from the maize fields came with a report that a similar fire had just been started and it was coming from all corners of the fields. The manager stood there listening to the reports that were coming from various foremen and supervisors.

By 4 am, visibility was becoming better and better.

"We are in trouble sir!" Jorum yelled from a distance.

"What is the matter Jorum," the manager was beginning to worry, and he was not sure what the issue could be. Surely the cattle could not have been burnt.

"Sir, all the dairy cattle are dead. They were killed by opening their stomachs. I have never seen such level of wickedness in my life. My wife and I are leaving, and we cannot survive in such a situation," Jorum remarked.

"Relax Joe, we need to make a police report. This is the work of the enemy," Simbarashe responded.

Michael woke to the sound of commotion outside his room. The farm manager was standing at Michael's door.

"Good morning boss, we have intruders. The wheat and the maize have all been burnt to ashes. Nothing left of commercial value. I have done a preliminary assessment around the farm, and it's a total loss Sir," the farm manager briefed him.

Michael was silent for a moment. He looked troubled but was not about to show weakness. He was deep in thought, not about the loss, but based on his personality. He probably wanted to know who had done it. He needed answers and he needed them right there.

Michael shifted his gaze to the manager.

"Do the guards know who did it? Make a full report and brief me. So we have made a total loss?" Michael asked casually as if it were an unimportant matter to him. Millions of dollars had just been destroyed, yet there he was calm and collected.

"Sir, all the Daisy dairy cattle were killed, 100 of them. Their stomachs were split open, and they died slowly and painfully. And there is more, all the heifers have been killed, all 600of them," the manager responded keeping a distance.

"The heifers were all killed, with no external wounds. If it were the rainy season, we could have been dealing with lightning, but not to the extent of 600 dying at once. Snake bites are also common killers, especially Black Mambas, but in this area we only have problems with pythons, besides Black Mambas don't kill the whole herd. I will take the water and the grass for lab tests," the farm manager explained while Michael was listening.

Michael was looking at the manager explaining and his heart was filled with deep-seated respect and awe for the farm manager. A man who was making millions from a farming business. Michael had regretted that he only knew crooked ways to make money.

There was a tobacco storage facility where the tobacco that had been packed and ready for delivery to the auction floors was burnt as well. The estimated value according to the manager was USD 3.9 million.

Michael was stunned that the thing that he used to do to others was now done to him. The problem was that he had too many suspects. And in most cases the perpetrator is much closer than you think or someone one wronged when they were powerless and eventually garner the power where it hurts the most.

"Sir, please do not lose heart," the farm accountants remarked noticed they were coming out of the Borrowdale police station to make a police report.

"That's very reassuring son. I lost millions and here you are telling me not to lose heart," Michael responded.

"Sir, if it's any consolation, we have insurance for fire, so we are likely to recover losses for all the crops and the tobacco. The poisoned cattle may strike a chance, but the dairy cattle, we do not know what the insurance company will say as the indications lead to a risk that is not covered," the accountant responded.

Michael was looking at the accountant, he was wondering why he was never taught how to do business as at a young age., That way he would have managed to do things the right way, he admired the accountant speaking up to him. In the world of business, professionals speak freely to their superiors unlike the drug and illegal land grabbers.

In the afternoon they went back to the farm and the head of security had finished running the CCTV, but the camera had not picked up anything unusual. This led them to believe that whoever did it must have gained access to the farm facilities during the day. Another run showed all the cars that went in. But when Michael was shown the video footage, he took ten hours looking at it and he demanded the details of a Toyota Hilux AFG 1947. The car was registered in the name of Bob Maheya according to the records at CVR. According to immigration records, Bob had left the country. Contact was made but he indicated the car was being used by an engineer colleague who had been in the United States for 10 years recovering from a terrible accident that almost killed him.

Something was unsettling about what Bob said, "An engineer friend who had been in the States for ten years, had an accident that almost killed him." Michael knew that he had many enemies in business and these were powerful enemies and in most cases intelligent.

Two months earlier Dr Engineer Makaza had come to the farm looking for a job at the Native Agribusiness. He worked efficiently and improved many roads and because he was elderly, he was never asked too many questions. He was allowed to start work immediately, and he was given access to every part of the farm.

Michael had an instinct that the perpetrator of the crime worked with an internal staff. All the staff members were summoned and questioned by the police. Dr Engineer Makaza moved slowly, holding a stick and when he appeared he had tattered clothes and what looked like mucus that flowed and was never wiped. The police dismissed him.

From there, the old man went to his room to rest. And exactly 10 Minutes later there was a thunderous sound all six cars that were in the parking bay were blown to pieces. The main plant where cattle feed and other farm accessories were stored was gutted by fire. There was a boom sound like that of supersonic concord plane breaching the speed of sound, the fuel reserves were up in smoke, in broad daylight and when Michael was there.

There was chaos and panic gripped the farm workers as many ran for cover.

Police came and interviews continued. This time, they were determined to investigate everyone. Michael might have had an idea of who would want to kill him and bring his business to its knees. This was not a rival gang. This was someone from the office who had coordinated the attack. How they executed the attacks in the early hours of the day and the during the day remained a total mystery to Michael. He was not sure what to think, who to accuse or how to process this. He had been used to being the top dog and the invincible. Threatened anyone who dared to speak or stand in his way. He did not know how to process any form of attack from rivals.

Detective Mike was called to the scene. He moved away from the entire scene, and he started taking notes before talking to anyone.

Detective Mike gestured to the farm manager.

"Who has access to the entire plant, offices, farm and drives?" Detective Mike enquired.

"Detective, where are you getting at, it's only me, Michael. The rest of the team requires approval to access certain areas," the farm Manager responded looking shocked and rather annoyed by the line of enquiry.

"Are you sure these are the only people?"

"Well there is an old man who joined us as an engineer. He is a bit confused but he has access to all the facilities, from cattle, farmland, equipment, boilers to fuels and the workshop," the manager responded while arms crossed and legs spread in an act of annoyance and frustration at the same time.

Detective Mike looked at the farm manager. "May I have his file?" Detective Mike demanded.

"The old man is more of a casual employee so we do not hold many details apart from his phone records," the farm manager responded.

"Can you call him, I want to talk to him," the detective demanded.

The farm manager sent for the Engineer. When he appeared, he was wearing a torn cap, a trousers with many patches and a faded shirt. Detective Mike was called to report to the office with immediate effect. He left the other detectives working on the matter.

The following morning, the Engineer did not report for duty.

Michael was trying to understand what was happening in his life. While at the office, he received a message that there was an explosion at his house. The fire department wanted the gate open to put out the fire but even then there was no way of reaching his fortified house. So it was, the house was burnt down.

Dr Engineer Makaza had bombed the farm using drones carrying makeshift petrol bombs that exploded on target. He had employed the same tactic and Michael was devastated but the property was no longer important, for the first time he feared for his life.

The insurance company called to indicate that they needed more time assessing the claim. They wanted to finalise their investigations. They were treating the whole situation as a crime scene and sabotage which the insurance companies do not pay.

Michael received a call with a hidden caller ID.

"Good evening Michael. How is life treating you?" the caller said. "Life is going on well, may I know who it is I am speaking to and why are you calling me?" Michael responded.

"I am the man you wanted to kill but failed. You wanted to kill me because of an environmental report that I had made and supported my decision to terminate the deal. So now that you got away with it, what did you achieve? I spent 10 years trying to recover from multiple fractures that you caused me. My family has suffered, spending every penny they had to get me into the best health facilities. You are a wizard, and I have come to kill you. It's a pity to have run out of luck my dear. This time you are going down," the Engineer remarked.

"I don't know who you are, but are picking on the wrong person, and will regret all these actions. I am a man capable of a lot of things," Michael ranted

"You see Michael your anger is clouding your judgment. Even the gods eventually die. I recommend you read a book called, "the gods above." The book will teach you how the mighty are eventually defeated. You had done well but greed and an insatiable appetite for power and dominance will destroy all that you have worked for," Engineer Makaza responded.

Michael had to admit that he had been outwitted by the Engineer. He had not seen this one coming. For a man who prided himself as a grand strategist, he had realised that there were loose ends. This was beginning to reveal a pattern. One that he was not clinical in execution, he was brutal, hungry for money, but was never meticulous in concluding his deals. The reason why most of the deals that he had involved himself in, landed him either in prison or at least in court.

Chapter 44

Michael was rattled by the recent streak of misfortunes that hit him. The losses at the farm, and the resignation of the farm manager. Michael was sure that he was never going to run the farm to the size and scale it had been before. He, however, did not want to pay compensation for the land.

There is a meeting on Thursday morning. Michael was the first to arrive, he had spent time with his wife the previous day and was in high spirits. The agenda of the meeting was to discuss the new housing project. There was a growing call from some powerful politicians from three main political players to take over the Native Agribusiness farm.

The meeting started at 07:35 am in Michael's office.

For the first time, the meeting started with a word of prayer. A surprising shift which may have been prompted by recent losses, attempts on his life, and the revenge from Dr. Makaza. Michael had shown a weakness that had never been seen before. He had been used to killing people, kidnapping, and human trafficking and he had not had a chance to feel what it meant to be violated in the manner he had inflicted on others. He was in denial. His mind failed to process how someone out there could be so meticulous and careful, in planning to burn down the whole farmland, the storehouse as well as bombing his house.

Investigations indicated that the house was burnt by makeshift explosives. A burnt drone was found at the scene and it was difficult to determine whether it was used in the arson attack or was part of Michael's property.

"We are under attack from all angles. Our enemies have been emboldened by the recent attack in Cape Town. You know, there is a cartoon I once saw where grasshoppers dominated the ants. And when one ant stood up against the chief grasshopper while addressing the ants, fellow grasshoppers asked their leader to let it slide as it it was only one ant. However the chief grasshopper took one seed and threw it to one grasshopper and asked if it hurt to which it responded with a loud laugh. Then the chief poured all the seeds and the grasshoppers were overwhelmed. The moral of the story is that if you allow one person to undermine us then you embolden the rest of our enemies to dare us," Michael explained.

There was silence in the room as people were trying to gauge Michael's mood. He was not angry, and he was not laughing either. He was in a crab-fraying mood.

Michael stood up, looking at each of the team members in the eyes before he spoke slowly. "I want Engineer Makaza's head. We will not be able to recover from this loss. We need information on whoever he is working with, pay whatever price we need to end the day on top of the situation," Michael left the meeting without telling anyone where he was going.

At 11 am, an urgent meeting was called for, this time in the boardroom. Michael did not waste time, skipping all the pleasantries, going straight to the point. We have gathered information that seems to suggest that the farm could be seized. I had been patiently waiting for the change of government to start selling the land in a different era. That way the new government will take time to notice, and we would have created massive gains in the front line. Michael opined.

"Yes sir," Timothy responded. He wanted something challenging to regain and repair his brutally wounded ego and pride when he was struck twice by Aunty Jo. He needed to manage something big.

The graphic designers went to work. A website was designed. Using their internal people they managed to have a master plan for the development of the land into residential stands. A provision for two high schools, two primary schools and three preparatory schools was made. There was a provision for a shopping complex, hospital, churches among others. Makokonyare and Madhini were the legal practitioners while One-way Real Estate was in charge of the sale of the stands.

The land preparations started, internal gravel roads were opened, and images were posted on the website daily. Aerial videos with voiceover videos were deposited onto the website. The stands were sold to the diaspora community and all five local newspapers reported on the advertisement of the stands. A place for a university was also reserved.

Native Investments managed to make significant developments in the six months that followed. This time they managed to have a walled and gated community system. They put in a mini sewer and water reticulation system, as well as, installed electric poles and paid for connections. This was done in one of the 10 phases. The starting price for the 2000 CM stood at USD 120000 sold on a cash basis with the money deposited in offshore accounts. The first batch was sold within a week of advertising. All the 200 stands were sold, raising USD 2.4 million.

Following the progress registered in phase 1 of the Gold Burg town. The deposits for the subsequent phases received all the way to phase 5 at a price of USD 180 per SM giving USD 180 000. Realising 3.6 million per phase bringing total revenue to 14.4

million and a total combined revenue of USD 16.8 million. Apart from USD 400 per stand for joining the resident's association, USD 50 site fee, USD 500 per stand for water and electricity connection, as well as routine road maintenance per household. The security fee was to be paid every month.

Zimbabweans had been battling with limited investment options after the collapse of the Zimbabwe Stock exchanges and the stagnation of the Victoria Falls Stock Exchange. The lack of land with proper title deeds has led to many falling victim of the Land Barons.

The months that followed saw growing unease among the prospective homeowners who had made payments to secure their land. Double allocations, changing of stand numbers without informing the owners were scams that Native Investments engaged in.

Chapter 45

It was a Monday morning, the sky was clear, birds were chirping from the trees dotted around the yard, and the day was promising to be a great one. At the Native Investments site office, a small queue had started forming. The staff members were aware that there had been growing unease among the clients.

By 9 pm, the reception was full, and some clients had to sit outside waiting for their turn. There was an unusual pattern forming where clients would not leave the office after they were attended to.

"An official came to the reception and made an announcement. "Good morning everyone, we are kindly asking that those who would have been served should make way for the incoming clients. We would appreciate it if we could clear the car park as well as we have limited parking space," the official requested.

There was a moment of silence as the clients were trying to process the announcement. There was a shadow of mistrust between the clients and the Native Investments officials. After some time, there were some murmurings, and the crowds that had started building up like vultures circling a dying animal, had started departing one by one. The departure was, however, unusual as conversations were taken outside and there was a lot of exchange of numbers. While it is not uncommon for Zimbabweans to network, normally there are united by adversity and necessity. They are usually divided people who cannot work together to achieve a common goal or a common good for society, whether at home or abroad. An opinion that some have refuted, while others have agreed to.

"Good morning ma'am," I have come to sign an agreement of sale. We made a payment last week and submitted our proof of payment via email," one Isaac, a client, demanded

"Good Morning," the lady at the reception responded revealing a "milk" white tooth. A diastema on the upper deck was visible, the lady wore a big smile revealing her clean gums that were spotless. Her dimples added to her beauty and a small chin dimple was quite a sight. She wore earrings that matched with her Rolex watch and the gold wedding ring on her finger. She had such a presence and served all her clients while maintaining eye contact. Her mannerisms made many admire her, she was a great listener. Never interjecting in a client, no matter how the client looks. Many men had asked her out despite the visible wedding band. She was an hourglass, with a waist, a great future behind her and a big chest, perhaps she was the war chest for Native Investments. She spoke softly, not fast, not slow. Her voice rightly pitched, she was alert, firm and fair in all her dealings. Many clients loved dealing with her.

It was said that when she went on maternity leave, there was a significant decline in the number of client enquiries. Many clients lagged behind with their residents' association monthly payments. This prompted Native Investments to cut her leave short, and she was given a five-months breast feeding where she would report for duty at 9 am and leave at noon. Candice was such a great asset to Native Investments.

"Good morning sir, how can I be of assistance today?" Candice responded.

"My name is Tinei, I made a payment for stand number 12 in the second phase, and there was a person on the stand already. I was subsequently moved to number 25 and again it belonged to someone. Last week I was promised that the matter will be resolved by Friday. Again, there was no solution offered. I would appreciate it if this matter could be resolved today. I have already spent so much time and I cannot continue taking time off from work," he explained. There was a sense of powerlessness and despair in the manner he described his ordeal.

Candice lifted her head. "I am very sorry to hear that you have not been assisted and I understand that it is frustrating to be moving up and down with no resolution to the matter. My understanding is that currently there is an ongoing audit that will be most likely to be completed in three weeks from now. I have made a note of your matter and I will include it in the high level report for allocation of stands earlier than the three weeks. As soon as we have stands that are not mixed up we shall be in a position to allocate you the first available stands," Tinei was devastated, but the bearer of the news made it easy for him to accept.

The next three clients overhead the discussion and decided to just leave the office and check after three weeks.

"I need a refund right now right here!," a client said. This caught Candice off guard as she had lowered her head picking up some documents from the drawer.

"Good morning sir, how may I help?" Candice replied while her hands were shaking though not visibly. The man did not respond for some time and a moment of silence followed.

"I need my money ma'am, I made a payment for USD 180 000 and signed an agreement of sale, and I am waiting for my title deeds. There has not been any development on the land and the slow progress that was there has since been halted," the man fumed with anger.

"Sir, may you follow me to the consultation rooms I want to allocate you someone who can speak to you," Candice suggested.

Candice retrieved a file for Norman Tavaziva. Sitting across from Norman, the man had calmed down somewhat, but his mouth was half open, perhaps he was ready to respond. Candice remained quiet as she studied the papers in the file and she briefly asked a waiter to bring some coffee for the client. Norman resisted somehow but when he realised that Candice did not insist on it he decided to agree. After some time Candice looked at Norman who was now totally calm and sank into the clients' easy chair.

"Sir, I have gone through your file, and I believe you have every reason to be unhappy with Native Investments. I want to apologise and ask for one week to find a definitive answer to this matter," Candice responded.

Norman looked at her as she was speaking, and when she was done, he looked around and then lowered his head and spoke in a whispering voice. "My dear, you are a very smart and beautiful employee who works hard and means well, but I need you to do yourself a favor. Leave this company at once, you need to leave now before it's too late. Here is my business card. If you ever need a job I will be happy to have you work for me."

Client after client, there was drama, and Candice was getting overwhelmed. When the office closed for lunch, she took all her things, and she never returned to the office from that day. She had called asking for permission to attend to her sick child. By 2:30 pm there was a huge crowd that had assembled further down east of the Native Investments site office. There was no commotion, but something was brewing.

"Ladies and gentlemen we need to be united in this matter. We need to look for a lawyer to represent us, we need representation," a man with a thin moustache was addressing the crowd that had left the Native Investments offices.

"I second that," an old timer yelled.

"Well there is need for a class action," another one responded.

Three police vehicles approached and asked the crowd to disperse as they were having an unapproved public gathering.

Native Investments was back in court again, this time, there was a class action. A group of home seekers who had various grievances had approached Mr Stephen Conley Attorneys, a law firm that was known for meaningful high-profile cases. There were whispers about ethical matters but there was no time for due diligence.

Chapter 46

Michael had travelled to Rome, he was one of the thousands of people who had gone to the Pope Benedict's funeral and came back for the Papal Conclave.

"Hey man can you explain to me this whole papal conclave thing? How does it work," Michael asked a one Martinez.

"My name is Martinez. I have been coming here for the papal conclave each time a new Pope is about to be ordained. A conclave or papal conclave is a gathering of the to appoint a new pope of the Catholic Church, and this happens after the death of a pope," Martinez explained, beaming with confidence and a desire to say more.

"Amazing, so what is the significance of the Pope anyway?" Michael followed up.

"Are you serious my friend?" Martinez responded while making a cross-like gesture.

"It is a widely believed position that the Catholics consider the pope to be the apostolic successor of Saint Peter and the earthly head of the Catholic Church. The pope is considered the leader of the Church," Martinez replied.

Each time Martinez spoke there was a deep sense of pride and an "I am happy to assist you pagan."

"How is the selection of the pope safeguarded from influence by global superpowers trying to shape the world order?" Michael asked casually while looking over the buildings where the whole election and where the cardinals were going to be meeting.

Martinez was capturing some scenes of scores of people flocking into to catch the vibe. The spiritual anointing that may perhaps come from being close to the appointment of the leader of the Catholic Church. He remained quiet for some time as if he had not heard what Michael had asked.

"My friend, you ask a very important question. Concerns around political interference led to reforms after the interregnum of 1268–1271. Pope Gregory X's decree during the second council of Lyons in 1274 that the cardinal electors should be locked in seclusion cum clave (Latin for 'with a key') and not permitted to leave until a new pope had been elected. Conclaves are now held in the Sistine Chapel of the Apostolic Palace in Vatican City," Martinez explained, eyes wide open, and a sense of ownership, pride, and belonging was visibly displayed.

"Really, dude? Locked up with a key? So what we're witnessing is a practice from t before Stone Age? This is an amazing thing to witness. The church must be very resolute in its handling of its practices," provokingly commented.

Martinez was unmoved by the remarks but took it as a time to teach.

"So hear this man, from the apostolic age until 1059, the Pope, like any other bishop, was chosen by the consensus of the clergy and laity of the diocese. In 1059, the body of electors was more defined, when the College of Cardinals was designated the sole body of electors. Since then, other details of the procedures have developed. In 1970, Pope Paul VI limited the electors to cardinals under 80 years of age in Ingravescentem aetatem. The current procedures established by Pope John Paul II in Universi

Dominici Gregis were slightly amended in 2007 and 2013 by Pope Benedict XVI," Martinez took time to explain.

Michael was impressed by the sound knowledge that Martinez was displaying, showing mastery in the manner in which the Church history had evolved. It was obvious that he was excited to be there and there was no question about his allegiance to the church.

"So how does the vote work? Is it just like the political votes where one who gets more than 50% votes will take the leadership role?" Michael asked again.

"No my dear, a two-thirds supermajority vote is required to elect the new pope," Martinez responded.

"You see, the procedures for the election of the pope developed over almost two millennia. Until the College of Cardinals was created in 1059, the bishops of Rome, like those in other areas, were elected by acclamation of the local clergy and people. Procedures similar to the present system were introduced in 1274 when Gregory X promulgated Ubi periculum following the action of the magistrates of Viterbo during the interregnum of 1268–1271," Martinez explained voluntarily.

Before Michael could comment Martinez continued. "The process was further refined by Gregory XV with his 1621 papal bull Aeterni Patris Filius, which established the requirement of a two-thirds majority of cardinal electors to elect a pope. The third council of the Lateran had initially set the requirement that two-thirds of the cardinals were needed to elect a pope in 1179. This requirement had varied since then, depending on whether the winning candidate was allowed to vote for himself, in which cases the required majority was two-thirds plus one vote. Aeterni Patris Filius prohibited this practice and established two-thirds as the standard needed for election," Martinez explained further.

"So if the Pope is the leader taking over from St Peter why is it that the process is now so mechanical and lacking the involvement of the Holy Spirit and God as the center of the process," Michael asked.

"It is believed that the running of the church was handed over to the apostles and hence God has entrusted men to run with his mission," Martinez.

"Before this new orderly Pope selection, what was the process like?" Michael asked.

"As early Christian communities emerged, they elected bishops, chosen by the clergy and laity with the assistance of the bishops of neighbouring dioceses. Cyprian (died 258) says that Pope Cornelius (in office 251–253) was chosen as bishop of Rome "by the decree of God and His Church, by the testimony of nearly all the clergy, by the college of aged bishops [sacerdotum], and of good men." As in other dioceses, the clergy of the Diocese of Rome was the electoral body for the bishop of Rome. Instead of casting votes, the bishop was selected by general consensus or by acclamation. The candidate was then submitted to the people for their general approval or disapproval. This lack of precision in the election procedures occasionally gave rise to rival popes or antipopes." Martinez Explained "I see that even though the church has kept its key history, many Popes have made significant changes to the practice of selection of the Pope. Michael commented.

"Since the 2005 papal conclave, the cardinal electors reside in the Domus Sanctae Marthae for the length of the conclave."

"In 1996, John Paul II promulgated a new apostolic constitution, Universi Dominici gregis, which with slight modifications by Pope Benedict XVI now governs the election of the pope, abolishing all previous constitutions on the matter, but preserving many procedures that date to much earlier times. Under Universi Dominici gregis, the cardinals are to be lodged in a purpose-built edifice in Vatican City, the Domus Sanctae Marthae, but continue to vote in the Sistine Chapel." Martinez responded.

There was a moment of silence followed by personal moments. Martinez made video recordings and took some photos. He also met some friends and talked about the convergence of the cardinals from all over the world and the possibility of black people and women participating in the Papal contest in the run-up to elect a new Pope.

Michael took the time to call home and check on things. He had missed his wife and children and was due to fly back home. There was a discussion about the nomination of a Munhumutapa day and paying of tribute to Munhumutapa in Masvingo. The Hills of the Great Zimbabwe was the chosen site, not too far and not too close to the sacred monuments that define the rule of Munhumutapa.

"So, before we took a break, you were about to tell me about the role of the dean of the College of Cardinal," Michael resumed the question and Answer.

"Several duties are performed by the dean of the College of Cardinals, who is always a cardinal bishop. If the dean is not entitled to participate in the conclave owing to age, his place is taken by the vice-dean, who is also always a cardinal bishop. If the vice-dean cannot participate, the senior cardinal bishop participating performs the functions." Martinez Explained

"So who makes the determination and announcement that the Pope is dead and is there a ritual." Michael asked.

"The camerlengo proclaiming a papal death Cardinals, bishops and priests attending the funeral of Pope John Paul II. The death of the pope is verified by the cardinal camerlengo, or chamberlain, who traditionally performed the task by calling out his baptismal (not papal) name. After confirming the death of the pope, the camerlengo pronounces the phrase "sede vacante" ("The throne is empty"). The camerlengo takes possession of the Ring of the Fisherman worn by the pope. The ring, along with the papal seal, is later destroyed before the College of Cardinals. The tradition originated to avoid forgery of documents, but today merely a symbol of the end of the pope's reign," Martinez explained, he was passionate about the church as seen by his response and articulation of issues.

"So are there instances when a Pope decides to resign from the office and duties of a Pope?" Michael asked almost immediately after Martinez had answered the question previously asked.

Martinez's phone rang, and he spoke in Latin. He stepped away for a moment and kept speaking in Latin then returned to Michael.

"Sorry I had to address something important. So, coming to your question, a vacancy in the papal office may also result from a papal resignation. Until the resignation of Benedict XVI on 28 February 2013, no pope had resigned since Gregory XII in 1415. In 1996, Pope John Paul II, in his apostolic constitution Universi Dominici gregis, anticipated the possibility of resignation when he specified that the procedures he set out in that document should be observed "even if the vacancy of the Apostolic See should occur as a result of the resignation of the Supreme Pontiff."

"In the case of a papal resignation, the Ring of the Fisherman is placed in the custody of the cardinal camerlengo; in the presence of the College of Cardinals. The camerlengo marks an "X" (for the cross) with a small silver hammer and chisel into the ring, disfiguring it so it may no longer be used for signing and sealing official papal documents." Martinez Continued.

"Insightful. So what are the grounds for resignation from the Papal office?" Michael followed up with another question.

"The idea is distinctly stated in his book, "Light of the World: The Pope, the Church and the Signs of the Times," Pope Benedict XVI espoused the idea of resignation on health grounds, which already had some theological respectability," Martinez elaborated. Though this idea had not been included as the basis giving way to the Papal Conclave, it was considered fair and practical.

"So now that the Pope is dead and the ring is destroyed what happens then?" Why not just have a vice Pope who takes over in the event of the sitting Pope passing on or resignation?"

"The cardinals hear two sermons before the election: one before actually entering the conclave, and one once they are settled in the Sistine Chapel. In both cases, the sermons are meant to lay out the current state of the church, and to suggest the qualities necessary for a pope to possess in that specific time. The first preacher in the 2005 conclave was Raniero Cantalamessa, the preacher of the papal household and a member of the Capuchin Franciscan order, who spoke at one of the meetings of the cardinals held before the actual day when the conclave began. Cardinal Tomáš Špidlík, a former professor at the Pontifical Oriental Institute and a non-voting member (due to age) of the College of Cardinals, spoke just before the doors were closed for the conclave," Martinez continued with the explanation.

Michael took a call that lasted 30 Minutes and while he was on the phone Martinez decided to take photos of different views, he also placed a video recording for his records.

Michael had struggled to reconcile the part where the Pope was supposed to be a church leader in the order of St Peter. The Romans were brutal and inconsiderate, even when Jesus was born, there was speculation that Jesus was supposed to be a messiah who was to relieve them from the bondage and oppression of the Romans. He wanted to ask but he was unsure of how Martinez was going to respond to such a question. So it was, wisdom led him to drop the matter and focus on the process.

While he was wondering, Martinez came back.

"So I was saying that on the morning of the day designated by the congregations of cardinals, the cardinal electors assemble in Saint Peter's Basilica to celebrate Mass. Then they gather in the afternoon in the Pauline Chapel in the Apostolic Palace and process to the Sistine Chapel while singing the Litany of the Saints. The cardinals will sing the "Veni Creator Spiritus", invoking the Holy Spirit, then take an oath to observe the procedures set down by the apostolic constitutions; to, if elected, defend the liberty of the Holy See; to maintain secrecy; and to disregard the instructions of secular authorities on voting. The senior cardinal reads the oath aloud in full. In order of precedence, the other cardinal electors repeat the oath, while touching the Gospels. Where their rank is the same, their seniority is taken as precedence. Martinez commented.

Chapter 47

Michael had received an invitation from the Ministry of Local Government to attend the crowning of Chief Nemwamwa. Michael decided that the meeting was to offer him a chance to have a discussion with the Minister of Local Government. Michael arrived by a helicopter in Masvingo, then drove to the venue of the meeting. The meeting was well attended by diplomats, senior government officials, members of the diplomatic community, civic society, members of parliament and senate academia Mayors of various towns.

Michael spotted the Minister of Local Government.

"Michael, what a rare pleasure to see you. I called your office the other day. Forget about today's meeting, I wanted to tell you that there are murmurings about your property development and how you are handling your clients. The matter has been brought to my attention by a lawyer of the defendants. There is a litigation brewing Michael and I hope you are on top of the situation." Minister Mushangwe reported.

"I heard, but am not sure about a group of home seekers who are planning to register a class action," Michael responded, his voice was a whisper. He looked around to see if there was no one in the ear short.

"What's going on Minister? Tell me?" Michael demanded.

The Minister looked around like a drug dealer who was about to disclose a certain classified drug operation information. His voice was a too low, much lower than Michael's.

''Look here Michael, there are a number of people who are not happy with the success you have been making. However the issue of the land is a hot one. There are questions over how you procured the land. The understanding from the Lands Ministry is that you were using government land for agriculture production and no one had a problem with that. The challenge however if that the recent development seem to have raised questions about the land ownership of the Land that you are parceling," the Minister explained to Michael who was neither happy nor sad, either moved or bothered. Michael did not want to give out his mood and he was very good at doing that.

"Minister what are my options regarding this one?" Michael was not aware that he spoke loudly.

"Do the right thing Michael, you have had a fair share of challenges and if you are to appease the class Action Team, then you have your chances of making it," the Minister responded.

The following day, the lawyer representing the complainants in a Class Action matter was called for business and had to travel to Cape Town. The following day, he concluded the transaction and decided to cool himself in a swimming pool. He drowned and his body was taken to the Mortuary. The circumstances surrounding his drowning were not clear but when the autopsy report was released, it indicated high levels of cocaine and heroin.

The head of the Class Action turned out that he was working for Michael in one of his newspaper businesses that he had purchased before. Oliver was his name. The following day he was transferred to work at Native as an advisor. He was offered a lucrative deal and when he accepted and started work at Native

Investments, he was accused of theft of trust funds. He was locked up, but Michael came in person and paid for the bail and asked him to think about dropping the habit of stealing and come back to work. He was also warned never to be involved in the affairs that could bring the company into disrepute.

Meanwhile the president Kufazvinei gave a speech at the crowning of Chief Nemwamwa.

"We are blessed to witness the crowning of Chief Nemamwa. We pay tribute to the chiefs, headmen, and various levels of governance in our country. The Sabhuku deals and councils offering land to Land Barons are ugly developments that require immediate, swift and decisive action against the criminals. Land barons are not investors, they are speculative greedy, unpatriotic and parasitic opportunists waiting to pounce on our land," President Kufazvinei remarked to wild cheers and applause.

Michael was disturbed by the remarks made by the president. He was aware that once the president has set a tone regarding a crime, the entire nation will follow suit, from judges, magistrates, the police and prison services. He was not sure what to make of the threat and derogatory remarks, which were being expressed by the President.

"My government will not watch while the entire country is being taken and parceled out for free and by a connected few. I am putting together a commission of inquiry and I am looking for answers and I need them." The president continued.

"Minister this tone from the resident, there will be a need for action from all security agencies. The Anti-Corruption will pounce on me even though I have not done anything wrong," Michael remarked as he looked intently at the Minister.

The Minister did not respond as he did not want to appear disrespectful to be talking while the president was giving a speech. He raised a hand to signal him to stop the conversation.

"We stand in the hills of the great and mighty Great Zimbabwe. The symbol of our nation's roots is firmly rooted in the spirit of Ubuntu the values of peace and tranquility. Prosperity and above all, a culture of honesty and integrity. The ruins are a steadfast and imposing symbol of the progress and prosperity that our forefathers enjoyed. The ruins speak of community building and a sense of purpose for a people that lived that time. It is our duty to preserve what our ancestors left behind," President Kufazvinei continued.

The great Zimbabwe is an iconic place, a reminder to those who doubt that blacks had a long history of being civilised with a great sense of leadership. The great tower inside the Great Enclosure at Great Zimbabwe is an imposing feature.

Chapter 48

While Michael raced against time to rally his allies and those in high offices to sabotage the President's directive against land barons, Timothy requested a week's leave. He cited that mental health distress was affecting his concentration. Michael initially disputed the request, arguing that Timothy still performed his duties well. But Timothy insisted that he was on the verge of a mental breakdown. A shutdown. With all the mounting trouble in Michael's businesses, he gave in. He realised that a mindful and present Timothy was a far greater asset than a sleepwalking Timothy or even ten substitutes. No one could replace him. He had stood by him through it all, in and out of prison. From the depths of the fiery furnace to the icy underworld deals across the globe, he remained loyal to him. He had all the intel needed to bring him down, but he chose loyalty. Michael appreciated that, though not in so many words.

Timothy and his wife headed for the Vumba Mountains. They spent four days touring and hiking the scenic hills in the area. The lush evergreen trees provided much-needed relaxation for the couple. Even in their middle age, they still had the *joie de vivre*. Helen, Timothy's wife, packed all the skimpy lingerie she could find in her drawers. She threw in a lot of polka-dot ones, her husband's favourite pattern. She disliked anything with dots, but they agreed to compromise here and there, as married couples do. However, their non-negotiable were exactly that: a no-go. Helen refused to share toothbrushes. It annoyed him so much that he lost his temper, but she stood her ground. Being married or close wasn't an excuse to erase personal boundaries. As for Timothy, he refused to have body art of any kind. During their honeymoon phase, she had asked him to tattoo her name, but he refused. The only other ink he had was for his college sweetheart. He had her name on his bicep. With remorse, he explained that he had acted out of foolishness and immaturity. Love is often blind in that way, leading people to do senseless things in the heat of the moment. One day, he would have it removed. But life always got in the way. Especially working for Michael, there were always more pressing priorities to deal with. A breakaway from work was a necessary detox. All the while in Vumba, Timothy's energy levels were unusually high, which unsettled his wife. Even in the weeks preceding it, he acted like his usual self, with no obvious signs of distress. But sometimes people mask their true feelings when troubled, especially men. She knew him well enough not to miss the signs. Then she realised he lied to his boss to get the leave approved. Still, she couldn't shake the uncanny feeling that something was off.

On the fifth morning of their trip, Timothy drove his wife to her parents' home in Honde Valley. She grew up in a pristine village bordering the Ngarura River. Overwhelmed with the joy of being home, she smiled and chatted the whole way. Then, two minutes' drive from their homestead, Timothy stopped the car.

He confronted his wife about her octopus tattoo. Startled, she dropped her phone. All questions about body art had been settled during their first two years of marriage. Why bring it up now, after decades of living together? Again, Timothy expressed regret over the tattoo of his ex-girlfriend's name, which he still had, but it was no secret how it came to be. He had been open about it from the start. On the other hand, she had told him she liked octopuses. It turned out Charles' claims were true. His wife had lied. She sat still in the passenger seat, her fingers twitching and twisting in her lap as Timothy spoke. Her eyes stayed fixed on the dashboard. For the first time in their marriage, she was speechless.

Timothy spoke to his wife, staring at her with steely eyes. He banged his fist on the dashboard, then switched off the radio. He told her everything except that Charles and his boss Alvaro had offered him to join them. When Charles called during the amateurish raid at the aquarium in South Africa, he later met up with Timothy. The leverage he held over Timothy was that he had damning evidence to bring both him and Michael down. Acting in his own best interest, he chose to protect himself. Michael had used him for far too long. At that secret meeting, Timothy demanded to know how he had survived the poison that night in October 2024.

He reminded his wife how he had casually mentioned the poison plan one evening. When he showed her the vial of poison, he never suspected she would turn against him. He assumed that she was too loyal to ever betray him. Before the deal at the restaurant that October, she had already swapped the poison for a fake dose. Timothy ended up giving Charles wine laced with a paralytic, not the deadly toxin he intended. According to Charles, Timothy's wife had secretly swapped the lethal tetrodotoxin with botulinum toxin, a paralytic that mimics death without causing immediate fatality. Unaware of the switch, Timothy gave Charles the fake dose, believing the plan had succeeded. Instead, he had slipped into a slow paralysis that made his body shut down, his breathing nearly stop, and his pulse undetectable. Paramedics, rushed and soon declared him dead. They didn't make a mistake, they were paid. Timothy's wife, Helen, a critical care nurse, had orchestrated the secret rescue, smuggling him out to a private clinic in South Africa. Charles' wife, Jennifer had been a trophy wife, who later remarried a mining mogul.

Timothy turned to look at his wife and said, "I'm telling you all this because you're the one who saved him. You did it because you were sleeping with the enemy." Helen's body stiffened and she bowed her head. Any word, and a bullet could strike her.

"The reason you were kidnapped that time at Olivia's spa was because, Rose, Charles' girlfriend, found out about your affair. I saved you, fortunately. And that octopus tattoo on your thigh, the one the whole world knows about? It was for your old boyfriend. You dated Michael before we met, yet you never mentioned it, even when you found out that he was my boss. That's in the ancient past. But Charles?"

Timothy paused, watching his wife sniffle and fidget as she clutched his hands. He continued, "This is where I paid my lobola for you. I'll leave you to think about what you want next. Rather, who you want. Me? Charles? Michael? The children don't have to know about this. You have my number." He drove to her parents' gate and helped her unload her bags. With that, he made a U-turn, leaving her sobbing at the gate.

Chapter 49

The Class Action for Gold Burn town had reached its final stages. The High Court heard testimonies from 22 witnesses, the arguments were strong and corroborated with the report for the commission of inquiry, this inquiry was an independent investigation that had been ordered by President Kufazvinei. The commission had concluded that a number of property developers had sold stands that did not belong to them. They had disregarded the legal notices issued by the government and used corrupt officials as well as faking and forging documents. They had managed to fool many officials into believing that the scheme of development was indeed legitimate. Michael was implicated on three occasions. While there was no concrete legally admissible evidence that he did fleece the government.

An extract from the Commission of Inquiry concluded that, "a number of property development companies had fraudulently developed areas that did not belong to them. In addition to that, they had offered false hope to the unsuspecting residents." Section 1000.96.3 of the Commission of Inquiry's report stated that, "Native Investments was involved in six irregular land developments where stands were sold to the public despite having no agreement with the owners of the land in question. In the case of Greendale town, Native was found to have breached the contract, leading to demolition of the properties resulting in loss of property and investment for the residents."

On the Goldburg matter, the high court had concluded that the Native Investments acted in bad faith, they were aware of their lack of capacity to develop the stands at the pace communicated to the home seekers yet they went ahead and collected the money from the unsuspecting prospective homeowners. There was commercial crime committed, and the directors were responsible for the criminal acts committed by their directors.

Speaking to Jotham, a reporter from The Morning Snail, after the High Court ruling on Goldburg, the complainants' lawyers were happy with the victory for the residents.

"Congratulations on a victory at such interesting times where the issue of the Land Barons has ravaged our society and led to loss of hard-earned income in the hands of dubious land developers," Jotham remarked, looking into the defense council who were still donning their legal wear and holding voluminous standing just outside the High court. In the background, the sound of the passing through Samora could be heard, but this did little to draw the excitement that was emerging from the High Court.

"This is a victory not only for the residents of Goldburg, but it sets the precedents for the many home seekers who have been fleeced. The Commission of Inquiry by His Excellency, the President Dr Kufazvinei has indicated that dire situation, as lawyers, we are ever ready to assist those in similar circumstances," remarked the lead of the defense council.

"So with this victory, what is the next course of action?" Jotham followed up.

"We have sued Onaway Real Estate the real estate company that was given a mandate to sell the stands. They violated the regulations of the Council for Real Estate by participating in an illegal activity which they knew was fraudulent. We have also submitted a request for cancellation of their license as well as approaching the Law Society to have the legal team that handled contracts for the fraudulent scheme," the defense council responded beaming with confidence and doing little to hide their excitement for the sweet victory.

In another case at the High Court under Judge Mushininga, Native Investments was being represented by Samusha and Chivhinga.

The matter was regarding the sale of stands on a land belonging to the City of Harare and subdividing the land for residential stands, for land reserved for road construction, specifically Harare Drive. Up to 200 stands now houses were facing demolition. Another Class action and in a shocking move, the case was concluded in three days.

It never rains, but it actually pours for Native Investments. In a shocking case, the Magistrate Mrs Maravi had found Native Investments guilty of parceling stands on a land belonging to a sports club and a school, respectively.

#

At 8 pm Olivia and Stone stopped by at Michael's house, they dropped one Aunty Racheal Paradzai. A teacher by profession was given orders to look after the kids and would receive further instructions.

"Michael, we need to move now or never," Stone's tone was sharp, commanding firm and final.

"I am coming with my wife," Michael protected.

"Negative Commander." She is very safe, She is a shareholder nor director and she will not answer to any of the issues about Native Investments. Stone responded.

"I need a passport and-,"Michael wanted to protest, but he was cut off by Stone.

Michael had a fleet of five planes, and that night four of them were due to fly into the country. Stone had handled the business. He had reported submitted an urgent application in various courts, arguing that his company was owed money by Native Investments. He fast-tracked the paperwork and submitted an order permitting his companies to attach the assets, based on services rendered that remained unpaid. The only asset was a Gulf Stream that Stone had attached at around 3 pm.

Stone was acting on intelligence from "connected" colleagues and he had been informed that a warrant of arrest was to be issued first thing in the morning. But his informer was behind, at 8 pm an urgent meeting was held, President Kufazvinei wanted examples, there was too much outcry, and they seemed to have been doing nothing to deal with the matter. The court rulings that condemned many developers pointed to a nation that was full of corruption. The President was looking for a spectacular example, he wanted to appease the public. The public anger was growing strong and fast, and the courts were treating matters relating to land fraud by Land Barons as urgent matters. The tone had been set by the leader at a national level.

At 9 am, a resolution was passed by, and a warrant of arrest was to be issued that night. Word went around that any Michael Paradzai should not be allowed to check in. The police were deployed at all the airports, and Michael was the subject matter.

As Stone drove towards the airstrip where the Gulf Stream was parked, he received a call from Timothy about the warrant and that changed everything. The plan to fly was still on course, but flight details had been changed. Stone made a U-turn and he was stopped three times before getting into town, all of them looking for Michael.

Social Media was awash with reports of Michael having been arrested. Stone parked in town and created a believable video of Michael sitting at a restaurant dismissing the rumors that he had been arrested. He even called the CID department asking them to clear the air on social media rumors that were circulating on many platforms. The officer who responded had just started duty and promised to call back.

There was a knock at the window, a police car had pulled up, and Michael was put in cuffs. He was arrested and put in police custody. The family was notified that Michael was arrested while trying to flee and that they would hear the breaking news.

Social media was awash with comments and many expressing happy emojis. The anger was appeased, the president was already asleep and it was anticipated that he was to give a press briefing.

The following morning, there was no news about what had happened. An order to freeze all bank accounts had been secured, but by the time the banks were served, Stone had emptied the accounts.

Turns out Michael was escorted by a stolen Police BMW all the way to the airport. He was holding a passport from Canada under Simon Whiteman. He was escorted through the VIP exit and right on time for boarding. He was the first to board.

There, the Air bus was taxing and just after clearance for take-off there was commission at the airport as the police, acting on a tipoff, tried to stop the plane but the plane was already in full speed and while they were arguing with the police the plane took off and in 40 minutes time it crossed the Zambezi river out of the Zimbabwean airspace.

The award winning book. Detective Mike tries to uncover the face behind the elusive drug lord, JBZ.

Detective Mike is at it again in this aviation thriller.

Elliot Chatima and Rumbi Chen

THE GODS ABOVE

A religious thriller of abuse of women

and girls in churches and society

By: Elliot Chatima and Rumbi Chen

Chapter 1

It was a cool Thursday morning, with patchy morning drizzle and light thunder showers expected later in the day, according to the MET department. Time really moves fast, the days are fleeting. The sound of New Year celebrations, the memories of Christmas cheer, the partying, and the bullet sound of firecrackers were still echoing in our ears. And yet we were already in the month of April. Noel Kasamba was having a glass of Amarula mixed with Ultra Heat Treated (UHT) milk, a mixture only for the lactose-tolerant. He was holding a giant marijuana cigarette which made choking smokes to those not used to such strong "medicine. Noel was a man with seven wives and 28 children. He had married the women when they were between the ages of 10 and 13 years. None of his wives was more than 15 years when they were "married". He had lost three wives and 3 children due to pregnancy and birth complications.

Susan, his first wife, was now 25 years old, a mother of 5 children. Each woman had been given a field measuring one hectare to farm, and they were to do so with their own children. In that sort of work, numbers mattered, and the one with more children had a lighter burden.

Susan entered Noel's chambers. She knelt down before him and waited for him to speak to her.

Noel cleared his throat and looked aside as if checking if no one was coming. He licked his lips with his tongue, lubricating his mouth with saliva, looking at her intently and started. "You know my heart beats for you, right? And there can be nothing difficult for me to do for a queen like you, my number one girl here."

Susan looked at him and started giggling like a little girl. "If you say so, there are times I begin to think that you have forgotten about me. These new girls keep you busy these days, and you have forgotten about me," she complained. "I am your first love, when I first met you we both had never been married, though I was young. How I wish things could have remained the same way," she continued.

"So you are still dreaming of the two of us only?." Noel demanded.

Susan looked at him. "You know how we were so pristine and we knew nothing about making love. I had to research a lot and it was great to see how much progress we made. When I was beginning to think that we were getting the hang of it, then boom another woman," Susan remarked

Noel moved closer to her, trying to bring her closer with his right hand but Susan was choked by the smoke from the marijuana. She backed off, and Noel laughed as he made aggressive pulls of the marijuana cigarette before coughing and releasing smoke into the air. He made two quick sips of Amarula before he spoke. "Pardon my bad manners, you requested to see me. What is it?."

Susan cleared her throat, looked at Noel as if trying to gauge his mood before she spoke. "My Lord," she started. "Angela, your seventh wife is heavily pregnant and from our assessment we believe she will not be able to deliver the baby in a normal way, we think it's a great idea to take her to the hospital."

Noel erupted from the bed, and like a possessed man, grabbed Susan by the throat and began to choke her, then threw her to the couch, narrowly missing the wall. He looked at her for a moment before he spoke. "The next time you speak to me like that, you will not be so lucky, I will kill you, and I will kill you dead!." Noel was shaking with anger, he was failing to control himself and in the end he ended up sitting down. There was complete silence. The silence was broken by a loud cry from the other room. They looked at each other before Noel shouted, "Go back and manage the situation. Even if the baby is crossing, she will deliver the same way others have. She will deliver here, call the lady from the next compound."

There was commotion in the next three hours that followed. Angela was given a homemade concoction to take, and it was a traditional mixture meant to induce a babe to come. After taking it, Angela started sweating and shaking, the other three of Noel's wives were holding her while the other one was wiping the sweat and calming her down. The Screams were loud, a call for help. She called her father and mother in a desperate plea to seek help. The screams were sharp and disturbing even the elderly midwife asked that Angela be taken to the hospital but that was a non-starter. Angela got married at the age of 12 and at 13 years she was pregnant. There was an unwritten law amongst the community of, "believers" that women would give birth at home and will never go for weighing scale or for vaccination. The idea was to evade jail, prison was not far.

Angela screamed one more time. Pushed and pushed, it was clear she wanted the baby to come out thus she used all the force she had, but to no avail. Everyone watched as she began to grow tired and powerless. Susan ran to Noel to alert him, but he was not in the mood. He did not entertain her.

Susan ran to Angela, raised her head and appealed to her to push one more time. "You can do it, my friend, please don't give up." Susan urged her. Angela summoned all the power and spoke. "I think my baby has crossed, he's not coming. I am tired, I am leaving you, and my body is getting cold. Tell my father that I love him and that I forgive him for what he did to me. Cutting my life at a developmental stage and handing me over to be rapped daily and left to die. Please make sure that you will treat your girls with dignity and that they will go to school." Angela looked at Susan while the midwife cast a lone and disturbed figure, thinking if she had been an evil person for assisting the women last minute. She wrestled with thoughts, and she did not realise that she was talking loudly and all the debate in her heart she aired out.

Angela looked at Susan, "I want to go vakoma (sister). I need you to promise me, I need you to avenge my death. At that point, everyone noticed that Lucia was in the room, because of the commotion no one had noticed, she saw and heard everything. Angela looked at Lucia, and with a weak hand gesture, she called her close. "Lucia my baby I am dying, you know and have seen what I went through. I need you to remember me and protect your sisters," she pleaded with her. At that point, Lucia was afraid and started screaming, went outside then she ran away from home, never to be seen again. Back in the room, Angela breathed her last. Her parents were informed, and the following morning, she was buried in a shallow grave in the compound. She was buried in an unmarked grave wrapped in a reed mat with a plastic on top and trees were planted on top of the grave.

Susan had nightmares few days that followed. Noel realised that his women were disturbed and called them. "I know what happened here has traumatised you. I could have addressed you before. The spirit had shown me that the evil one shall come and will sit in the midst of the family. That person will bring foreign ideas, but I prayed that none of that would happen. Angela was used by the devil and her death is a defeat to the powers of darkness, we have conquered," Noel charged. All the women looked at Susan for approval and whoever Susan approved, everybody would follow without question.

Susan had not gone to school, but she was intelligent. She had mastered the art of deception, but she still had flaws as an uneducated person, and her skimming would actually be foiled. Susan looked at everyone and looked at Noel who was now portraying a face of a hungry puppy begging for food. She looked down and blinked first, closed her eyes as she presumably tried to shake off the loud screams and the plea for help by Angela. In the end tears flew effortlessly and when she spoke, her voice was low but audible.

"Indeed, as our father and husband has said. We were under attack by the evil spirit. This event, the death of Angela, was Satan's doing, and we must be united in prayer that the evil departs from this house and from our lives forever." When she was done talking she was shaking and gritting her teeth. All the other women responded with an "amen." But Noel was not to be fooled, she saw the pain and trauma in Susan.

The following day, Noel and his six wives prepared for church. It was a Passover meeting, and they were going to be gone for six days. They were part of the Mission Critical Church of Apostles. The name sounded like some government department responsible for espionage and other secretive missions. But nevertheless, the church had existed for 85 years.

The members wore blue and white uniforms from time to time. They camped in Buhera, and instantly the place became a business hub. Women were responsible for making food, providing hot water for their husbands and making tea as and when it was needed.

Noel was a high-ranking member who sat on the church's leadership council. They each took turns preaching to their congregants.

The sitting arrangement was weird, the men sat in front facing the young girls. The boys sat behind their fathers while the mothers sat behind their daughters.

A time for prophecy came, and all the leaders started speaking in tongues. "Hiririririri CD Ramachksaakada aaaaa bullshit yematatya."

The first one was the leader of the church, and there would be a second person to repeat what they had said. "The spirit has shown me a family that will perish tonight, but there is nothing to fear, as all has been revealed to me," he said to wild cheers. The congregants were aware of what was about to happen. "Spirit has said unto me, if I take the daughter in marriage, the death will be averted and the entire family will be saved from harm." He continued, looked at the young girls, barely 12 years and pointed at one of them and asked her to stand up. The family approached the leader and knelt before him. They grabbed their daughter by the hand, and without emotion or question, they handed her over. There were loud cheers and applause, with women immediately erupting into songs of "praise and worship. The act was considered sent by God.

Next was Noel, he had taken marijuana and his famous Amarula, his tongue was a borderline circus, and in the end he too prophesied. "Zvanzi nemweya (The spirit said) there is a girl sitting in front of you, that girl, you are to pray for her and she will be promiscuous. Sorry, meant prosperous, she must come to you." Mothers urged their children to run, and the one that came to him was the one he wanted, he had stood right in front of her. When the girls stood before him, he continued, "the spirit said you shall bear fruit and be wealthy and prosperous in my house You shall be my wife from today." The young girl was shocked and she attempted to run away but her parents grabbed her and handed her over to Noel. Susan looked at the scene and Noel cast a gaze in her direction, as if to show that he was the man and did whatever he wanted.

So it was that Noel had taken another, "wife" a thirteen year old girl. The girl shed tears and fought hard. She cried and begged to be allowed to go to school, but all the begging fell on deaf ears.

As the church meeting was coming to an end, Edith was happy that she had survived the forced marriage arrangements, she was an intelligent child always coming first in her class. She had escaped to her uncle's house trying to evade the church camp meeting, but the plan did not work, as her father demanded that she come home without wasting time.

As the people were folding the tents and preparing to leave, Edith was called by her father with the mother joining her.

"Edith, you are a beautiful girl, and I don't doubt that you are going to be a great wife. Always listen to your husband and don't talk back, you must do everything he asks of you," Edith smiled and responded, "Yes Mom, one day, when I finish school, I will meet someone I love, get married and start a family," she responded. "You do not have to wait for all that long my daughter," the mother interjected. "We have already found a man for you. Look at him he has fields, businesses and he will be taking care of you." A man in his late forties was approaching the parents he cleared his throat to announce his arrival. "Good evening brothers and sisters in the lord, I hope I am not interrupting an important conversation," he asked.

There was an awkward silence, revealing that there was unfinished business. He figured out that there was a discussion to hand over the girl that he had been promised when the parents had failed to repay a debt of USD 200. The parents had borrowed over time, hoping that they were going to be paid for the work the husband had done for someone, but that did not materialise.

The creditor ran out of patience, he stepped forward and grabbed Edith like a shepherd carrying a kid. Edith wiggled and screamed as she was taken away but that did not help, the parents had mixed emotions. They wanted their daughter to finish school, but it was too late, the agreement they made could not be reversed. And so it was.

The following morning, Edith's father, Samson Mabwe, went to a man he had done work for and managed to get USD 220 after narrating the story. But when they visited Murindagomo, the man whom they had offered Edith as settlement for the debt owing, but the man was adamant..

The man refused to budge, stating that Edith was very intelligent and he needed her to run his businesses. Murindagomo had sent Edith to a boarding school after her plea to finish school. The man, however, refused to let them know where Edith was, stating that she was his wife and he had a right to send her anywhere he wished. He would not be pushed to disclose what he was doing with his wives at his homestead.

On the other hand, Noel took the girl he had "prophesied" about. They all drove home in silence in the family minivan. As they got home, Noel's wives did what was once done to them. They tied Natasha's hands and legs and sent her into one of the bedrooms. They gave her a lecture about being intimate with a man and how difficult life was going to be at her newly found home.

An hour later, dinner was brought, but Natasha refused to eat.

At midnight, Noel entered the bedroom and unbound Natasha, he was holding a glass of Amarula and a cigarette of marijuana.

"You smoke?" Natasha asked. Noel did not take kindly to any questioning, but he decided to move with the flow. "Yes I do and I smoke too," Noel responded. Natasha looked at him. She moved closer to him to dispel the notion that she wanted to run away. "Can we drink together and possibly smoke together?" she asked.

Noel looked at her and had to admit that she was intelligent. He looked at her then walked to the kitchen to take another glass, much to the surprise of the other wives who were eagerly waiting to know how and when he was going to violate the new girl as he had done to them.

That night, Natasha and Noel drank Amarula until almost 4 am. There were screams coming from Natasha's bedroom. Noel had turned into an animal as he did with other girls when he brought them. He repeatedly raped her. She cried for help, she wanted out, she wanted to go but nobody could hear her. This went on for days and into weeks till she got used to it and till she was totally brainwashed and till she was filled with rage.

Just after her 14th birthday, she discovered that she was pregnant, and that's when she became suicidal and hatched a plan to destroy Noel. She intended to destroy the whole family, blot out Noel's name, and anything that was related to him.